P9-DGQ-132

MAN UP

KIM OCLON

TRISM BOOKS
Turning Pages. Growing Minds.

Man Up
Copyright © 2020 by Kim Oclon

All rights reserved. This is a work of fiction. All characters and events in this publication, other than those clearly in the public domain, are fictitious and any resemblance to real persons, living or dead, is purely coincidental. No part of this publication may be reproduced in whole or in part, stored in a retrieval system, or transmitted in any form or by any means, electronic, mechanical, photocopying, recording, or otherwise, without written permission of the publisher.

Man Up / Oclon, Kim

ISBN 978-0-9993886-3-1

[1. LGBTQ – Fiction. 2. Baseball – Fiction. 3. Self Esteem – Fiction. 4. Friendship – Fiction. 5. Bullying – Fiction.] I. Title.

Printed in the United States of America
10 9 8 7 6 5 4 3 2 1

Trism Books, Deerfield, IL, USA
www.trismbooks.com

To Virginia
You make me so very happy

PROLOGUE

I came out to my dad at the hottest part of the day in the middle of last summer. Standing at the grill, he turned to ask me how I wanted my burger done.

"I'm gay. Medium well is fine." The sun's rays beat down on my baseball cap as my arms and legs were sticky with sweat.

My dad's neck and back twitched. He didn't say anything, just angled the spatula and flipped two burgers. The top half of my body tried to go back inside, but the bottom half was super-glued to the patio. Dad didn't turn around after the last flip. He just stood in front of the grill, letting smoke get into his eyes.

I had to ump a Little League game later so when we were all seated at the table, I wolfed my food down in less than five minutes. My mom said something about staying hydrated since it was still so hot and I knew she had this tight smile on her face, wondering why everyone was being so weird. Well, Robert, my little brother, wasn't being weird. He went on and on about this homerun derby fundraiser thing for his travel team.

Dad managed to avoid me for two days. Even though it seemed impossible for us to not see each other in our small two-bedroom house, it was actually pretty easy. He got up early to get some work in before the sun began to broil him while he measured boards for a deck he was building for a neighbor's friend. And maybe I left a little early for the games I had to ump. When I got home, my mom claimed Dad was already asleep, the door to their bedroom closed. Being outside in the heat all day must have made him tired.

Or maybe he couldn't even look at me because he fucking hated me. I actually thought that.

On the third day, I came home to find Dad sitting on the front step, sipping a beer, wearing his reliable after-work uniform, shorts and an old White Sox T-shirt from their unbelievable World Series run. I turned off the car, forgetting to put it in park. It heaved forward like it was about to throw up, reminding me to shift gears. My dad continued to sit, elbows resting on his knees like he was still waiting for me to come home.

My hand froze on the door handle. Maybe he wasn't even going to let me back in the house.

When I finally got out of the car, we didn't say anything to one another for a few moments. I just stood there, slightly off to the side of the porch, aware of the mosquitos swarming around my legs.

Dad leaned forward to put his elbows on his knees. He looked at weeds growing through a crack in the pavement. "When I told your mom what you told me… she was relieved."

I wrinkled my eyebrows, asking a question without having to say anything.

"She said that with the way I was acting, she thought I was going to tell her that you were sick. Like you had cancer or something like that." Dad spoke slowly, still avoiding eye contact with me. Now, he focused on setting his beer down on a ring of condensation that was already on the porch.

"I'm not sick," I said, feeling like I had to peel the words from my mouth.

"Are you still going to play ball in the spring?" Dad finally looked up at me with one eye.

"Yeah," I said, surprised by the question. "Why wouldn't I?" The summer night drone of insects and birds seemed to get louder.

Dad picked up his beer and moved over so he sat on the condensation ring. He gestured for me to sit down with his eyes. Baseball was a good subject for us. I sat next to him.

"I didn't know if you would want to or if you had some other plans," Dad shrugged. "You know, because you're..."

"Gay." Dad needed me to finish the sentence but not because he hated me. How long had it taken me to say a little three-letter word? I could see him hearing the word and absorbing it.

I put a hand on my dad's sweaty shoulder. "I'll always play baseball, Dad. Being gay has nothing to do with it."

The outline of his head nodded in the orange glow of the lights on the front of the house. "I don't know how this works, David." He patted my grass-stained knee.

"Me either." It was true. I had no idea. But for now, I didn't have to. So we just sat on the porch together, my dad with his beer and me with a sports drink, until the mosquitos threatened to eat us alive and my mom called us inside.

CHAPTER 1
DAVID

Something invisible hovered over me on the first day of Open Gym. It pushed down, preventing me from lifting the bench press bar that wavered above my shaking elbows. There was no need to be nervous about making the team or playing time. I made varsity my sophomore year and started all of junior year. My spot was guaranteed providing I didn't lose a leg or arm in a freak accident. But no matter how much I grunted or sharply inhaled, the bench press bar didn't move. I only tasted the sweat, steel, and rubber that always hung in the weight room's air. The cement walls somehow absorbed the stench because it even smelled that way over the summer when no one used it.

"Come on, David! Come on, David!" Mike, my best friend, yelled. He put his hands under the bar, ready to guide it back to the original slots.

I arched my back, breathed in again, and managed to straighten my arms. The bar settled in with a loud clang of steel on steel.

"I think you were able to lift that with one arm last season," Mike razzed me as I sat up on the bench, swinging my arms to loosen them up.

"You barely got the bar up when you tried." I sat on the bench for a moment so the blood could drain from my head and settle back into place. "Good thing I was spotting you." As the pressure slowly faded, the gymnastics team glided into the weight room and began a regimen of push-ups and sit ups.

"Something's about to come up." Mike raised his eyebrows, pointing his eyes at the leotards and leggings. "Right?"

Forcing out a laugh, I fixed my focus on the free weights and rolled my shoulders forward and backward a few times. "Come on. Bi's and tri's." I grabbed a fifteen-pound weight and my muscles burned after three quick reps of curls.

Mike let his weight fall and it bounced off the rubber floor that sucked up the smell of wet dirt and sand from the various playing fields. The gymnastics team added chalk and hairspray to the mix.

I took off the Lincoln High School baseball cap I'd gotten freshmen year and reshaped the beak. Almost four years of use changed the bright red to something that looked kind of pink. Sweat stains darkened the inside along the brim. I switched arms and took a deep breath, preparing for the next set of reps.

Mike lingered on the girls' tight ponytails and pointed toes, as they slowly lowered themselves into a center split. The more flexible ones easily slid into position and bounced a little against the floor as if that would help them stretch even lower. "Jesus Christ, David, relax. It's not like we're going to the World Series tomorrow," Mike said. "Fucking hot, right…right?"

I followed Mike's gaze to the girls who were facing each other in a full center split and holding hands so they could pull one another into a deeper stretch. My shoulders tensed as I forced a tight smile and said, "Yep." I looked away and put all of my attention into holding the weight above my head and bending my elbow, quickly feeling the burn in my triceps.

There were a bunch of times when I almost told Mike. Almost blurting it out but swallowing the words. He'd ask, "Want to go to the batting cages?"

I wanted to say, "Sure. By the way, I'm gay."

Or maybe when we were being lazy in his basement, sprawled out on this huge couch, Mike would suggest we play video games. "What do you want to play?"

"*MLB MVP*, of course. I'm gay."

Or, it should have been easy when he thought it would be a good idea for me to go out with one of his girlfriend's, Carrie's, friends. "She's really cute and I heard she kind of likes you."

"Well, I don't like her. I'm gay."

I had already gone on a double date with Mike and Carrie two times. I spent the whole time at the movies eating the biggest popcorn they had so I could keep my hands busy. The whole two hours. At one point, she settled for trying to put her head on my shoulder, but I got up to go to the bathroom at that moment. There was no second date.

"Dude, take a break," Mike said, breaking my trance. I must have done a double rep because my arm really burned. "We don't have anything to worry about this year."

I switched arms, staring at the cinderblock wall in front of me. Eventually, the little craters embedded in it came into focus. "Keep sitting there and Coach will take that "C" off your jersey." I smiled a real smile so Mike knew I was joking.

"Wouldn't Kevin and his crazy-ass dad love that?" Mike took his eyes off the girls and began to work his triceps. "No more of this co-captain shit."

I slowly pulled my elbow behind my head, feeling the tension begin to subside. As I stretched my other arm, the heavy door to the weight room scraped the floor and banged against the wall. The gymnastics team nearly fell out of their wall-sit. Kevin Kaminski, the other captain and ace pitcher, snaked through the bench presses, free weights, and machines, taking a detour to strut past the girls. Most ignored him, as their legs began to shake, but a couple managed to toss their ponytails and flash him a smile.

God dammit.

Kevin, wearing long basketball shorts and T-shirt with the sleeves cut off, sat near us on a crate used for box squats. "Hey faggots, just getting started?"

I turned my face, reminding myself that was the way Kevin greeted everyone. Most of the guys knew Kevin was an asshole but tolerated him because he started throwing a killer curveball in Little League. Private pitching lessons have that effect on a young player.

"We were just finishing." Mike rolled his eyes. "Nice of you to join us."

"Talk to me when you sign a letter of intent to a D-1 school." Kevin folded his arms with this stupid smile on his face, probably giving himself a mental high-five and a pat on the back.

"Really? Where?" I asked, trying to hide my jealousy even though I knew for a while that a bunch of colleges were interested in Kevin and his curveball.

"U of I."

Mike looked as if he suddenly caught a whiff of one of the football player's armpits. "I thought you had to be smart to go there."

Kevin jumped off the box. "What the fuck is that supposed to mean?"

Mike stood up too. "It means not everyone who applies gets into that school so back off."

"My cousin was in the top ten percent of her class and she didn't get in," I said, glad I could back up Mike.

"Well, there you go," Kevin said as if it was obvious. "She."

"Yeah, because we all know girls don't go to college." Mike rolled his eyes again.

"Not to play baseball they don't."

"You got me there." Mike threw up his hands as if defeated in a battle of insults.

"Yeah, well where are you going to play?" Kevin moved the pin in a weight machine down a couple notches and sat down to do a leg press. "Hope to be a walk-on at Sinni like Patrick?" He looked at me, shoving his legs forward with a grunt. The College of Northeastern Illinois was dubbed Sinni by everyone who went there, probably even the teachers.

"Patrick's going there?" I asked, recalling the catcher's slightly massive body blocking the plate for a close play at home. I shrugged like I was the one who had just signed a letter of intent. "Good for him."

Kevin snorted. "It's not like any other place else is going to take him." He bent his knees to lower the weights and then glanced at Mike.

"What about you? Maybe some shitty D-3 school?"

"Maybe," Mike said even though I knew the schools on his wish list.

He could get into and play for any of them.

Kevin grunted his legs forward again, scoffing at me. "You're going to be a charity case." He closed his eyes and stuck out his hand, holding an imaginary paper cup. "For the poor, for the poor."

My face felt hot and something in the pit of my stomach went from simmering to boiling.

"Stop being an asshole," Mike said, stepping in front of me. He finished stretching his arms and followed me to the weight room's exit.

"Stop being a fag," I heard Kevin say as we left.

"You've still got that school in Minnesota, right?" Mike asked me as we walked across the field house. "Not exactly as awesome as U of I, but not shitty D-3 or Sinni either."

"I'll take any school that will give me a scholarship," I said. Mike already knew that. When Coach Kelly told my parents I was good enough to play in college, they told me baseball was the only way I would get to go. Four years ago, my dad lost his job at the construction company where he had worked for fifteen years. We'd barely been getting by on my mom's part-time salary and the side jobs Dad sometimes found. Right now, he was in the middle of installing, sanding, and refinishing hardwood floors for a neighbor. "I mean you're still waiting too."

Mike and I paused at the edge of the indoor track so we wouldn't get run over by approaching members of the track team. "Yeah. Kansas. Missouri. I got in touch with South Carolina for the hell of it."

A small pack of runners glided by in perfect unison, as if their legs belonged to the same body. Tyler jogged in front, leading the pack with his natural stride that made running look effortless. He waved to catch my attention and for a moment all the crap about college was forgotten. "I'll meet you outside after the cool down."

I waved back to show I heard him, my stomach doing a little flip at the same time.

"I didn't know you hung out with Tyler," Mike said.

I shrugged. "He lives by me. Sometimes I give him a ride home."

"He's gay, isn't he?" Mike followed the pack approach the next curve as if something in their running would give him the answer to his question.

I started to cross the field house. "Yeah. I guess. I don't know. We've never talked about it." I did a couple of quick shoulder rolls to shake the tension and tightness that returned to my muscles.

I waited for Tyler in my car, hoping the heat would kick in soon. It was an old car, practically the size of a small boat, the color of muddy pond water, and paid for after a summer of umping Little League games. Despite its appearance, the car worked well. It was worth every yell about a close play and every stare I got after a game when a parent felt their child was somehow wronged in the world of Park District Little League.

Rubbing my hands together, I put them in front of one of the vents even though it still blew icy air. It stung the way a foul ball would when it hit the bat during the season's early games. Just as the air was warming, I saw Tyler approaching through the foggy window.

"Nice hat," I said as Tyler plopped into the passenger seat.

"Thanks. I got it over the weekend." Tyler shook his head so that the little puffball attached to the top of his striped knit hat bobbled from side to side. "Along with a pile of running gear."

As I waited to make a left turn out of the parking lot, Kevin sped into the lane next to me in the SUV his dad handed down to him when he bought a new one. He managed to hit a huge puddle of slush and spray my car. Tyler ducked and covered his head as if the tidal wave of muck would crash through the window.

Kevin's car lurched and the brake lights glowed bright red. He stuck his head out of the window. "Hey, David, I knew your car was a shitbox, not a homo-bile!" He skidded off, a half a second before another car came rushing by.

"What a dick," I muttered, turning on the windshield wipers at high speed.

"I've heard worse," Tyler said, settling back into the seat.

I double-checked the road before making my turn. "Can you believe he's going to play ball for U of I?"

Tyler sighed. "Figures. I'll still have to deal with him." He had gotten in his applications early and knew where he was going since November. "At least it's a big school."

I decided to slow at the yellow light rather than race through. A drop on the windshield slid in a curved path as if it needed a special map to get to the bottom of the window. The road and the light went out of focus and the drop came into clear view.

"Screw him. There's a team looking for a sexy second baseman. They just haven't found you yet," Tyler said as he placed his hand, palm-up, on my knee.

I smiled at Tyler's hand. As I laced my fingers through his and squeezed, I felt how smooth his hands were while mine were rough with callouses from the hours spent in the batting cage over the years.

"UW-Parkside offered something, but it was only for half of the tuition," I said, remembering the hollowness I felt after reading the news. Not wanting to release Tyler's hand, I flicked the turn signal with my driving hand, letting the car steer itself for a half second. "There's still Mankato. This D-2 school in Minnesota." Coach Kelly had also reached out to Mankato on my behalf, telling the coaching staff about the speedy second baseman that could leg out a well-placed bunt and stop any ball hit his way.

I swung the car into Tyler's driveway and put it in park. Tyler reached to take my other hand. The first time we held hands in my car we almost burned our arms on the console because the car had been baking in the heat during our morning workouts this past summer. "You're going to get to play. Even if it's some place far away like Minnesota."

"Thanks." I smiled and struggled to lean over the center console. We still had time. And my car. Our little world consisted of this old brown boat with bad defrosters and a seatbelt that didn't unclick the first time I tried. I kissed Tyler, my lips sliding over the Chapstick he just put on his lips.

CHAPTER 2
TYLER

I walked into my house to find my mom leaning against the island in the kitchen, flipping through the mail. She still had on her gray skirt and jacket from work so she must have just gotten home.

"Can you believe this?" She tossed something on the kitchen table so I could see it.

A guy in a tux with a toothpaste smile grinned up at me.

"Prom season already?" My mom gestured to the advertisement from the tux rental place in the mall. "Don't they know I need time to slow down as it is?" She sighed dramatically.

"Hi, Mom," I said. She did this on an almost daily basis, finding some reason to get all sad because of all the milestones approaching.

"Hi, honey." She stopped her fake tears and gave me a squeeze on the shoulder and picked up the tux ad. "Do you want me to hang on to this for you?"

"No, that's okay." I walked over to the pantry, pretending to be busy looking for something to eat even though any appetite I had just left.

"Are you two going?" my mom asked. "Maybe you could get matching tuxes." She smiled like she had just thought of the cleverest thing in the whole world.

I shrugged, scanning the boxes of cereal and protein bars my dad liked. "I don't think so, Mom. You know David isn't really out and I don't think prom would be the place for us to make our first public appearance."

She took a couple pots down from the hooks hanging by the stove. "I didn't think about that. I'm sorry."

"It's okay." I ended up grabbing a bag of pretzels and headed for the stairs. "I'm gonna do some homework."

But when I got to my room, I dropped my bookbag on the floor and flopped on my bed to scroll through my phone. There were a ridiculous number of selfies of David and me, most of which were in my room or in his car. A couple were taken on the swing on the front porch.

Hidden hands. Secret kisses.

This wasn't exactly what I thought it would be when David and I got to know each other last summer. I would run laps on the track in the morning before it got too hot and David would spend time in the weight room. Our paths crossed at the water fountain outside the field house. And then he gave me a ride home one time. I didn't think that old car's AC would work but I underestimated it...and him. I didn't think I'd find a serious boyfriend when I started at Lincoln High School sophomore year. It was hard to tell if there were any boyfriends to even find.

I didn't need to go to prom in order to prove that David and I were together. But I would have liked to hold his hand in the parking lot before we got to his car. Or maybe give him a hug when he came by my locker every morning.

He came close a couple times. But what would have happened if David didn't pull back? What if he just went for it?

I ignored my bulging bag of AP textbooks, contemplating the answer to that question.

CHAPTER 3
DAVID

A few days later, as I was setting up a physics lab that would test the velocity of matchbox cars released at various inclines, a student worker delivered a pass telling me to go to Coach Kelly's office. I automatically knew something was up. Coach never sent for any players during academic classes. Some of the guys would huff when asked to miss a few minutes of lunch and Coach would ask if they devoted as much attention to their classes as they did to the cafeteria.

As my shoes squeaked through the silent halls, I figured this summons had to be about college. The topic followed me everywhere these days. The weight room. My mailbox. My car. Mankato probably got in touch with Coach Kelly and told him "thank you but no thank you" and now Coach had the unfortunate job of telling me there would be no college ball in my future and because of that, no college either.

I smirked to myself, recalling Sinni was still an option. A letter about the school's athletic programs arrived the day before. I barely skimmed it before stuffing it into the middle of my collection of college brochures, all advertising perfect campuses with freshly turned fall leaves and bright green grass in the courtyards. All the kids in the pictures looked like being able to study outside was the biggest thrill of their lives.

I nodded at the secretary, Mrs. Carlson, when I walked into the athletic office and sat in a chair across from her. Not all coaches were so lucky to have their own office, but Coach Kelly was also the assistant athletic director.

"You can have a seat. He'll be with you in a moment." Mrs. Carlson gave me what appeared to be a sympathetic smile, motherly eyes of concern and slightly upturned corners of the mouth, which confirmed my suspicions about the reason for the pass.

Maybe Parkside could still be an option. Maybe I could get two jobs this summer. Work somewhere during the day and ump at night and do doubleheaders on Saturdays. Sundays could be for me and Tyler. Loans weren't an option. My parents wouldn't be able to cosign for one because they were late on so many mortgage payments before they decided to sell our old house and found a smaller to rent.

The door to Coach Kelly's office wasn't fully latched so I heard fragments of his telephone conversation. "I haven't even had a chance to talk to him yet and I won't be able to if…" He sounded as if he just got cut off, sputtering a stream of incomplete words, only a scattering of isolated consonants and vowels.

From behind Mrs. Carlson, the rows of photographs of Lincoln alumni who moved on to college athletics made fun of me and my nonexistent plans. Confident smiles posed with a piece of equipment to signify the sport, some faded from years of sun exposure, others brand new having just been hung. A particular corner of the office was dedicated to Carl Howell, a player who signed a minor league contract the year before I got to high school, but it was still all anyone could talk about. Everyone was so sure they were going to be the next Lincoln player to go pro. Last I heard Carl was being promoted to Triple A this spring.

I heard Coach sigh a goodbye and hang up. The door fully opened as Coach Kelly firmly said, "Catherine, don't put through any more calls from…" Coach stopped speaking when he saw me staring at him. "David," he said a bit too loudly. "I didn't know you were here already."

I always thought it was weird to see Coach during the school day because he wore dress pants and a button-up shirt, as opposed to the T-shirts and sweats during practice. "I got a pass from you." I held up the little piece of paper.

"Yes, I know." Coach always seemed uncomfortable in his "Assistant Athletic Director" clothes. He undid the top button of his shirt as if it were strangling him. He tried to pull up his sleeves but must have forgotten that they were buttoned at the cuff. "Umm, come in. Come in."

Coach Kelly ushered me into his office and made sure to close the door behind him before striding slowly to his desk. Since his belly was on the large side, he couldn't push his chair in all the way. Many of the guys on the team ribbed him about it sometimes, asking him about his due date, and he always took it well, saying how he'd name the baby after anyone who hit for the cycle.

That Coach Kelly was not the Coach Kelly sitting before me. The one who just folded his hands and strained a smile. "I see you've been putting in some time in the weight room for the preseason conditioning. Glad someone is taking advantage of this time."

"Yeah. Mike's been there too." I wished he would just say that I didn't have a future so I could go back to playing with the cars in physics.

"Good." Coach nodded. "He's going to do great things this season."

"Is something the matter, Coach? Is everything okay?" I figured I could be the one to move the conversation along, letting Coach know it was okay to just say it.

Coach rested his hands on his belly and moved them around in order to find a comfortable place. If Mike were there, he would have whispered to me that Coach was trying to feel the baby kick. "Me? I'm fine. I'm doing fine." The nodding turned into a slight rocking. "How are you?"

"Uh, I'm doing pretty good. Excited for the season." Actually, I felt like I was either going to throw up or cry. I'd end up embarrassed either way.

"Good, good." Coach continued to rock as I squirmed in a brown plastic chair. It would have been impossible to get comfortable in it regardless of the conversation.

Behind Coach Kelly's desk hung a series of photos of all the baseball teams he had coached during his time at Lincoln. The most recent two photos featured me front and center. I hit my growth spurt later than the rest of the guys and was a little on the short side, so I had to sit or kneel in the front row of team photos. In Little League photos, Mike often posed in the front with me, each of us holding a bat or a glove and ball. By high school, Mike moved on to one of the middle rows.

"David, I have to talk to you about something."

This was it. No college. Dreams shattered. Was it too late to start researching other options? A lot of people hadn't made a final decision yet, right? "I know, Coach. I-"

"Now, I am not sure how to bring this up." Coach tried to shift in his chair but got stuck by the armrests on either side of him. "You got a big season coming up and I know how much you need to focus on that."

Big season? Maybe my last season. "Yeah. I'm waiting to hear-"

"What I'm trying to say is," Coach plowed on, "there's no easy way to say this."

If Coach would just shut up for a fucking second I could tell him to save his breath. "You don't have to," I tried to cut in. "I'll just-"

"So, I'm just going to say it."

"No need, Coach. College-"

"David," Coach sucked in a breath through his teeth, "are you a homosexual?"

Wait. What?

I couldn't breathe. It felt like someone punched me in the chest. Was I having a heart attack? Did kids my age have heart attacks?

Tension didn't spread from my shoulders, it instantly consumed my whole body and twisted every muscle. "What?" I had heard the question and didn't need a repeat but I asked anyway.

"I didn't want to ask, and I wouldn't have." Coach Kelly shifted again in his chair, not finding any spare room. "But I've been getting these calls from some parents who don't want their kids to play ball with a queer."

I winced when Coach said that word. It sounded different when he said it.

My tongue was stuck to the roof of my mouth. Parents? No one knew except for my family, Tyler, and Tyler's parents.

"I told them I would ask so we could just forget about the whole thing, so that's what I'm doing." Coach Kelly's neck was red despite undoing the top button. Plus, for being a big man, Coach didn't really sweat off the ball field, but now little droplets clung to his forehead.

"Parents are calling you?" I stuttered on the "p."

"Well, I guess a parent is more accurate. I know it's crazy, son." Coach shook his head at me like I was a T-ball player who didn't get to play the position he wanted. "It's Kaminski's dad. You know how he is." I knew what Coach was talking about. Everyone knew what Coach was talking about.

Kevin's dad had been a member of the school board for the past six years, starting when Kevin's older brother was a sophomore. He was the reason why money was set aside for new dugouts last year and why we were able to go to a tournament in Florida two years ago. However, he was also part of the reason why *Catcher in the Rye* couldn't be taught anymore. Apparently it wasn't a baseball story, just the ramblings of a drunk kid who couldn't stop swearing.

"I know uh, he has an opinion about a lot of things." This was not the way it was supposed to be, with Kevin's dumb ass dad forcing me to talk to Coach about this. I was supposed to be in physics, with the matchbox cars, waiting to see my boyfriend who no one knew about, at the end of the day.

Glancing back at the wall of team photos, I noticed that even when we were kids, Kevin usually got to stand in the center of the back row, the place where everyone immediately looked. He wore the expression that most guys have in any sort of sports photo: slightly looking down at the camera with the head tilted back, mouth in a firm line, like it would be totally wussy to even think about smiling.

Shit.

Shit. Shit. Shit.

I could tell Coach Kelly was expecting an immediate denial and that maybe the two of us would have a laugh because Scott Kaminski was being his usual stupid self. Now it was turning into a very uncomfortable conversation for both of us.

Hell, I didn't really want to have the conversation with anyone… yet. It was something I was still getting used to myself. All I had to do was get through the rest of senior year by glancing at Tyler in the hallways during school, and then giving him rides home after workouts and practices.

I liked the fact we had a secret. I liked our rides home and weekend nights, most of which were spent in Tyler's bedroom because he had a TV and no little brother to share a room with. It was our safe world, just the two of us.

When Mike had asked me if I would take his girlfriend's friend to the Homecoming dance, I had lied, saying my cousin was getting married that weekend. Instead, me and Tyler watched the Steve Prefontaine movie, *Without Limits*, and *The Natural*. We both fell asleep during *Field of Dreams*. The last scene I remembered watching was when Moonlight Graham stepped onto the field to take his only at-bat in the big leagues.

"I told him I'm sure it's not true and there must be some sort of misunderstanding." Coach jolted me out of Tyler's bedroom and back into the stiff plastic chair in the athletic office. "Kevin says he saw you with someone from the track team, in your car, and you were…" His neck got redder as he dropped his eyes.

Were what? Watching a pile of slush spray my car? There was no way he could have seen Tyler lean into my lap. And even if he did, that didn't automatically mean anything except that asshole sprayed shit all over my car.

Coach Kelly continued, almost talking to himself. "You know, maybe Kaminski's just seeing things. We all know he likes the spotlight and can be a little dramatic. Remember that time last season when he cried about having to carry the bat bag and the helmet bag?" He chuckled slightly and tried to loosen his collar by moving his neck around.

That was ridiculous and funny. I tried to force my mouth to smile but I still couldn't move.

"His bad eyes are no reason for his dad to cause a ruckus, right?" Coach sounded like he thought the conversation had come to an end.

Lying would be easy. All I had to say was, "right" but the words were clogged in my throat. All I had to do was simply nod, but I couldn't bring myself to do that either. I felt like I was back on the bench press, struggling with a lift that was too heavy and threatening to crush me, only this time Mike wasn't there to spot me.

Coach Kelly blinked a few times, waiting for my response. "I know he can be a lot to handle sometimes but Kaminski is one hell of a ball player. He's our ace pitcher with a curve that has gotten better in the off season. Did you know he led the team in RBI's last season?" Coach might as well have been talking to a new assistant coach. And I did know about the RBI stat. Everyone knew. "And you," Coach pointed at me with his whole hand. "You are one of the fastest players I've ever had. You can get to anything on the ground hit your way."

"Thanks, Coach," I said, unsure if I was being paid a compliment or not.

"Here's the thing. We have the chance to go far this year. Really far. I'm talking all the way to State."

I was able to nod. "I know."

"I need everyone on this team to be able to…focus. Completely." Coach looked at me like he expected an answer.

"Uh huh." That was all I could manage. Coach was doing a great job of dragging this out.

"Yep, that's what we need," Coach nodded firmly. "Focus. Complete focus." It was like he just revealed a secret play.

"Okay." Was he going to keep me here until I gave him the answer he thought he was going to get?

"We can't be…distracted. By anything off the field or anyone on the field." Coach said. He was looking over my head. It was like he was talking to himself. "There's a lot of players on the team and I can't have one of them being distracted by someone else. That could pose a big problem."

I sat upright, bashing my heel into one of the chair legs. "You're saying I can't play?" I wasn't sure if that was what Coach meant by his sudden concern about someone lacking focus but that was what it sounded like to me. Kevin. His dad. All that crap. The thought of not being able to play never crossed my mind.

"No, no. Of course not." Coach Kelly held up his hands as if to prove he was unarmed. "No, I'm not saying that at all. I'm just saying that, there's, uh, there seems to be a lot going on. I just need to know that you're going to be able to focus on the game."

I wondered if I was the first gay guy that Coach had ever encountered. Probably not. Just the first that he knew of. He was talking to me like he didn't know about the three successful seasons I'd already had at Lincoln. "I've played on varsity for two years already, Coach. You know I'm focused."

"I'm just thinking about all you have riding on this season. Between all this and college. Do you know where you're going yet?"

I glanced to the side of Coach Kelly's head, seeing a pile of basketball uniforms that were probably turned in the week before. "Not yet. Still waiting." It was too much to think about at one time. I didn't want to have a college talk and this talk mixed into one.

Coach sighed. "I was hoping I'd be able to tell Scott Kaminski he was getting all worked up about nothing. As usual." Coach's eyes darted to me as his expression changed. "Not that this is something. Or anything. I just thought I'd be able to tell Kaminski his son must be mistaken."

My gaze went back to the gray, slushy track as I imagined Tyler in his hat with the little puffball and wind burned cheeks rounding the corner and approaching the straightaway.

"I know." Those two words scraped my throat. I did know that was what Coach wanted to do. He'd probably come across dozens of gay people, he just never knew it before.

"Maybe that's what I should do." Coach's tone wasn't menacing. His voice went up a little at the end, like he was asking my opinion about whether or not to change the time of practice or cancel a game due to rain. "If you think that's an option."

I tried to come up with something to say but my brain couldn't communicate with my mouth. I just shrugged and shook my head. A cross between "I don't know" and "no."

Coach looked at the phone on his desk like he expected it to ring at any second. "I'd like to say he's going to shut up about all this after today," he said, "but we both know that won't happen." He narrowed his eyes to the wall and muttered, "One more season of his shit. I swear."

I wasn't sure if he meant for me to hear or knew that I did. I had one more season of this shit too.

Coach moved the phone a few centimeters away as if that would protect him from it. "Well, I guess you should go back to class. Physics is an important class." He shifted some papers around on his desk. "I hope to continue to see you at Open Gym. Add some weight next time."

I rose from the chair, feeling as if I had been sitting for the past eight hours instead of just a few minutes. I didn't know where this left everything but didn't want to sit in that chair for a second longer. I left without saying anything. Even though I knew it wasn't a heart attack, I still felt like someone was jumping on my chest.

As I made sure the office door latched closed, the clacking of the secretary's keyboard stopped. "I don't mean to be so forward," she said. "I'm sorry."

I turned to her. "Are you talking to me?"

"Yes," she offered another sympathetic, motherly smile. She really did look like she was sorry for the way Coach Kelly ambushed me. "Here." She handed me a pamphlet. I glanced down at it to see

Support and
Acceptance for
Freedom of
Expression

Each line a different color ink: blue, green, yellow, and red.

"Maybe you'd like to talk to them," Mrs. Carlson said. She was just trying to be nice, even supportive, and I really did feel like I should have been grateful for that since it wasn't clear if Coach was on my side or not. Instead, I crumpled the pamphlet into a little ball and flicked my wrist so it landed in a nearby wastebasket. "Nope."

CHAPTER 4
DAVID

The paralysis that left me stupid in Coach Kelly's office disappeared when I entered a hallway filling with students as the bell rang to signal the end of the period. Even though I'd never been one to throw a punch, not even when this asshole slid into me with his spikes up last year, I felt like I was going to hit the first person that looked at me in any way, friendly or not. For everyone's safety, I ducked into a bathroom.

I threw myself into the last stall and climbed on top of the toilet into a squatting position so no one would see my feet, burrowing my head into my hands. Damn this school for not putting fucking doors on the stalls in the boys' bathroom.

I hid in the stall until the bell ricocheted in the close quarters of the bathroom, louder in the small, empty space than in a full classroom. With the bell still ringing in my ears, my feet took me to the cafeteria where hundreds of conversations finally drowned out the noise in my head. That was all it was: noise. Like the static when the TV's not working. As I waited for my turkey sandwich in the deli line, a list of commands separated themselves from the cafeteria buzz:

1. Ditch Pre-calculus.
2. Go to the library.
3. Find Tyler.
4. Talk to him.

I set the flimsy paper plate on the ledge by the cashier so I could take my lunch card out of my wallet. A piece of orange plastic with my name and picture on it and a series of x's crisscrossed the other side of the card, one for each day that I received a free lunch. Mom had applied for it a year after Dad lost his job. The first few times I had to dig it out, I felt self-conscious, like the lunch lady was judging me. That feeling was magnified by a million today.

"You can get chips with the sandwich." The lunch lady smiled at me from under her hairnet and tan visor. "Don't you want chips?" She indicated to the display near the register.

"No, I'm fine." I managed to keep the edge out of my voice as I took the card from her hand and slipped it back into my wallet. I spotted Mike at our usual table, consuming almost half a piece of pizza in one bite and skimming a thin packet of paper. Just for a second, I debated whether or not to sit down, feeling like Mike would just know everything by looking at me. Know that Coach talked to me. Know that I had been keeping a huge secret from my best friend.

The debate ended quickly. If I decided not to sit with Mike, he'd ask why. Creating a simple lie seemed too complicated so I stepped towards the table with a shake of my head and shoulders like I was about to step into the batter's box.

"What are you working on?" I sat down like it was any other day.

Mike's eyes remained on the packet as he scrawled some words. "I totally forgot this debate paper was due today. They always seem to come up on me." Mike devoured the rest of his pizza, leaving behind a bit of crust. "We talk about the topic in class. We watch a news story about it. And I always forget to write the fucking thing."

"What's this one about?" I had government last semester and knew Mr. Ritter assigned several debates during the semester.

"This one is about health care. Privatized or government-run." Mike moved on to a boat of French fries drowning in barbeque sauce. "I got government-run."

I focused on tearing the corner of a mustard packet and creating an abstract painting on the layer of turkey. It would have been so easy to keep talking about Mike's homework or that afternoon's workout, but

I sensed an opportunity. Maybe this was a sign. "Hey, did you do the paper about the baker and the wedding yet?"

"The guy who didn't want to bake a cake for two dudes getting married?" Mike asked, wiping his hands on a crumpled napkin before turning a page in the packet.

I nodded, certain my voice would shake if I talked.

"Yeah, that was the first one. I got the freedom of religion side."

"I got the other side." I searched Mike's face or posture for something that would indicate he had made a connection between the paper topic and that I was the one who asked about it.

Nothing. Mike just stuffed the last of his fries in his mouth and gulped a nuclear colored drink.

During the debate in my class, three students ignored the actual topic and used their time as a platform for why guys marrying guys and girls marrying girls shouldn't be able to marry in the first place. As the students talked about that being the real problem, my heart literally hurt. Not the same as when I was having a heart attack in Coach's office. More heavy than hurt. I had never thought about whether or not I wanted to marry Tyler or if he wanted to marry me but I knew I wanted to be a dad and teach my kid to play catch. Mr. Ritter had to bang his little gavel on his desk and remind the students of the topic and the two sides of the debate.

Since I had already brought it up and Mike seemed distracted by the paper he needed to write, I decided to press forward. "What do you think about that?" I treaded carefully, as if stepping on to a frozen lake when my dad took me ice fishing once.

"About what? The guy and his stupid cake?"

I nodded again, almost swallowing a piece of my sandwich without totally chewing it.

Mike shrugged. "He makes cakes. Just make the fucking cake." He might as well have been asked if he thought putting ketchup on a hot dog was blasphemous.

"Really?" I leaned forward so quickly, I knocked the table, causing Mike to scribble down the margin of his paper. "So you're not all freaked out about two guys getting married?"

"Yeah, I really don't care. What someone does in their house is none of my business. Just don't involve me in it." Mike went back to his paper.

"What do you mean by that?"

"I guess as long as I don't have to see it, then I don't care."

"What if I were gay?" I don't know how Mike heard me above all the noise in the cafeteria.

Mike's pen stopped in mid-word. He slowly turned his head like a robot. "But you're not."

My heart beat in my ears. "Okay, not me. What about someone on the team?"

"What? Like Kevin?" Mike smirked.

"Anybody." I kind of had my answer but I wanted a real one. A firm one. One that would tell me Kevin and his dad were bigger assholes than we thought.

"Honestly, David, I'd rather not know. If you know something, keep it to yourself. Let me finish this, okay? I'm almost done." He tossed the empty boat of fries and crumpled napkins into a garbage can before turning the page in his notebook and giving me my answer.

My effort to blend in with the crowd of students entering the library failed. Students were supposed to sign in and present their ID to the student working behind the check-in desk during that given period. With only four other students waiting to get into the library, it was impossible to sneak in. Since it was a month into the semester so the student worker and the librarian probably had a good idea who the regulars were and who was ditching class.

I stood on one side of the library's sensor that tattled on students attempting to take something without checking it out. If I even stepped near it, I had a feeling it would siren, complete with flashing red lights, blaring to the entire school that I was somewhere I wasn't supposed to be.

"Do you want to check in?" the girl behind the counter asked. I'd never seen her before. She had pretty eyes and a soft voice, with brown hair that was really short and almost buzzed at the back and sides, but a little longer on top. She wore gray skinny jeans and a plaid shirt with a T-shirt of some band I never heard of. A bunch of other kids wore the exact same thing only they had different band shirts on. I usually stuck with jeans and a hooded sweatshirt in cold weather and jeans and some sort of baseball T-shirt in warmer weather.

"Uh, yes," I blurted. "I mean no." I took a step back from the telltale sensor when the librarian glanced over her shoulder at me.

"That doesn't really answer my question." The girl smiled.

I leaned on the counter that separated us and whispered, "I need to talk to someone."

"Who?"

"Someone. Please."

She surveyed the library. Students playing games on computers. Students typing papers. Students sitting in front of a stack of books, playing on their phones. Groups scattered about at tables, socializing rather than studying and having a hard time keeping their voices at a whisper. Her gaze lingered in the back corner of the library. Without looking at me, she picked up the scanner used to register IDs. With a pull of the trigger, a hairline of red swept the empty counter.

"You're all set to go," she said to the books piled in the 'return' bin.

"What?" I asked, not catching on immediately.

She picked up the small stack of books. "Have a nice day." The girl walked the books over to a pushcart a few feet away.

The sensor didn't acknowledge me as I stepped over it like dog shit on the sidewalk. Since Tyler actually used his study hall to study, I knew he spent the time at a table by himself in the back of the library in the non-fiction section. No one ever went there unless their teachers insisted they use an actual print source and not only rely on the library's database of online articles for research. I took a quick detour past the magazine rack and scanned the titles without reading them and then picked a paperback book off a rack that spun. If the girl at the desk was still watching me, I didn't want her to see where I was headed.

And then I saw Tyler hunched over a thick textbook at a secluded table in between two bookcases. One held ancient encyclopedias courtesy of a variety of publishing houses and the other stored two copies of every yearbook printed since Lincoln High School opened in 1973. Tyler had one hand ready to turn the page while the other quickly scrawled something in a spiral notebook. Even though I couldn't see his face, everything stopped for a couple seconds as I imagined him chewing on the inside of his lower lip. I remembered when I pointed it out to Tyler one time, he said he didn't know he did that when he was really focused.

I suddenly realized I didn't know what I expected Tyler to say or do. He had been so understanding and good to me since the beginning, allowing me to come by his locker before school like we were two friends simply hanging out before first period. Holding my hand on the center console of the car. Waiting to kiss me until we got to one of our houses. We never really lied to anyone, it's just that no one ever came out and asked, "Is he your boyfriend? Are you dating him?"

Even though most of my weekends were spent with Tyler, sometimes I hung out with Mike or some guys on the team. When the conversation would turn to girls and Mike would complain about how Carrie gave him a hard time for spending so much time with the guys or somebody else would talk about a girl and how her clothes hugged her body in a way that caused all of them to stare, they'd ask me which girl he was into. Who did I think was cute? It wasn't lying to say, "I'm not really into anyone right now."

Just because I didn't want to lie didn't mean I was ready to make an announcement over the school's PA system either.

I slinked into a seat across from Tyler. "Hey, what are you doing here?" he whispered, smiling in surprise. "I told you during second period that I don't need a ride home tonight, right? Late practice because the wrestling team needs the space after school?"

"Yeah, you told me already." I fidgeted, wondering if all the chairs in the school were always this uncomfortable.

We didn't plan on taking Art Appreciation together but were excited when we compared schedules the week before school started. I wasn't really into art but did appreciate the excellent view I got of the back of Tyler's head everyday because I sat two rows behind and one over from him.

"So, what's going on? You want to talk some more about hidden messages in The Mona Lisa because I think that little grin means she might have had a thing for girls or knew some secrets about Da Vinci." He softly laughed but quickly stopped when I didn't hint at a smile. I wished we were back in Art, talking about Da Vinci conspiracy theories before physics and everything in my world was normal.

"Coach called me out of class to ask me if I'm gay."

"What?"

"It was Kevin Kaminski." My stomach flipped the way it did when I saw a set of spikes coming toward my face during that game. "He saw us together. He told his dad. His dad told Coach. Coach asked me if I'm gay." Short sentences were easier because I was breathing like I had just completed the running regimen Coach made use do when we committed errors. Maybe I was hyperventilating.

"Slow down. He saw us?" Tyler looked like I just spoke to him in a foreign language.

I just shrugged, not sure what to say next because I didn't know anything else.

"But where? How? How would he know?" Tyler didn't wait for me to answer. "I don't understand how he would know."

"I don't either. He sees you in my car and that automatically means something to him?" For the first time since my conversation with Coach Kelly, I really thought about it. What the hell did Kevin see?

"Well, what did you say?" Tyler's voice calmed a little as he inched his foot forward so the toes of our shoes touched, my scuffed gym shoes against Tyler's black canvas shoes with red laces, the closest we'd ever come to being public about our relationship. Even though several layers of leather and cotton separated our feet under the table, it felt like we were on Tyler's bed with our arms and legs wrapped around each other.

"Nothing. Which is probably an answer all on its own." I wiped the back of my neck with a clammy palm and gave Tyler a quick summary of my conversation with Coach. Or rather, the one-sided conversation.

"That's crazy," Tyler sighed. "Sounds like he just wanted you to deny it so it would go away."

I looked away from Tyler. "He said some shit about me being

distracted by the guys on the team. Like I wouldn't be able too…" It was too embarrassing to say it out loud. "Like maybe he might have a reason to cut me this year." My voice cracked and I couldn't believe that out of everything that happened today, the thought of not playing baseball was what was going to make me fall apart. I covered the toe of Tyler's shoe with mine.

"What are you going to do?"

"What would you do?" I curled my fingers into a fist, pretending they were wrapped around Tyler's hand.

"I would tell Kevin Kaminski to fuck himself." His pale skin pinked with each word. "The queers are here. Get used to it."

"I've already thought about that." I said, grateful to have Tyler and that he didn't mind ducking into corners of the library, surrounded by dusty books that no one cared about.

"I can't believe this is happening at our school." Tyler hung his head and held it in his hands.

"Why?" I asked, talking to Tyler in a way I never had before. "Because we don't hear about little faggots getting beat up on their way home from school or walking in the hallway?" Tyler winced. "Because everything is just fucking perfect?"

"I don't think everything is fine. But I did feel like things are better now than they were when I first moved here," Tyler said calmly and quietly.

"Is that because of fucking SAFE?" My voice actually rose as I thought about the naïve secretary who thought all of my problems would go away if I joined the other gays in their gay club.

"Hey, this is a library." A voice came from between the encyclopedia shelves.

I felt like I was holding my face over a burner. Anger mixed with embarrassment. I looked in the direction of the voice and saw the student worker with the skinny jeans and short hair organizing the magazine rack. We made eye contact for a split second before I looked away.

"Keep it down, will you? People are trying to talk over there." She gestured to the tables where a bunch of people sat and walked off. I heard the smile in her voice but that didn't make the heat subside.

"Just because you call it 'safe,' doesn't mean it is," I whispered to Tyler as loudly as I could.

Instead of touching my hand, Tyler traced the outline with the tip of a pen. "Where do you feel unsafe?"

A montage of moments flickered in my memory: Kevin's love for the word "fag" and all its forms. The football meatheads saying "no homo" as they patted each other's asses, assuring one another the gesture was purely platonic, and miming anal sex to those who didn't say it fast enough. The two girls who wanted to go to the Homecoming dance together last year and were sold two single tickets instead of a double. Students during the debate in Mr. Ritter's class insisting that there was something wrong with people who felt the same way as I did.

Mike telling me he'd rather not know.

"Kids at other schools have it way worse," Tyler pointed out. "I'm not saying that to make you feel better or that what you're saying isn't true. Sometimes it just sucks."

"Here, it's like this unspoken thing, but it's there."

"Sometimes you think you're safe some place and you find out you're not the hard way." Tyler stood and ran a hand across the encyclopedia bindings as if they were piano keys. "A lot of teachers don't stop the students from saying a homework assignment is gay. Sometimes they say it too." He wiped dust on his jeans. "But not Ms. Larson. She actually tells kids to find another word to use."

"I had her for biology my freshmen year. We need more people like her." The anger in my throat was starting to subside and now I just felt tired. Had I really talked to Coach only a couple hours ago?

While stacking his textbook, notebooks, and binder, Tyler brushed his hand over my clenched fists. "We just need each other."

Going to the weight room was the last thing I wanted to do after school. Well, going home was also near the bottom of my list. I didn't want to see my parents yet. But Mike was expecting to see me there and right now, my short-term plan was to pretend that I never had that meeting with Coach, which was probably his strategy as well. Talking to Tyler and just being with him made me feel better but that didn't mean I knew what was going to happen next or if I even wanted to know.

The door to the weight room felt extra heavy and I needed to give it a hard yank because it got caught on the corner of a mat. The room smelled like the door hadn't been opened in a year and the stale stench immediately made me feel like I was going to throw up. Mike appeared to be oblivious to the odor as he slid weights on the bar for the bench press. "I was thinking we should add some weight. What do you say?" he asked.

"I don't think I can do this," I said, lying back on the bench.

"Give it a try." Mike gripped the bar, ready to help me guide it out.

I immediately felt the added weight. As I slowly lowered the bar, the heaviness spread from my biceps to my shoulders and chest.

CHAPTER 5
TYLER

I hadn't felt like every whisper in the hallway was about me in a long time. When I first moved here it was ridiculous. It was like some of these people thought gay people only existed on TV.

"Did you hear?"

"Fag alert."

"I change in the bathroom during PE now."

"I would too."

I knew I wasn't the first openly gay student to walk the halls of Lincoln High. And there was Adam, SAFE's president. He came out a little before I did. The worst was when we were walking down the hall together.

"Are they going out?"

"Probably. They're both gay."

"Homo squared."

"If one of them hits on me, I swear…"

The hallway was nearly empty as I scanned the contents of my locker, looking for my copy of *The Grapes of Wrath*. When I found the book and saw the cover with an old jalopy puttering down a dusty road, the memory of a run at dusk on a limestone path crashed into my head and then hit me between my shoulder blades. It began to throb at the memory of feet slapping on the path in an uneven rhythm and the sound of villainous laughter assailed my ears. I slammed my locker and stood up in one motion.

The noise shook the memory out of my head but must have triggered something inside of me. My feet carried me to room 1335 as if it was something I did every day after school instead of regularly during my sophomore and junior year.

The way I marched right up to the door made me think I would have simply gone right in but instead, I peeked through the narrow vertical window at the side of the door. A smile filled my chest at the familiar sight of a small group of students pulling desks into a lopsided circle. They always added too many so some had to be taken away. Adam, dressed in his uniform of a collared shirt and sweater vest, stood at the board, writing an agenda. Each item was written in a different color, as was tradition. It was business as usual and the group carried on regardless of how many people were present or whatever was going on outside this classroom's walls.

Ms. Larson stood at the opposite side of the room cleaning up from the day's science experiment, putting away beakers and Bunsen burners. When she turned to grab a stack of rulers, her eyes meandered to the door and she did a double take before waving me into the room with an excited smile. I took a step back and waved my hands in front of me, hoping to convey, "I'm not sure." I guess I just wanted to see room 1335 and the people in it, not actually go inside.

But Ms. Larson didn't appear to understand my message. Her wheat colored ponytail bounced from shoulder to shoulder as she walked toward me. "Hey guys, look who's here." Ms. Larson opened the door but I waved at the small group from the hallway.

"Tyler! I haven't seen you in forever!" Anna, a junior who wore something rainbow inspired every day, leapt off a desk she was sitting on and threw her arms around me as if I was a long-lost sister.

"Hi," I said, stiffening in Anna's overzealous embrace.

"Look what I made for everyone." She held up her arm, proudly displaying a black wristband with a rainbow knitted into it. I noticed her shoes also had rainbow laces. Because of her affinity for all of the colors, many students at Lincoln constantly asked Anna if she was a dyke. Anna usually responded by either saying, "You wish," if a girl asked or "Sometimes I wish I was," if a guy did.

"Nice job." I smiled. It was hard to stay upset around her.

"I would have brought more if I knew you were coming but you haven't been to a meeting in forever." Anna walked back to the desk she was sitting on and hopped on it.

I took a tentative step over the classroom's threshold, like walking through the door was committing to something, and I wasn't even sure what I was doing there. I didn't recognize the other students in the room. A small boy with a swoosh of dark hair in his eyes, two girls, one little and blonde, the other tall and dark, and the girl from the library.

Adam turned from the whiteboard, leaving the final agenda item unfinished so that it read "Gay pro."

Anna laughed. "Are you a professional gay, Adam?"

"I've been practicing for a while now." Adam scrawled an orange "m." He turned back to me. "Hey," he said. His eyes looked welcoming, but I could tell there was a question lingering in them. Adam had asked me a couple times why I stopped coming to SAFE meetings and I just blew him off, saying that I was busy training or something like that when I actually wanted to spend any minute outside of school with David, but I couldn't tell Adam that. I doubt he would have told anyone if I did, but still.

"Oh, 'gay prom'." Anna exaggerated the "m" sound. "Now, I get it. Is Lake Park hosting one again this year? We need to go because my mom wouldn't let me go last year." She looked at Mrs. Larson.

"I got an email from their GSA sponsor and I'll share all the details when we get there." Ms. Larson wheeled her desk chair into a vacant spot in the circle. "Let's start with introductions so everyone knows who everyone is."

"Good idea. Tyler doesn't know everyone and they might not know him," Anna said. "I'll start. I'm Anna and I'm a junior." She pointed both index fingers to the boy next to her.

"Uh, hi. I'm Will and I'm a freshman." He paused and tossed his head so that the hair on his forehead revealed his eyes for less than a second. "Do I have to say anything else?"

"If you want to," Ms. Larson said.

"I'm good." Will settled back into his chair.

"I'm Stacey and I'm a junior," said the blonde girl.

"I'm Monika and I'm a junior too," said the one next to her.

"Allie. Senior." The girl with short hair waved with a small flick of her wrist. "Library ID scanner."

"A senior?" I asked. "I've never seen you around before this year."

"Yeah, I moved here at the beginning of the year."

Anna leaned forward. "At Allie's old school, the GSA had like twenty members and they held an event once a month during lunch hours to talk to people about LGBT issues. Isn't that awesome?"

"Pretty awesome," I nodded, trying to imagine how a LGBT panel would be received at Lincoln. I pictured Anna behind a table with all of her rainbow creations, a smile on her face like a little kid who started her first lemonade stand. And then Kevin Kaminski invaded, leading a pack of students and calling Anna a dyke before ripping down the rainbow SAFE sign that hung in front of the table.

"And you all know me. I'm Adam and I'm a senior." Adam turned to read the agenda he'd written on the board. "Well, the Day of Silence is coming up in a couple months and we need to plan how we are going to get the word out this year and encourage people to participate. Plus, we need to plan something better for 'breaking the silence.' Allie was saying that her old school had a pizza party afterwards."

"Add Tyler to the agenda so we make sure to have time for him to tell us why he's here." Anna smiled at me. "You've been gone all year so something major must be going on."

I knew this was common practice at SAFE meetings and not Anna being nosy, which she was sometimes. If someone had something they wanted to share, their name would be added to the agenda. Sometimes Anna would bring up the hate speech she heard the football coach telling the players. Or, when he first came out to his parents, Adam shared how they kept asking him if he was sure.

With a shrug, Adam wrote my name on the board with a purple marker. "Okay, about the Day of Silence. Do we have the cards from last year that we had students show their teachers?"

Ms. Larson nodded. "I have the files from last year. I'll make sure to print out copies in time."

I tuned out the other points of discussion regarding the Day of Silence, remembering how I participated my sophomore year. I was out and everyone knew it, but all I accomplished was giving this idiot from my Geometry class a reason to jump in front of me at any given chance, wave his arms in a bad impersonation of a ghost and howl, "Oooo, look at me. I'm a fag and I can't talk. Oooo."

But there were some who asked why people weren't talking and when they glanced at the card that explained the cause, they smiled, said, "Cool." A couple even said they were going to participate next year.

"Okay Tyler, you have the floor." Anna interrupted my thoughts.

"No, that's okay." I waved my hands in front of me like I didn't want a ball thrown at me. "I just thought I'd come by to see how everyone was doing. I have track late today since the wrestling team had a couple guys advance to State and they need the space to practice."

"So you're just killing time with us?" Anna bit her lip and wiped a fake tear from her eye.

"No. I wanted to…uh," I searched for the right words. "I just wanted to make sure you guys were still here."

Adam looked confused. "Of course we're still here." He began erasing the board in lopsided swipes so little specks of marker remained. "Same time, same place."

"I know." I curled my toes inside my shoes, imagining David's foot touching mine, just like we did in the library. "It's just that something happened today and I needed to remind myself that SAFE existed. I needed to know that some people in this school are different and not everyone sucks."

"If you're looking for different, I'd say you came to the right place," Ms. Larson laughed.

"What happened today?" Will asked, swooshing his hair off his eyes with a toss of his head.

Monika put a hand on Will's desk and looked at him like she was his mother. "You know he doesn't have to tell us if he doesn't want to, Will."

Will folded his arms and slouched. "I know."

Anna leaned as far forward as she could without falling off her desk. "But, you know you can. If you want to. Nothing leaves this room."

I knew that and other people had shared stuff way more intense than what was on my mind. "I'm just worried about my…" I didn't know if I should say it. If I did, they'd want to know who I was talking about. And what about David? I started to feel that even being here was some sort of violation of his trust. But he was in this position because we kept everything a secret. "My boyfriend," I finally said. The feeling surprised me. That cheesy one that fills your chest when you think of your boyfriend after only going out for a couple weeks. I'd never said the word "boyfriend" out loud at school before. I don't think I'd even whispered it to David in the halls.

"You have a boyfriend?" Stacey asked, twirling her hair around a finger. "How long have you guys been together?"

"Uh, about six months." No need to give the exact date, time, and location of when we made it official.

"That's a long time," Monika commented.

"What's wrong with him?" Anna got the conversation back on track. Of course.

I could feel Ms. Larson's concerned eyes on me. Eyes I was very familiar with from my year and a half as a consistent and loyal SAFE member. "He's worried…" I chose my words carefully. "Someone made him feel like he can't be some place because he's gay." So vague and not even completely true.

"Like church?" Stacey asked.

"Nobody likes going to church," Will scoffed.

"Some people do," Allie said.

"What is it?" Anna pressed.

"I…I don't think I want to say." More questions meant more details. "He doesn't know I'm here and he's not out to that many people."

"So he goes to Lincoln?" Anna asked.

"Yeah," I said without thinking.

"This sounds like something that happened at my old school." Allie unknowingly rescued me. "This guy's dad made him quit the show choir because he thought the whole group was made up of gay guys."

"How ignorant," Anna said.

"What's a show choir?" Will asked.

"We have one here," Anna said. "Adam's in it."

"That I am." Adam nodded.

"Cool," Will said.

"Wait a second." Monika put down the phone she had been glancing at all meeting. "You said no one knows he's gay?"

"Some people know," I clarified. "His family and stuff."

"No one here?" Monika asked.

My silence was enough of an answer.

"Wow," Anna said to herself.

"If I couldn't kiss my boyfriend at lunch everyday, I would die," Stacey said. "Or dump him."

That pierced me in a way I didn't expect. "It's okay," I said.

"It's not as easy as that you guys." Allie looked at each person in the circle.

"Who is it?" Anna asked.

"Anna." Adam got his point across with a glare.

"Sorry, really. I'm curious." Anna meekly ducked her head.

I wanted to say his name. Because I should be able to, especially to this group of people, but I couldn't. I couldn't do that to David. I told him it would be fine. I thought I would be fine.

Ms. Larson looked at the clock ticking towards 4:00. "Why don't we call it there, guys? I have a meeting tonight so I can't stick around like I usually do."

"But what about Tyler and his problem?" Anna asked.

"Tyler," Ms. Larson turned to me, "you know our door is always open. Come back and see us again."

"I'll try," I said, knowing this would be my last SAFE meeting. With the outdoor season starting up, I wouldn't be able to come even if I wanted to.

Adam swung his messenger bag over his shoulder. "We'll get the details about the prom at Lake Park next week. The dance isn't for another couple months anyway." He turned to me before walking out. "See you around." He held out his hand and as we shook we clapped each other on the back.

Stacey and Monika waved as they walked out of the room connected to the same phone by sharing earbuds. Will and Anna put the desks back in their rows. They bundled themselves up in puffy jackets before leaving. "Tell the track team to have a late practice again next week," Anna tugged a knitted hat on her head.

"I really don't have a say in things like that," I said.

"Bye." Will followed Anna out of the room.

When the door latched behind Will, Ms. Larson stopped moving piles of paper around on her desk. "I'm glad you stuck around."

"I don't know how to help him," I said, surprised by the prickly sensation in my eyes. I turned my head and blinked a few times.

"Is your friend in danger?" Ms. Larson asked. She walked around to the front of her desk and leaned against it, half sitting.

"No," I said.

"Is a student doing something to him?"

Ms. Larson had a way of asking people questions that inevitably led them to share what they needed to share. Despite knowing this, I didn't move or make up an excuse to leave. "Kind of," I shrugged.

"Is it in one of your friend's classes? Does the teacher know?"

"No and kind of." Another shrug.

"Do you want me to talk to the teacher?"

"No and kind of." I felt a corner of my mouth smile.

Ms. Larson smiled too and put a hand on my shoulder. "You know where to find me. Or, maybe your friend would like to come to one of our meetings. I know Anna is a bit much sometimes, but maybe it would help him to talk about it and see that there are people in this school who support him."

I imagined David coming to a SAFE meeting with Anna pouncing on him as he walked through the door and shoving one of her rainbow wristbands up his arm. Would Will be in awe of the varsity baseball player in his presence or care less? Did Stacey and Monika know who he was? What would Allie think of him? Adam had several classes with David over the years but knew nothing about us being together. "That's probably not going to happen, but thanks for hanging around for a little bit. I know you have to get to your meeting."

Ms. Larson smiled and walked back behind her desk. "Oh, there's no meeting. Sometimes I just have to move things along." She sat down and uncapped the green pen she often used for grading. "Come see us again, Tyler."

"Thanks, Ms. Larson," I said as I gathered my book bag and jacket, feeling a little lighter than when I first approached room 1335. But back in the hallway with the door closed behind me, the heaviness instantly returned. Kevin Kaminski sauntered towards me from the far end hallway. Even though he couldn't see me, I had a feeling he was on his way to the locker room so I fought the urge to throw one of my spikes at him and decided to walk through the library and cafeteria, taking the long way instead and I hated myself for that.

CHAPTER 6
DAVID

One of my elbows locked while the other one gave out as if the bone suddenly disappeared. "Jesus Christ, David." Mike scrambled to lift the side of the bar that was no longer supported by my arm, but my rib cage. The bar fell back into its slots with a loud clang that echoed in the almost empty weight room. No gymnastics team today. And no Kevin either, yet.

"I'm sorry." I sat up, rubbing my side. "Maybe I'm sore or something."

Mike gave me a questioning look from under the brim of his cap. "Let's move on to free weights. Maybe that will be safer."

"Sounds good." I stood up, walking over to the free weights with an extra bounce in my step to prove to Mike I was fine.

"Is that one going to be too heavy?" Mike raised his eyebrows at my fifteen-pound weight.

"Asshole," I laughed as Mike grabbed a twenty-pound weight. We began doing a regimen that would work out the individual muscles in our arms. I tried to focus on the repetitive motion of my raised arm bending at the elbow and going up and down behind my head, imagining how this would add speed to my throw and snap to my bat.

Up, down, up, down. Exhale, inhale, exhale, inhale.

The sound of the heavy door scraping against the floor caused my stomach to churn and I tasted the remnants of a partially digested turkey sandwich. My shoulders and neck felt like a four -hundred- pound fat kid had just sat on them to play a game of chicken.

Another one of the football regulars strode across the room to join two of his friends who were doing squats. They managed to jam backwards baseball caps on their square heads, and each had on a homemade muscle shirt made from the PE uniform we had two years ago. They cut so much of the shirt off that it looked more like a wrestling singlet. One of the guys positioned himself behind the one that was doing squats. Each time the guy lifting squatted, so would the one behind him and he would do an exaggerated thrusting motion, complete with sound effects.

"Yeah, that's good. Do it again." The thrusting guy fed off the laughter of his friends.

"Cut it out, man," the guy doing the lifts said, trying to give the thruster a look but he had a hard time since the bar was resting on his neck.

Why the fuck did I come today? My arm shook even though I was only halfway through the regimen. Fuck it.

"Where you going?" Mike asked as I picked up my sweatshirt and flung it over my shoulder.

"I gotta go," I said.

"What?" Mike dropped his weight and followed me to the door. "Seriously?"

"Yeah, I…" A simple lie wouldn't form as I reached for the weight room door, but it opened before I touched it.

Kevin barged in and stopped when he saw me. He squinted his eyes and pretended to look through a pair of binoculars. "David, is that you? Or am I just seeing things?" He adjusted the imaginary binoculars. "Nope. I think it's pretty clear."

"Oh good," Mike sighed. "You're here again."

My legs wanted to run out of the weight room while my fists clenched, ready to punch that stupid smirk off Kevin's face. Instead, I just stood there.

"Of course I am." Kevin nodded his head back at Patrick, our catcher, who walked in behind him. "I'm going to try and get Fatty here back in shape."

"You didn't get me here," Patrick shook his head. "We just walked in at the same time." He always insisted he was "husky" not fat, and that the extra girth allowed him to block more of the plate. "Besides, I think a couple more pizzas would really give us an advantage. The super-supreme kind. Think of how much of the plate I could block with this." He turned to the side and puffed out his gut as much as possible so that it looked like his baby might be due shortly after Coach Kelly's.

Mike laughed while I couldn't force a smile on my face. My brain told my legs to move but they wouldn't.

"If you get too fat, Sinni's not going to want you anymore," Kevin smirked. "And I don't know where you go after a community college turns you down."

"Shut up, Mr. Illini," Patrick said. "We all can't be as awesome as you." He picked up a medicine ball and began to do a twisting exercise with it. "Gotta work the core for all the homeruns I'm gonna hit."

As Kevin turned to me, I finally got my legs moving somehow. "David, maybe you'd like to help Patrick with those balls."

"He seems to be doing fine on his own," I said, shoving my way past him.

When I got home, I realized I was alone and hoped no one else would be home for a while. My dad started doing some basement remodel so that should keep him busy. This was the last job that Dad had lined up and he was hoping it would turn into a referral to do another basement. Everyone in our family always knew when Dad was working, when he wasn't, and when he was waiting for something to come along.

I guessed my mom was at work. She was a caregiver at a nearby nursing home and had been picking up any hours she could.

My brother, Robert, had his first travel ball practice today. From the way he talked about this team, anyone would have thought Robert was the one just awarded a much-needed scholarship instead of getting the honor of paying hundreds of dollars to play for a team. My parents said Robert could only play for a travel team if he somehow paid for it himself so he sold a ridiculous number of chocolate bars to my friends and Mom's coworkers and mowed anyone's lawn who would pay him to do it.

Even though I hadn't eaten anything except half of the turkey sandwich at lunch, I felt full. Like I had made a meal out of all of the nerves and they were sitting in my stomach like old pizza for breakfast.

The muffled opening notes of "Thunderstruck" by AC/DC came from my backpack and I had to dig my phone out of the small pocket where I kept extra pens, pencils, and a protractor I hadn't used since geometry my sophomore year. It was a text from Mike.

What happened 2 u?

I fell into one of the chairs at the kitchen table. *Had 2 go. Sry.*

More notes from "Thunderstruck." *Y? You left me alone with Kevin!*

It was amazing what kind of debate you could have in your mind in the nanosecond it should take to answer a friend's question. If we were actually on the phone there would have been a weird silence but I couldn't ignore the question for long. I felt like I was in one of those old cartoons when a character has a devil and an angel on each shoulder, only I had Ballsy David and Cowardly David. Ballsy David sat with a stern look and folded arms, wanting me to spill everything about Kevin and his dad to Mike. To not be afraid of what might happen if he did and just do it already. Cowardly David sat at the edge of my shoulder, sheepishly looking at me in quick backward glances. He thought it would be best to pretend my phone ran out of battery so I could put off Mike's question for a few hours, at least. Ballsy David demanded I text, "I'm gay god dammit!" Cowardly David suggested throwing my phone in the garbage.

Another buzz from AC/DC. *He went on and on about baseball camp at U of I. Sounds gay, right?*

That stung more than it usually did. I picked up my phone. *Lots of hw. Essay due 2morrow.* A lame excuse, I know, but it was all I had.

Hw?!?! We're seniors!

I was a senior who had no idea what his future looked like when I got up in the morning and now the picture was looking even more blurry. *No colleges pounding on my door. Still gotta study.*

Adding weight next time 2 make up 4 your lame ass. U gonna make it?

Might have an extra credit physics lab.

Mike responded with an emoji that looked like it was throwing up.

It was funny. I even smiled for a second.

I sat with the phone in my hands, dwelling on the workout in the weight room I cut short. It wasn't like I'd be able to leave practice if Kevin continued to be even more of an ass than he already was.

He wasn't going to keep his mouth shut for an entire season and just let this go away because I didn't give Coach a straight answer to his question. Literally. Kevin's under-the-breath comments would first come out of the corner of his mouth, when only I was in earshot. Then, he would be packing up his equipment with Patrick, notice me doing the same outside the dugout and comment on how the team we just played were a bunch of fags. "Let's ask David what he thinks. He's an expert."

A drop of water fell on the kitchen table and I looked up at the ceiling to see if there was a leak somewhere but there didn't seem to be anything out of the ordinary. A typical white ceiling. No signs of water damage, leaks, or cracks. Another drop fell on the table and started to merge with the other one, looking like a diagram from biology class for the stages of mitosis. When I inhaled through my nose, it sounded like I had a cold and that was when I realized I was crying. Seriously, I was crying? I had held it together with Coach, with Mike in the cafeteria, with Tyler in the library, even with that dickface Kevin.

Scraping the chair back, I swiped the tears off the table and pawed at my face, trying to prevent more from coming. I stomped around the kitchen, opening cabinets only to slam them shut. My dad made them so they were definitely strong enough to survive. I kicked the wall with a socked foot and immediately felt my big toe pulsate with pain. "What the fuck is wrong with you?" I drew my leg back, getting reading to kick the wall again, leading with my throbbing big toe, not caring what kind of damage I did.

"David!"

My mom dropped the bag of groceries in her arms. The only sound came from the short hiccups of breath that made my chest hurt. Her eyes looked so sad. Cowardly David and Ballsy David went at it again. "Tell her you got a bad grade on a test," Cowardly David advised. "You're going to go crazy if you try to keep this up," Ballsy

David warned, trying to swat Cowardly David off my shoulder. "You already are."

"What's wrong? What's going on?" My mom sounded like she was about to cry.

"Nothing," I hiccupped. "Everything's fine."

"That's not true," Mom said as she walked towards me like she was afraid I was going to break into a billion pieces right in front of her.

I backed into the countertop on the opposite side of the small kitchen and put my weight on the foot without the throbbing toe. Little rings of color faded in and out of my vision as I rubbed my eyes.

"Please talk to me, David." My mom sat down in her usual seat at the dinner table. Worry deepened the slight creases on her forehead.

I limped past her and out of the kitchen. "I'm just mad, that's all." I grumbled like I had just gotten called out on a close play because of a blind umpire.

"What are you mad about?" Mom called but she didn't follow me.

"Just some stuff." My voice was louder and angrier than I intended as I closed the bedroom door and slumped next to the stack of college materials I began piling on the floor between my and Robert's bed. The first arrived in the middle of my junior year.

I heard footsteps shuffle through the thick carpeting in the hallway. "I have to go pick up Robert."

I didn't say anything. She wasn't making any noise, but I could tell Mom still stood on the other side of the door. "We'll talk when I get back," she said. It was more of a question than a statement. Her voice went up at the end of the sentence.

A few seconds later, I heard the front door open and close followed by the slamming of the van door. I balled up my fists and rubbed my eyes with my knuckles. Maybe if I rubbed hard enough, I wouldn't think about how I couldn't stay in my room forever and that Ballsy David was shaking his head at Cowardly David who seemed very pleased with himself.

CHAPTER 7
DAVID

The letter I received the other day from Sinni seemed to be making fun of me, with its crinkled corner of plain paper standing out among the glossy brochures. That was all I needed in addition to all the other shit that happened today was for my mom or dad to somehow find that letter and declare it was what we've been waiting for. It was probably sent to every athlete. Even though the letter actually had my name at the top instead of "Dear Student," it wasn't anything special. It simply asked if I had ever considered becoming a CNEI Bobcat and if I was aware that they offered athletic scholarships in addition to academic ones.

No, I wasn't aware. And no, I never considered becoming a Bobcat.

I turned my head to the left and settled in on the poster of the 2005 White Sox team that hung on the wall between the two beds. It was taken on the field after they had won the World Series and everyone looked like this was the happiest moment of their entire lives. My baseball days hadn't even begun at that time but my dad loved to remind me how he and I watched every game together. Whenever a game went into extra innings, he'd remind my mom how he had to beg her to let me stay up to watch one of the World Series games that went into extra innings. I didn't make it past the top of the tenth.

With the throbbing in my toe subsiding but the image of my mom's sad and confused face fresh in my mind, I imagined a different sort of press conference taking place after the locker room was hosed down with champagne. Would that season have been any less incredible if one of the guys on that team were gay? Would the fans say it didn't matter that they went 11-1 in the postseason because it was a gay guy who made a diving catch or scored a game-changing run?

It would be on the front page of the sports section for a few days and a topic of conversation on ESPN's various shows, but no one was going to take away a World Series ring or say the team didn't deserve it, right? When an NFL player came out after he had left the game, it was all anyone could talk about. Commentators expressed concern about the future of the league and the game itself if a gay guy was the one doing the tackling or putting his arms around a teammate in a huddle. Somehow, groups of fans still gathered around the television every Sunday during the fall and winter for a marathon day of games. Apparently, a few years ago a top draft pick came out and coaches did say his sexuality would have nothing to do with them picking him for a team or not.

But I wasn't a top prospect in the NFL draft and I didn't have a World Series ring, and definitely never would. I'd never have to worry about major league locker rooms, but there were still high school ones, and hopefully college ones, to navigate.

I heard the front door open and my dad exhale a groan as he dragged his steel-toed booted feet through the door. Two grunts and two thuds followed, one for each boot being pulled off and dropped on the floor.

"David?" Dad called.

For a second, I thought my dad might think I wasn't home from school yet if I sat very still and held my breath. But then I remembered my car was parked on the driveway.

Dad's sweaty feet streaked across the kitchen floor and stopped in front of my closed bedroom door. "David?"

"I'm writing a paper, Dad." My voice sounded like I had just woken up.

"Good job." A few moments later, the shower turned on. In a few minutes, I knew Dad would emerge in his post-work uniform: a pair of sweats and a White Sox T-shirt, probably one commemorating the 2005 season. They were faded and stretched out but he still wore them.

The usual sounds of an evening in my house sounded different from behind a closed door. The stove clicking on. Pots being taken out of the cabinet. Water coming from the sink. It had been about ten hours since Coach called me to his office. About eight hours since I talked to Tyler and about forty-five minutes since I lost it in front of my mom.

"Where's David?" I heard Mom ask Dad when she and Robert came home.

I kind of woke up when I heard her voice, like I had fallen asleep with my eyes open or been in some sort of trance from still staring at the White Sox poster.

"Writing a paper in his room."

"Did you talk to him?"

"Not really."

"How did he sound?"

"Like he was writing a paper."

I imagined my mom holding her hair in a ponytail. I was familiar with "the ponytail hold" as if her long hair in her face prevented her from thinking clearly. "He was a wreck when I came home earlier."

I rolled my eyes at Mom for exaggerating. I should have gone into my room when I got home.

"What? What's going on with him?" Dad asked.

"I don't know. He wouldn't tell me anything. He just went to his room."

Heavy footsteps got louder as they made their way from the kitchen to my door. "David?" A firm knock on the door. "What's going on?"

"Nothing is going on." I didn't even sound believable.

"Can we come in?" Mom asked.

A third set of feet came down the hallway and stopped in front of the door. It had to be Robert. "I told you Stevie said his dad said something was wrong with David." Stevie was Kevin's little brother and somehow, Robert's best friend.

The rage that boiled over earlier in the kitchen returned without notice. I sprung up from the floor and flung open the bedroom door. "What did you say?"

Robert backed up and looked like he was being held up against the wall even though I was still standing in the bedroom with my hand gripping the doorknob. I hadn't yelled at Robert, really yelled at him, since he called the White Sox a bunch of fags for having a really shitty season last year. "Stevie heard his dad talking."

"About what?" I yelled.

My parents looked at Robert, waiting for his answer, more interested in what Robert had to say than the fact I was shouting at him. Robert just shrugged and looked nervous. "I don't know. He just heard his dad say something about how you might not be able to play baseball this year. But I told Stevie there was nothing wrong with you and that you're fine."

"You're not playing?" Dad asked. "What's he talking about?"

"Go ask Kevin and his stupid fucking dad." There had been many close calls, but this was the first f-bomb I ever dropped in front of my parents.

"David!" My mom's mouth dropped.

"You wanna know what's wrong?" I looked from Mom to Dad. "Coach Kelly wanted to talk to me today."

The concern on my parents' faces was replaced with confusion.

"Hey, David,'" I said in a bad impersonation of Coach. "Are you a fag? Just asking 'cuz Kevin's dad wanted me to, so…"

I didn't know what my parents' faces looked like because I turned and sat on the bed with my back turned to them. My chest hurt like I just did a bunch of wind sprints.

My mom came in and sat down at the end of the bed. "That happened today?"

Dad crossed the threshold. "David, you're going to have to back up a little bit." He sat down on Robert's bed, which was parallel to mine so it was impossible not to look at him.

Robert stayed in the hallway, cowering into the wall.

Just like I did with Tyler in the library earlier that day, I gave my parents the short version of what Coach said to me. His dad's knees bounced up and down, the speed increasing as the story progressed. "That prick!" He finally exploded. "That fucking prick!"

"Greg!" My mom used the same tone she did when telling Robert or me to watch our language. "That is not going to help anything."

He stomped out of my room, almost running into Robert. "I am going to call that asshole right now. No, I am going to go to his fucking house." I heard Dad pacing through the kitchen and family room causing a shelf of trophies to rattle. "You think you don't want your son to play ball with mine. Well, fuck you buddy. I never wanted my son to play ball with yours."

It felt good that Dad was saying all the things I wanted to. Mom must have been thinking the same thing, which is why she stayed on the bed, not trying to calm him down.

"The thing is, there is something wrong with your son." The shaking trophies meant Dad was still doing laps around the kitchen and family room. "He's a goddamn fucking asshole, just like his dad."

Mom shook her head before resting it in her hands. "We'll just let him finish." She squeezed my shoulder so hard it kind of hurt. I'd seen Dad pissed: when he lost his job, when Robert broke a power tool he needed for a side job that day, when I skipped school because Tyler was home sick. But I'd never seen him completely lose it before.

The trophies stopped rattling, and we could no longer hear any heavy pacing doing laps through the house. Since Robert was still glued to the hallway wall, my mom looked at him with a question mark in her eyes. He looked to his side and said, "He's sitting on the couch."

"I'll go talk to him." She took a couple of deep breaths, like she was giving herself a pep talk.

I slightly turned my head, looking at Robert out of the corner of my eye. "Are you going to stay out there all night?" I asked, attempting to let him know I wasn't mad at him. Robert was just a messenger who didn't know he was carrying a message.

Robert pushed himself off the wall, but didn't take a step forward. "I thought Stevie was talking about when you sprained your wrist."

"My wrist is fine."

Robert slid into the room but still stood by the door. "Stevie's not like Kevin or his dad."

"Not yet," I said.

CHAPTER 8
TYLER

Late practice meant I had to wait for my mom to pick me up. I sat on a parking block hugging my knees wondering what David was doing at this exact moment. I often wondered that, but it was more than usual today. I missed my hand off in the relay and Coach made us do it three more times before he was satisfied.

I reached into my bag and took out my phone, scrolling through David and my text conversations. He needed time. I knew that. Sometimes, it was worse when people bothered you with phone calls, texts, or whatever to offer bullshit, regurgitated advice.

My mom tried that night. She kept asking questions, but not the right ones. The ones that allowed her to linger on the porch for too long.

I had sat hunched on the stoop, thinking my parents might go to bed soon and I could sneak upstairs and wake up tomorrow, not remembering anything about that day. It was late, but not that late. Too late for a run down the path in the forest preserve.

"How far did you make it?" she asked when she came outside.

"Not too far." I couldn't look at her. The scrapes on my shins and knees started to burn like someone poured peroxide on them.

The silence was too long. She had to know something was up by the way she kept asking questions.

"You can try again some other time, right?"

"Don't you think it's still so hot out?"

"Are you going to sit out here all night?"

"Are you okay?" she finally asked after a series of one-word answers.

"Fine," I said.

David didn't need me to pretend like I had the right words to say and knew the right questions to ask. Not only did I not have anything profound to say, the only thing I had was something I didn't think David was ready to hear. When we first officially got together I had told him we could take things as slow as he wanted.

I thought about Stacey at the SAFE meeting, saying she'd die if she couldn't kiss her boyfriend at lunch. A kiss at lunch was impossible, mainly because David and I didn't have the same lunch period. But a kiss at my locker in the mornings would be nice.

Better than nice. Absolutely amazing.

If anybody did or said anything, at least we would have been together.

CHAPTER 9
DAVID

When my alarm went off the next morning, I felt like I had closed my eyes only a few moments before even though I went to bed early. Robert grunted, as he did every morning. "Turn it off," he mumbled over the sound of a tornado test siren.

My hand fished its way out of the mass of blankets and jutted out into the cold hanging in the dark room and slapped the snooze button. It took me a second to remember why I woke up with my stomach feeling like I was in the middle of a rollercoaster ride, one with a series of hills so the feeling kept repeating itself. Coach folding his hands and resting them on his desk. Kevin's shit-eating grin. My mom coming home. My dad yelling. The toe of Tyler's shoe touching mine. We only needed each other.

The tornado siren ripped through the room again. Before Robert could grunt, I switched off the alarm and threw the blankets off, all the way to foot of the bed so it wouldn't be so easy to scramble to cover myself back up.

The only reason I even thought about going to school was to see Tyler. The possibility of staying home crossed my mind. My parents would probably let me. Mike would applaud a ditch day after my lame excuse to leave the weight room. But, I was upright, almost shivering in an old umpiring T-shirt and flannel pants. It was the first step.

I got dressed in the dark, as I did every morning. It was easier than listening to Robert complain. If he didn't get to sleep in for his extra twenty minutes he grumbled about hating to share a room and how unfair life was. I groped through the clothes hanging in the closet, and sifted through the hangers until I felt what must have been my favorite black hoodie with a White Sox logo that filled the front. It was easy to tell because the stitching was coming undone at one of the cuffs and the frayed ends of the hood strings. Plus, this hood felt thicker than the others. I grabbed the top pair of jeans from a nearby dresser drawer and managed to pull them on as I walked out of the bedroom.

The smell of coffee hung in the air already. Dad was probably working his way through the pot. He always drank a large mug before leaving the house and filled a huge travel mug for later. Mom preferred tea and the kettle was just starting to whistle as I walked into kitchen.

It took me a second to notice my parents seated at the kitchen table since the only light came from the barely rising sun and the weak light above the stove. They looked like they spent most of the night sitting across from one another. Dad with his hands wrapped around a mug like he was trying to warm himself by a small fire, and Mom with her hair in a lazy ponytail, hugging a purple robe around her. Their hushed conversation stopped when they saw me. It was pointless to ask what they were talking about so I went to the freezer to dig out a box of frozen waffles. I put two in the toaster and stood in front of it, watching the insides gradually glow orange. It felt like being up to bat in the bottom of the ninth with two outs feeling every eye in the stands staring at the name and number on your back.

I heard a chair smoothly slide across the floor. My mom poured water into her mug just centimeters from me but didn't say anything. Then, she knocked on the bedroom door. "Ten more minutes." Her voice sounded scratchy, like she was coming down with a cold.

"Twenty." Robert's muffled reply.

The waffles sprang up a perfect golden brown, and the inside wires gradually lost their orange glow and returned to gray. I pinched the edge of the waffles and dropped them on a plate so I could lather them up with super crunchy peanut butter and stick them together to make an extra thick waffle sandwich. Still standing in front of the toaster with my back to the kitchen table, I took a bite and focused on chewing.

Then Dad stood right behind me, filling his travel mug. He put a hand on my shoulder. "Are you okay?"

I looked at him for the first time that morning. My dad dropped his hand from my shoulder like it stung him. "Sorry. Stupid question," he said, taking a long sip despite the swirls of steam. "Your mom and I were thinking of talking to your coach today."

I struggled to quickly chew what was in my mouth and swallow. "You don't need to do that."

"I think we do."

"No, Dad, you don't," I insisted. "If Coach does find some stupid reason to keep me from playing you can do whatever you want to him. I think he's just never met someone who's gay before. You should have seen the look on his face." I recalled how Coach wriggled in his chair, completely taken by surprise.

"What about Asshole and Asshole Junior?"

"You think the whole school knows, Dad?" I asked, ignoring Dad's question and imagining walking into school with everyone really looking at me instead of me just thinking their eyes were pointed in my direction. "I'm not ready for the whole school to know." I'd already told the people I wanted to and started to get pissed all over again that Kevin thought it was something he could blab about to his dad. I didn't tell the whole school when Mike told me he started going out with Carrie.

"No, David," Dad said. "I don't think the whole school knows."

He sounded so certain, I couldn't help but believe him.

Tyler's locker was in the middle of the sophomore hallway because he came to Lincoln High School in the middle of freshmen year and whoever registered him stuck him in the wrong hallway by mistake. Last year, he was embarrassed, being a junior in the freshmen hallway. This year he didn't care because it meant I could drop by his locker almost whenever I wanted to. None of the sophomores would notice two people who never spoke to one another in the two and a half years they had been in high school together were suddenly spending many passing periods at one another's side.

I kept my gaze focused on the figure at the end of the hallway that wore a pair of gray jeans and black and red striped sweater. Tyler pulled the knit hat with the puffball off his head, and some strands of golden hair stayed standing up even after he put the hat in his locker. "Hi," I said.

"David." He looked me over as if my clothes would somehow indicate how I was doing but it was the same thing I wore almost every day. "Are you okay?"

I shrugged because I honestly didn't know if I was okay or not.

Tyler reached out to me but quickly balled his fist and put it stiffly at his side. "I really want to hug you right now." The fist at his side tightened. "I want you to know how much I'm here for you."

"I know you are." I wanted to hug Tyler too, and if we were in my car or in Tyler's bedroom I'd have no problem, but I already felt like there was a spotlight on me.

I looked around at the hallway traffic of sophomores lugging full backpacks, unwrapping scarves, taking off hats, stuffing coats into lockers. No one paid any attention to the misplaced senior boy and the other boy at his locker. We looked at each other for so long that all the hallway traffic seemed to disappear. I tried to telepathically tell Tyler how much I appreciated him and all he had done for me.

"Do you have practice after school?" I asked.

Tyler nodded. "Just a light workout since we're in between the indoor and outdoor season."

I nodded. "I forgot. You told me that already."

"Are you going to open gym?"

I shook my head. "The weight room isn't open today."

"Oh yeah. I forgot."

"That's okay." I wanted to hit myself in the back of the head. It felt like the conversations we would have through the chain-link fence that surrounded the track before Tyler finally asked me for a ride home one day and our arms touched when we both rested them on the center console.

A bell rang, informing everyone that we had five minutes before first period started. I hadn't been to my locker yet and still wore my heavy coat and carried a bag full of books I didn't open the night before. "I'll see you second period."

"I like to call it 'our place,'" Tyler said, hinting at a smile.

"Our place," I said to myself, feeling a smile in my chest. "I thought you just liked looking at all the pictures."

"Pieces. They're pieces of art," Tyler mimicked our teacher. "I mostly try to look at you."

I gave Tyler a mental hug, hoping he could feel it. Despite the second hand ticking around the clock, I didn't make a move toward my locker.

"I don't know what's going to happen next, David, but it always seems messy at first." Tyler closed his locker and slid a bag over his shoulder. "Well I don't know if it is always messy but from personal experience and from what I've heard, messy is the norm."

"I've never liked messes," I said. "Ask Robert about how I nag him about his side of the room."

True, the words in front of me were written in a foreign language, but I'd been taking Spanish for five years now and the dialogue for a fake travel show really should have been easier to memorize. All I had to do was recite the lines, listen to everyone else recite theirs, and then loiter at the side of the gym while everyone else in my class took the annual PE Dodge Ball Tournament very seriously. It would be the easiest part of my day, pretending like I was about to throw someone out when, dammit, I got hit in the leg with a ball and would have to wait on the sidelines until a teammate caught a ball, giving me permission to rejoin the game. Hopefully there'd be lots of butterfingers today.

Everything else about this day had been hard.

I was able to avoid Mike during lunch because I really did have to work on that essay for *1984* since I didn't do anything for it the night before. I got my usual turkey sandwich and stopped at the table to tell Mike I was going to the library.

Mike had been intently punching buttons on his graphing calculator. "I decided that I'm not going to do trig homework at home anymore. I'm going to get done what I can at lunch and if I finish, I finish."

He put the calculator down to write something down. "If I don't, I don't. I really don't think I am ever going to use this stuff anyway." He managed to gnaw on a pizza crust while working on a problem.

"I was going to the library anyway," I said, balancing my sandwich and a drink in addition to his books. "I'm stuck on this paper."

Mike nodded knowingly and swallowed. "I told you, man. We're seniors. We're going to be out of here before you know it. Once the season starts, it's going to go so fast."

"Uh huh," I said, setting down my drink so I could eat my sandwich standing up.

Mike picked up his second slice of pizza and was about to take a bite when he paused, his nose centimeters from a string of melted cheese. "You know, there might not even be time for homework then." He shrugged. "I'll write the papers and study for tests, but homework? We'll see." With that, half the slice was gone.

"But we're not there yet. So, yeah, this paper." I nodded a good-bye to Mike and left the cafeteria.

"Smooth sailing in just a couple weeks, my friend," Mike crumpled up the large napkin he was using as a plate and tossed it into a nearby garbage can. He gave himself a congratulatory smile before returning to his work.

At the library, I settled into a chair at an empty computer at the end of a long row, which meant there was a wall to my left and thankfully, an empty seat to my right. I managed to type my name, the date, and class period and come up with the title *1984 Essay* that I centered at the top of the page. After thumbing through the book a few times, not really looking for the part when Winston finds out who O'Brien really is, I absently searched online and began half reading baseball news sites. First looking to see if the White Sox had made any moves with spring training starting up. No new news since I last checked a couple days ago. Then, I searched for MSU Mankato and navigated my way to the site for the baseball team. I scrolled through team photos and action shots of guys sliding safely into home or making a diving catch.

I continued to click through the pictures even though I was no longer looking at them. As the impressive plays flickered by, I couldn't believe I was so sure it would be easy to make it through senior year with a secret boyfriend. It seemed so stupid now that I said it to myself. A secret boyfriend. Shit, I sounded like some seventh grade girl. This was high school. Things never stay secret forever. I should consider it a miracle that no one knew about me and Tyler after being together for over six months. Even so, I wasn't ready for this.

And in Spanish, I wasn't ready to recite my travelogue when my teacher called me to the front of the classroom. With one last useless glance at the paper, I slid out of the desk.

"Whenever you're ready," Señora Fannin smiled at me with a nod of her head.

"Uh," I cleared my throat. "Hola. Bienvenido…" A knock on the door and the door opening interrupted me.

A cheerleader-type girl bounced into the room with a long ponytail swinging from side to side. "Here you go." She handed Señora Fannin a couple small pieces of paper.

"Gracias," she said, glancing at slips of paper as the girl bobbed out of the room. She waved one at me. "Señor David Lukas, you have been saved by a pass."

"Seriously?" Relief washed over me as I went to retrieve the pass, but it was quickly replaced by anxiety as I remembered yesterday and the last time a pass called me out of class. Odd how many times in the last twenty-four hours I had completely forgotten about being in Coach Kelly's office.

I didn't look at the pass until I was in the hallway and stood outside the door for a moment remembering when I was a freshman and got jealous of the kids who got a small break from class when a little piece of paper told them to go somewhere. I always wondered why no one ever called me out of class. This time, the pass told me to go to a small alcove of a classroom in the library. I didn't even know that students were allowed in those rooms. Most of the time they were dark and empty. Only on a few occasions did I see a small group of teachers gathered in there, looking like a cluster of students working on a project for a class. I thought about not going, not having any idea who would be waiting for me in that tiny room and why they wanted to meet me there.

Maybe it was just something counselors and deans did for seniors as they began the home stretch of their final semester of high school. That had to be it.

"You're here again," said the girl behind the library check-in desk. The same one from yesterday, only today she wore black skinny jeans and a button-up shirt the color of grape juice.

"So are you," I said.

The girl shrugged. "I have a couple free periods during the day. I'd rather hang out here than in the cafeteria."

I showed her the pass and handed her my ID, for real this time, so that my whereabouts could be properly registered in the computer. "Oh yeah, Ms. Larson is in there waiting for you." She pointed to the back corner of the library on the opposite side of the non-fiction section.

"Ms. Larson?" I asked, sliding my ID back into my wallet. "I haven't talked to her since freshman year." While I headed toward the designated corner of the library, I tried to connect the dots between Ms. Larson and me, coming up with nothing. I had her for biology, got B's both semesters, and hadn't really seen her since.

I approached the door and saw her sitting at the table. She didn't have anything with her. No paper, grade book, not even anything to write with. "Hi, Ms. Larson," I said, opening the door.

I recognized her welcoming smile from the first day of school my freshmen year. It was the same one she gave me whenever we crossed paths in the halls. "David, hi. You knew it was me waiting in here for you?"

"Yeah, the girl working at the desk told me you were waiting for me."

"Allie gave me away, huh?" Ms. Larson motioned to the empty seat around the corner from where she sat.

"Allie? I didn't know her name," I said, sitting down in the chair Ms. Larson had indicated. "So what's going on?" I showed Ms. Larson the pass I just received.

"Don't you just love a mystery?" Ms. Larson smiled.

I shifted in the plastic chair, making it squeak. "Not lately."

Ms. Larson folded her hands on the table and leaned in my direction. The playful smile disappeared and was replaced by soft eyes and a concerned mouth, just like Mrs. Carlson from Coach Kelly's office. "David, a concerned person at this school asked me to speak with you."

With that sentence, I made the connection, pushing my chair back and standing up. The plastic chair fell over and hit the wall behind me. "You're in charge of that group." I looked down at Ms. Larson. What the fuck?

"I am," she calmly said.

"So why are you talking to me?" The room was already small and I felt like it was getting smaller.

"Because someone asked me to."

"Who talked to you?" I continued using an accusatory tone. And then made another connection. "It was Tyler wasn't it?"

"Tyler?" Ms. Larson asked, her head cocked to the side.

"I know you know who he is." I had never talked to a teacher like this. I rarely talked to teachers, period, and now they all want to discuss my personal business with me.

Ms. Larson's eyes widened. "You're Tyler's boyfriend?"

On the field, I was known for keeping it together. If I made an error, I could shake it off and turn a double play without missing a step. If I struck out on a bad call, I didn't take it with me on the field. Any evidence of the calm and collected David was not there in the tiny library room with Ms. Larson. "How could he tell you?" Luckily the thick door and brick walls of the library suffocated my words.

Ms. Larson stood up but stayed on her side of the table. "Tyler didn't tell me anything."

"Then who did?"

She regained her composure. "Someone who is concerned about you."

"No one knows there's anything to be concerned about besides Tyler and Coach Kelly and I know he didn't talk to you."

"I just wanted to make sure you knew that there are people in this building you can turn to if you feel like you need a safe place," Ms. Larson said.

Safe. There was that word again.

I wasn't looking at Ms. Larson or even really listening to her. I was looking at the woven threads of library carpeting, a tangle of black, gray, and white. Tyler told Ms. Larson. Tyler told Ms. Larson. Tyler told Ms. Larson. It wasn't that she knew. It was that Tyler told.

The bell rang, signaling the end of the seventh period. I shoved my chair under the table. "I have to get to my next class."

"I do too." Ms. Larson slowly pushed in her chair like it needed to fit into a specific space. "If you ever need to, you can find me in the same classroom."

"I don't want to talk to anyone and I'm sick of people talking to me." I walked the step and a half to the door and flung it open.

I made my way to the boys' locker room with my head down, my feet somehow avoiding a collision with packs of students herding through the hallways. The thought of ditching PE crossed my mind but I was already lucky that my pre-calculus teacher must have not noticed my absence yesterday because there was no call home about it and he didn't say anything in class when he greeted me at the door.

As I tugged on a pair of red shorts and slipped on a gray T-shirt with "Lincoln High School" generically stamped on the front, I tried to imagine the conversation that involved Tyler telling Ms. Larson. Did he plan it? Did he mean to do it?

The second hand on the clock reminded me that I had less than a minute to join my class that was most likely sitting in a semi-circle around the teacher, anxious for the dodge ball tournament to continue. My excitement for the tournament was at a six when it first started and now it was in the negative numbers. The only thing that annoyed me more than Kevin Kaminski were people who took PE games way too seriously. It wasn't like I could count on a college to reward me with a scholarship due to my exceptional dodgeball skills.

CHAPTER 10
TYLER

I've always paid attention in class, never daydreaming or looking out the window. Well, maybe to gauge the weather and see how many layers I'd have to wear to practice that day. The only time I did drift away was last year, the day before the State finals. The bus was leaving at the end of seventh period and I spent my entire English class looking at the minutes change on the digital clock in the corner of the classroom.

But after seeing David again in Art Appreciation in the same White Sox hoodie I'd seen him wear so many times, I spent almost the entire AP Chemistry period thinking about him. Sure, my mind drifted to him throughout the day everyday but never like this. I actually imagined us going to prom together.

Girls were already showing each other pictures of their dream dresses. I'm pretty sure some guys were beginning to plan elaborate, ridiculous ways to ask the girls they already knew would agree to go with them. I never got caught up in it. For one, I never had anyone I wanted to go with.

Two, I always assumed David and I would spend the night in my room. Or maybe a hotel room. I didn't know. We hadn't talked about anything yet.

But it would be incredible to go with him. Sure, the student council wouldn't sell a couple's ticket to those two girls last year. But, just because we bought two single tickets didn't mean we couldn't go together, walk in together, and spend the whole time together.

It would be a lot to put on him. I knew that. So as my teacher droned on about some practice AP test we were going to take at some point next week, I decided that maybe this weekend I would try to convince David that even though Kevin Kaminski was the biggest dick to ever walk the halls of Lincoln High School, maybe his dumb ass actually served a purpose for once.

CHAPTER 11
DAVID

My team was in second place by the end of the period, behind the team that had developed a strategy for double and even triple teaming the opponent so that there was no chance of them catching or dodging the ball. When a small herd congregated and raised their Nerf balls, aiming for me, I let go of the ball I was holding and waited. Less than half a second later one ball hit my chest and two others hit me in the legs. I was more than happy to go to the end of the line of four people waiting to rejoin the game. They crouched on the floor like professional basketball players, anticipating the moment when the ref would call for a substitution. I could barely move to begin with because it felt like I had weights wrapped around my ankles.

After class, I headed toward the sophomore hallway, reaching Tyler's locker just as he was opening it. "Looks like you made it through the day." Tyler smiled as he pulled a duffle bag full of track clothes out of his locker.

"Barely," I stiffly said.

Tyler swapped out a couple textbooks in his bag for some stacked at the bottom of his locker. "I'm sorry if it was tough."

"It was okay," I shrugged. "Until I got another pass in the middle of seventh period."

"What? Another one?" Tyler almost dropped a textbook. "Did your coach talk to you again?"

"Not from Coach," I shook my head and folded my arms. "Ms. Larson. My freshman year biology teacher. Why the fuck would she want to talk to me?"

"Ms. Larson?" Tyler looked like he tasted something that he couldn't quite place the flavor of.

"You know her?" I asked, faking surprise.

"You know I know her," Tyler said. "Why did she want to talk to you?"

"You already know." I knew he was confused and hurt by my tone, but I didn't care. Kevin did what he did because he was a dick. But with Tyler…this was ours. He told me he would never…

"I don't know." Tyler's voice was quiet and it was hard to hear him over the students slamming their lockers and racing down the hallway so they could leave school as quickly as possible. "It's not like she has automatic gay-dar."

"Unless someone tells her," I said. "How could you tell her?"

"I didn't tell her. I didn't." Tyler reached to touch my arm but I took a small step back, just out of his grasp. "I went to the SAFE meeting yesterday because I didn't know where else to go before practice."

"You haven't gone in a while."

Tyler's face relaxed and his eyes smiled. "I don't need to. I have you."

I got that feeling inside of me when we first started going out and I'd see Tyler's name on my phone when it rang. "You didn't tell me you were going," I said quietly.

"I didn't get a chance to and I didn't know I was going to."

The hallway started to empty. The barrage of slamming locker doors were replaced by squeaking sneakers fading down the hallway. A teacher's high heels clacked towards us and then disappeared as she turned a corner that headed towards the staff lounge. We were the only two left. My anger receded from my chest and dropped into the depths of my stomach in a ball of regret mixed with the realization of a new fear. If Tyler didn't tell Ms. Larson someone else did. But until yesterday, no one really seemed to care about me and who I liked.

"Are you there?" Tyler waved a hand in front of my face, giving me a full smile this time.

"Yeah," I said absently. "Just thinking." When I looked at Tyler, I felt like I was seeing him last summer when he was rounding the track and heading towards a straightaway. It was the first time I felt something more than physical attraction and a casual *he's kind of cute*. I wanted to know him. I wanted to be with him. Tyler looked so strong and confident. He still looked strong and confident.

"About what?"

I looked around the hallway. A boy dragged his feet towards us. I kept my eye on the boy's striped hooded sweatshirt, watching him get slowly closer and closer. "About how I wish we weren't at school right now. How I wish you didn't have to go to track. How great it would be if it was last week when it was just you and me in my car and none of this happened." The boy in the striped hoodie was getting closer.

"We could, you know." Tyler hesitated, standing straighter. "Right here. We could. Say fuck 'em."

"I don't know," I said.

"Okay." Tyler looked down.

I wanted to ask Tyler if he was sorry for being with me. If it was too much of a pain in the ass and he wanted to just say fuck it. But I didn't, not only because I was scared of his answer but also that boy was a few steps away. I could tell the hoodie was black with thin turquoise stripes running horizontally across it. He had his hands jammed in the pockets and with each step, the dark swoop of hair over his forehead and eyes bounced up and down. I decided to wait for the boy to pass.

But when he saw Tyler, I noticed the boy's slow gait gained a slight bounce. "Tyler, hi." The boy stopped in front of us.

I had no idea who this kid was, but he acted like he knew Tyler pretty well.

"Hey," Tyler paused, looking the boy and up and down. "Will?"

"Yeah, Will." Will smiled, tossing his head so the swoosh of hair uncovered his eyes for a millisecond. "Are you coming to the next SAFE meeting?"

"Uh, I'm not sure." Tyler glanced at me. "It depends if I have a late track practice or not."

"You should," Will went on. "It was cool to have someone else there."

"It was nice to see Anna and Ms. Larson and everyone," Tyler nodded.

Will stood off to Tyler's side. "Ms. Larson is so awesome," he continued. "I think she's the coolest teacher here."

"She's pretty great," Tyler agreed, glancing at me just in time to see me raise an eyebrow and shake my head. This kid needed to leave.

"Hey, I'm Will." Will turned to me.

"David." My tone did nothing to send him on his way.

"Are you Tyler's boyfriend?"

"What?" I'd never been punched in the face before, but this had to be what it felt like. I even brought my hand to my cheek since it felt like it was throbbing.

Will seemed oblivious. "Tyler told us about you yesterday."

"Will!" Tyler said.

I glared at Tyler as hard as I could but he wouldn't look at me. My calves felt sweaty and my jeans were sticking to them. "I don't know what you're talking about."

"I don't mind if you're gay," Will said to me. "I might be. I don't know yet. But I like going to SAFE."

"I, uh," I stammered. Tyler told Ms. Larson and then lied to me about it. This kid needed to fucking leave now.

"We're going over a project for class, Will," Tyler broke in. "What do you say you let us finish up? I have to get to practice soon."

"No problem." Will took a step back and jammed his hands back in his pockets. "You really should come to another meeting. Think about it."

"Okay," Tyler nodded

He turned to me. "You should come too. Anyone can come."

"I've been hearing a lot about it lately," I said, certain Will didn't pick up on the sarcasm in my voice. "You did tell them," I hissed a whisper at Tyler as soon as Will was out of our peripheral vision.

"I didn't. I swear."

"No? Then what the fuck was that kid talking about?" I'd never talked to Tyler like this before. Our biggest fight to date was when we had a miscommunication about whether or not Tyler had practice after school and I left without realizing he needed a ride. Tyler had to wait almost an hour for his mom to pick him up on her way home from work.

The apologetic tone left Tyler's voice. He spoke evenly and firmly. "I just told them I was worried about my boyfriend. Because I am. I didn't say your name. I didn't say anything about Kevin or your coach or baseball or anything."

"That asshat is going to tell everyone in your group, and they're going to tell everyone in the school." I imagined the news spreading from person to person like a huge game of telephone with everyone lining the hallway with their hands cupped over an ear. "It's pretty obvious that they can't keep their mouths shut."

Tyler took a step forward so that his face was inches from mine but there was nothing affectionate in his face or posture. "I told them what little I did because I needed to tell someone. Because I thought maybe they would understand or that Ms. Larson could help somehow. Maybe if you knew, really knew that not everyone in this school is an asshole you wouldn't go through your day worried that Kevin Kaminski was going to pop out from inside a garbage can and out you to the whole school. Maybe it's finally time for you to do that for yourself."

I slammed Tyler's locker door with such force that the latch didn't catch and it bounced off the frame. I felt like I was standing in the middle of a sauna. Somehow, heat rose from the ground and encircled me. "I can't believe you would say something like that now." The teacher with the loud high heels came back down the hallway, hugging a stack of stapled packets. Her small figure gradually got bigger. I turned back to Tyler. "We can't do this here."

Tyler leaned against his locker like he was waiting at a bus stop. "Why not?" He shrugged. "Someone might hear us? I don't mind. The whole school knows I'm gay."

The heat rising up around me circled my head and I began to feel shaky. I guess I didn't need to ask Tyler any questions about him wanting to be with me. That pretty much said it all. He was right there in front me but couldn't have been further away.

The teacher slowed up as she approached Tyler and me. "Everything okay here, gentlemen?"

"Yup," I said, unable to look at her.

"Fine," Tyler said.

The teacher gave us a long glance before continuing her trek down the hall. "Well, then, get out of here. It's Friday."

Tyler put his duffle bag over one shoulder and his messenger bag over the other. "I have to go. Practice." He shut his locker, staring at me, like he was waiting for me to say something.

I still had my hand on the row of lockers for support. Anything I thought about saying was mean, desperate, or pathetic. "If you have to go."

Tyler nodded. "I do." He turned away from me and quickly walked away.

I kept my eyes on Tyler's black canvas shoes with red laces. The soles of his shoes were red too. I watched the quick flicker of red until Tyler turned down the hallway that led to the boys' locker room. The heat began to subside and dissolve and I was able to take my hand off the lockers.

Good thing it wasn't a weight room day. Mike would have given me shit for being so weak. Plus, I didn't feel like talking to Mike or anyone else. It would be nice for no one to want to talk to me either.

As I trudged to my locker, I kept my eyes on the floor, dragging my feet over scuff marks, trying to erase the black smudges. The flight of stairs felt like the summit of a mountain I should have trained for in order to climb. I went through the school day trying to remember which classes I had homework in. Pre-calculus? Maybe. Physics? The lab report. That English paper that I really did have to write this weekend.

Flurries taunted me as I walked to the car. Any other year, the swirling white dust would have made me antsy. When would the team get to practice outside for the first time? Was the first game going to be cancelled, like it usually was? When would we finally get to play?

I kicked up some loose gravel with the toes of my shoes. The car door creaked open like it would fall off if I closed it too hard. I didn't wait for the vents to blow lukewarm air before I shifted the brown boat into gear and sped out of the parking lot. On the way home, I found myself taking the route to Tyler's house. I almost pulled into the driveway before realizing that Tyler wasn't sitting in the passenger seat, bobbing his head along with the radio so the little puffball attached to his hat danced around.

CHAPTER 12
TYLER

I barreled through the hallway as much as someone lugging a bag of textbooks and another stuffed with practice clothes could barrel. With each step, the corner of one of my books hit me in the leg. That was not how it was supposed to happen. I was supposed to tell David that we could do this together and I would be right here for him. If he wanted to rent a skywriter, I would have given him the money. If he wanted to do it quietly, telling Mike first and whoever else, I would have been by his side. But, that was before he said *I have no idea what you're talking about.*

It stabbed me in a way I wasn't expecting. You'd think I would have been ready for something like that given our in-school charade the last six months. Six months, two weeks, and three days.

And to think I was going to talk to David about prom this weekend.

He couldn't even be honest in an empty hallway. He was going to walk into a room full of people with me? Bullshit.

Taking loud, deep breaths in an effort to calm the volcano that was about to erupt in my chest, I flung open the door that led to the athletic locker rooms and offices. It slammed against the cinderblock wall and closed with a bang that echoed in the rank halls that looked and felt more like a dungeon than an area of a high school devoted to athletics.

As I passed the athletic director's office, I ran right into someone, hard. Our bodies ricocheted off one another. My messenger bag, weighted with books fell into the crook of my elbow and threw me off balance. I stumbled back a few steps in an effort to stay on my feet.

"What the fuck?" the other person yelled as if someone squirted ketchup all over his brand-new shirt.

"Sorry. I wasn't looking where I was going." I managed to regain my balance and swung my arm so the bag repositioned itself on my shoulder.

"Too busy thinking about your boyfriend?"

The volcanic feelings that coursed through me only a moment before were replaced with ice. Kevin Kaminski stood with his arms folded, looking down at me with this twisted smirk. His dirty blonde hair stuck out from a fitted backwards Yankee cap and stuck to his forehead in little points.

Too many people cowered in the presence of him. David among them. I was not going to be one of those people. "Actually, I was. Not that it should matter to you." I stepped to the side to go around him.

Kevin grabbed my arm and pulled me towards him so he could growl in my ear. "Yeah it matters to me when I have to be in the same locker room as someone who likes dick." He glanced at the door to the athletic office and dragged me a few feet down the hallway to a nearby bathroom.

"Get the fuck away from me." I flapped my arm in an effort to loosen Kevin's grip, but it only made him clamp his fingers down harder. For the second time in two days I was thrown back onto that limestone path in the forest preserve going for a run at dusk.

Kevin flung me into the wall. I tried to catch my balance before banging into the blinding white blocks, but my arms were tangled in my bags and I banged my head on the hand dryer. I managed to stay on my feet and rubbed my forehead, trying to extinguish the firecrackers going off behind my eyes.

"If Coach Kelly doesn't think it's appropriate for him to make decisions about his players based on who they like to fuck then I'll say it." Kevin stood over me so it was impossible for me to get around him. "Tell your boyfriend to sit this season out." He sneered and adjusted the backpack on his shoulder, which looked rather empty considering it was the weekend. "Maybe he should go out for the track team. Bunch of fags running in circles so you can check out each other's asses."

Only a couple sparks remained of the fireworks display going off in my head. "I think he would prefer to play baseball." I pushed Kevin off of me.

"Prefer?" Kevin said the word as if I used it to mock him. "I'd prefer for him to keep his gay ass away from me."

I couldn't get away that night, but this time I was going to. "I have to get to practice." With my head throbbing, I tried to slide past Kevin. He sidestepped to block my path. I couldn't go the other way because the sink was in my way. If I stepped further to the side, Kevin would only block me again.

"Indoor track, huh?" The smirk on Kevin's face made me want to rip it right off and flush it down a toilet. "Even gayer than regular track."

"Watch out," I warned, using the comeback I'd used before. "If anyone were to walk in here and see the two of us together they might start thinking things."

"Fuck you," Kevin said, grabbing me by the back of the neck and bashing my face into the rim of the sink.

I closed my eyes, bracing for impact but it still felt like something in my head exploded. Maybe I was disoriented, but I swear I heard maniacal laughing echoing through the dungeons of the athletic area as my arms flailed, unsuccessfully trying to find the floor before my head hit it.

CHAPTER 13
DAVID

With Robert at yet another practice for the all mighty Rebels, my dad finishing up the basement job, and Mom doing a very early shift at the nursing home, I had the house to myself on a Saturday morning. It was something that rarely happened, which is why I spent most of my time at Tyler's house. Plus, he had his own bedroom.

I would have texted to tell him to come over to my house for once, praying it was possible to ignore the twin bed on the opposite side of my bedroom but I didn't. I couldn't. If Tyler wanted to break up with me, he was going to have to officially do it. Besides, he should be the one to get in touch with me. He was the one who stabbed me in the back…twice. Telling everyone at SAFE and Ms. Larson. And then throwing that shit in my face about him being out and everyone knowing.

The open laptop on the kitchen table reminded me that my stupid English paper still needed to be written. I would have finished it last night if Robert didn't come into our bedroom with a loud sigh, demanding to know when I was going to be done. He explained that he had to go to bed because he had an early and important practice in the morning. My response was an equally loud exhale as I closed the laptop and shut the light off as I left the bedroom, leaving my little brother standing in the dark.

I drowned a bowl of shredded wheat in milk and carried it over to the table. Rather than finish the paper, I checked my phone to see if I missed anything. What a dumbass. The last text came from Mike last night who had asked me if I wanted to go see a movie with him, Carrie, and a couple of Carrie's friends.

With a mouthful of cereal, my hands hovered over the keyboard as if there was something my fingers were anxious to type but my brain wasn't sending the message. Using only my pointer finger, I searched *gay baseball player*. I was looking for a name. Maybe a name I would recognize from a lifetime of following the White Sox and learning about countless other major league players. There was a story about a basketball player, the NFL player I heard the news story a couple years ago, the NFL draft pick who came out, and a few articles about a player in the seventies that claims he was the real first professional athlete to publicly come out. I quickly scanned the links and saw headlines that read *I Know I had a Gay Teammate*, *I Would Welcome a Gay Teammate*, and *MLB Ready for First Openly Gay Player*.

The results were much more positive than I expected. I thought the first few links would be message boards devoted to gay bashing and locker room fears. When I got to the bottom of the page, I cleared his search history, shut the laptop, and brought my cereal bowl to the sink.

It should be easy. It should. The major leagues were ready, or so they said, so why wasn't I?

My phone rang and vibrated so it moved along the edge of the table, playing the opening notes to the White Sox fight song of 1959. I kept it as one of my ring tones because Robert told me it was stupid.

With a knee buckle and neck jerk at the sudden noise, I engaged in a staring contest with my phone, willing the picture of Tyler in the puffball hat to appear on the screen. This had to be him. I couldn't think of anyone else who would text me before noon on a Saturday. But, when I finally looked at the screen I didn't see any picture, just Mike's name.

Found tokens to Grand Slam! Wanna go?

That was the batting cage Mike and I spent most of the off season at. *Score! When?*

Whenever. Just gotta meet C for the big 10-month anniversary later.

Carrie loved to commemorate each month anniversary. *Sounds special.*

Her idea.

I glanced at the clock. Dad should be gone all afternoon and Mom was going to pick up Robert on her way home from work. *Wanna go now?*

B there soon.

I sent him emojis of a bat and a ball and set the phone on the counter. It would feel good to hit something hard over and over again.

CHAPTER 14
TYLER

There was no hiding it from Mom and Dad this time. The gash on my forehead and swollen face. The fact that I needed to call Mom at work so she could come pick me up. I stayed in the bathroom until she came, telling her to text me when she was out front.

She wanted to take me to the hospital. I told her home would be fine. My dad wanted to call the police. I told him we would take care of everything later. They asked me if they should try to reach David.

I told them no.

CHAPTER 15
DAVID

Ready to get out of the silence, I sat on the couch nearest to the front door and occupied myself by tracing the tiny checked pattern on the couch. It was hard to trace one square without touching the ones next to it.

I unzipped my jacket, which I had put on as soon as we made our plans. Chances were that Mike just got up and didn't eat anything and still needed to get dressed. I probably had at least ten minutes before he got here. Maybe I should text Tyler. Something lame about how practice was, just to let him know I didn't hate him for literally turning his back on me. I was madder at him than I was at Kevin. But Tyler was acting like I should be thanking Kevin for being a douchebag and an asshole.

A car honked as if its goal were to wake up someone sleeping at a red light. That was definitely Mike. I grabbed my equipment bag, threw my phone into it and left the house. Since the backseat was so clean, I felt like Mike's mom would yell at me for dirtying it up with my bag, but the car was Mike's. It was only a few years old because his dad "happened" to be in the market for a new car at the same time Mike got his driver's license. It was silver and small, and still really clean. Pretty amazing considering Mike had already driven it through a baseball season.

"Hey," Mike said, putting the car in reverse and speeding down my street.

I had to twist to click my seatbelt. "How was the movie last night?"

Mike shrugged. "It was all right. The good guys won and the world didn't end. Spoiler alert."

"I had a feeling that's how it turned out."

"Kevin showed up to the same show at the same theater. What are the odds?"

"Yeah?" I shifted in his seat. The whole point of going to the batting cages with Mike was so I wouldn't think about Kevin. And thinking about Kevin made me think about Tyler, which was weird. I didn't like the two of them being connected in my thoughts.

"He was there with Elise. Apparently they're together now."

I looked out the window. "I thought she was smarter than that."

Grand Slam Baseball Center smelled like the weight room. Rubber that somehow managed to soak up the stench of sweat. A slight odor of burning plastic mixed in because of the balls that zipped through the pitching machines. The various bats making connections with balls sounded like they were people attempting to clap together but kept coming in offbeat. The batting cages were to one side and an open area of fake turf was on the other. A variety of equipment designed to increase bat speed and precision was scattered about the area.

Only two people were having private hitting lessons today. A boy, who looked to be about nine years old, retrieved balls that were strewn around this net he was hitting into. His batting helmet wobbled on his head like it was a bobble head. The other guy looked like he was probably in high school. He had swung at a ball on a tee and froze on the moment of connection. His instructor circled his frozen figure and appeared to be offering critiques of the guy's hips, feet, hands, and the angle of the bat.

"Here, check this out." Mike moved off to the side of the door we walked into the entryway and dug into a pocket of his equipment bag. He held up a sandwich bag sagging from the weight of a handful of batting tokens.

"That's pretty awesome," I smiled at the bag of dull coins. The sound of the balls zipping out of the pitching machines energized me and I felt a ping of anticipation before hearing the bat connect with the ball. Even the stale air made me feel better. I hadn't been to Grand Slam since last spring when Mike and I spent a rainy Sunday afternoon there, adjusting the speed of the machine without the other one knowing it so that the ball either came in like a parent pitching to a small child or like the ball was shot out of a rifle. We had little success with either speed. Then we switched to adjusting the height of the pitches so the batter wouldn't know if he would be golfing or playing tennis when the ball came whizzing by. The day definitely didn't do much to help our form and technique, but it was a lot of fun.

Mike and I zigzagged around parents, children, and several people who also appeared to be antsy for the upcoming season. I recognized several caps from neighboring high schools, all of which Lincoln defeated last season. We set our bags against a bench and removed the bats from our bags, making the sound effects of swords being taken out of a scabbard.

"Your tokens, your turn," I said holding aside the net that led into the batting cage.

Mike inserted one of the tokens into the slot and stepped into the cage, rushing through a few practice swings as an orange light above the pitching machine warned him the first pitch was coming. He swung and hit a line drive up the middle. "Yes!" Mike congratulated himself. "Not a bit rusty."

"The shortstop would have had it," I said, pretending to be unimpressed.

"Shut up." Mike realigned himself with home plate, ready for the next pitch.

I sat on the bench, waiting for my turn. All of the batting cages were being used, with the exception of two. Softball cages were on the other side and only three of those were occupied. One by two small girls, about ten years old and someone who seemed to be their dad, another by two older girls, maybe in high school, wearing helmets that had a slot for their ponytails to slide through, and the other by a guy taking swings by himself. He had a thin frame and a good batting stance as he slightly waved a purple bat above his head. Navy blue workout pants and a yellow T-shirt hung from his body. On the next pitch, he hit a ball on the ground that probably had enough power to make it through the infield. I shrugged at the sight. Maybe the guy played for some intramural league at a college or something. You don't see that many guys in the fast pitch cages. Maybe an old guy in the slow, high-arc ones because those guys took their recreational league very seriously, but that was it.

"Your turn." Mike stepped out of the cage and flopped on the bench next to me.

"Cool." I dug a token out of the baggie.

"Hey batter, batter. Hey, batter, batter," Mike yelled.

I shook my head and quickly completed my pre-pitch ritual of a swing and a final alignment with the front corner of the plate. The orange light above the pitching machine fully illuminated and a ball dropped into the machine. In the nanosecond it took for the ball to reach me, I stepped, pivoted, swung, and squarely connected with the ball. It sailed a few feet above the pitching machine before hitting the net and sliding to the ground.

"Nice," Mike said, opening a bag of cheese curls he had just bought from a nearby vending machine.

While they might not have been homeruns or even base hits, I was pleased that I made solid connection on each of the pitches. On the last one, the image of Tyler's shocked and hurt face when I pretty much told that Will kid that Tyler wasn't my boyfriend flickered in my memory. The bat sliced through the air and I heard a dull thwack as a little yellow ball rolled by my feet.

"Whoa!" Mike stood up, pretending to watch a ball sail high into the air and over a fence. "It's still going."

"Shut up." I kicked the ball so it could get eaten by the contraption that would carry it back to the pitching machine.I undid the Velcro of my batting gloves and leaned my bat against the bench as Mike geared up for his second round in the cage.

"That was a pretty sloppy swing."

I turned in the voice's direction with a wrinkled eyebrow and saw the guy from the softball batting cages standing off to my side.

"It wasn't very good," I agreed and turned back to watch Mike take his swings.

"You totally dropped your hands and had a weird a follow through."

"I know." I narrowed my eyes, seeing the navy blue pants and yellow T-shirt standing a few feet away. Like I needed some random person to tell me my swing sucked, especially when it was obvious what I did wrong. I thought about the boyfriend who seemed to take the side of the biggest asshole in the school.

The guy took off his helmet and set it on the bench near my bat. I saw something familiar in the short hair and small smile. It was Allie, the girl from the library.

"Oh, hey." I wasn't sorry for my short responses but I did feel bad for not recognizing her.

"Allie," she said.

"I know. I didn't recognize you with the helmet on."

"I didn't know you played baseball," she said, sitting down.

"I didn't know you played softball." I nodded at the softball cages. "You scanning, or not scanning my ID in the library didn't leave much time for us to talk about our favorite sports."

"I played at my old school," Allie hugged one of her knees to her chest. "Second base."

"Me too. I play second," I said. "Softball tryouts are the same time as baseball's. Are you going out for the team?"

Allie shrugged a shoulder. "I don't know yet. Probably not." She retied a shoe that didn't need to be retied, or maybe she didn't like the feeling of her shoes being loose.

"Yes!" Mike yelled from the cage as he made a solid connection. He pumped his arms a few times before getting ready for the next pitch.

"Ms. Larson seemed pretty upset after she talked to you," Allie said.

"Yeah?" I redid the Velcro of my batting gloves, ready to go back in the cage even though Mike had only hit four of the fifteen balls.

"I guess you didn't look too happy either."

"I wasn't." I stood, hoping to indicate to Allie that I didn't want to talk about this.

"How come?" Allie said it carefully and with a little hesitation.

I lowered my eyes. "She thought I needed help with something." Spending all that time with Ms. Larson must have had an effect on Allie. She seemed to have a gift for getting people to say things they didn't want to.

"Well, that sucked." Mike stepped out of the cage. "The last three were all infield flies. Patrick's fat ass would have ran on them and there's two outs without even trying." He slipped his bat into his bag. "I'm going to get something to drink. You want anything?"

"I'm good," I said.

Mike noticed Allie sitting on the bench. "Hey." He greeted her like he had to, like when my aunt got married a couple years ago and my mom made me say hi to each of my family members. I'd never seen most of them before.

"Allie. I'm in your government class."

"Yeah." Mike looked from me to Allie and back. I could see the question in Mike's eyes. "Well, I'll be right back."

I dug through the baggie of tokens even though all I had to do was reach in and grab one. "Why are you talking to me?"

"Because I recognized you. Because you're one of the few people I've met at school who didn't call me a dyke or something along those lines within the first three seconds of meeting me." Allie stood up. "So, thanks for that."

I lowered my head in shame on behalf of every person who was ever mean to Allie. I was sorry for my body language during our conversation, standing off to the side, not looking at her, wishing she would go away.

"I like girls," Allie said. "Don't think I'm hitting on you or something. I haven't hit on a guy since fourth grade when I sent Tony Sorini a ridiculous Valentine."

"Did it work?" I asked.

Allie shook her head. "It was short lived. We got two swings next to each other at recess but Marissa Thoms got the one on the other side of him." She dramatically sighed. "If only I would have gotten the middle swing. Then maybe Marissa and I would have gotten together."

I couldn't help but laugh a little at the thought of a fourth grade

Allie possibly leaving Tony for Marissa. "I didn't think you were hitting on me. It was just a really rough ending to the week and I was trying hard not to remember it."

Allie pulled a hooded sweatshirt that was emblazoned with a ferocious looking tiger's head and the name of a school I had never heard of. "Is the batting cage helping?"

"A little," I paused. "Not really." Nothing was going to help me get rid of what Tyler said and how he looked when we last talked yesterday.

She pulled on a winter hat that had long flaps that covered her ears. "Whatever it is, you're not going to stop thinking about it until you deal with it."

"You are so wise," I said sarcastically.

"Not the most profound piece of advice, I know. But it's true." Allie put the bat she was using into one of the slots that lined the wall and hung the helmet on a hook.

I shrugged, thinking it was strange that here I was, sort of talking to Allie about what was going on. If we were somewhere else, maybe I would have told her everything. She probably would have some profound advice.

Allie put her hands in the pocket of her sweatshirt and nodded a goodbye. "If you need to get into the library, you know who to come to."

"Thanks for that, the other day," I said, feeling self-conscious. "I really needed to get in."

"I could tell. See you later." She turned and dodged two boys who were trying on extra large helmets and trying to walk around in them without running into anything.

Allie and Mike crossed paths as he also had to take a small detour around a bench to avoid the kids. He had a cup in his hand that looked like it could hold a liter of liquid. When he took a sip, a neon yellow beverage shot up the straw. Mike took another look behind him as Allie walked out of the batting cage section of Grand Slam and made her way to the doors.

"I'm your best friend. Were you going to wait until the wedding to fill me in?" Mike grinned.

I shook my head. "She and I talked in the library a few times. She was just saying hi."

Mike grinned like a big brother who wasn't going to let his little brother off the hook that easily. "Quite a long hello if you ask me. Were you planning your next date?"

Part of me wanted to believe Mike would be giving me a hard time if it had been any girl who was talking with me. The other part of me didn't want to believe that Mike was giving me a hard time because of what Allie looked like and what must be common knowledge that she was a lesbian.

And then I remembered our conversation in the cafeteria. Allie definitely didn't allow Mike to "not know."

"I don't think I'm her type, man," I said, which was something I'd said in the past when Mike asked why I wasn't going to go out with one of Carrie's friends, even though she thought I was really cute.

"No shit," Mike laughed. "She wouldn't know what to do with a wiener even if you hit her in the face with one."

I stepped into the cage and put the token I had been holding for the past five minutes into the slot. Now my hand smelled like money kept in a sock drawer for the past decade. "You sound like Kaminski." Mike had no idea how much of an insult that was and how much it sucked.

"Ouch," he said, taking a step back like I had just shoved him and laughed again.

CHAPTER 16
DAVID

On Monday, I walked past the first flight of stairs so I could see if Tyler was at his locker. Ever since we'd been together a whole weekend never went by without seeing each other, let alone without talking. At some point on Sunday, while I was watching a spring training game with Robert, I realized it made me kind of happy to know that Tyler thought that much of me to call me his boyfriend in front of other people. It was why guys and girls walked the halls holding hands, stopping to kiss each other at classroom doors. You didn't have to say you were together, everyone automatically knew. I never thought of that. Tyler still wanted to be my boyfriend even though I asked him not to tell anyone about it. Except his parents, but that doesn't count.

It was that look Tyler gave me when he said the whole school already knew he was gay that still bothered me. Like he was ready to go back on what he told me the day before school started. We were on his bed, making out. Facing each other all sweaty and red, I had asked him if he was okay with keeping us a secret. If he could do it. And he had said, "Of course. I would do anything for you."

The memory made me whip my phone out of my pocket and press Tyler's photo before I had a chance to convince myself otherwise. This was worth actually saying not just texting. The phone rang twice and went to voicemail and I hung up before getting through Tyler's greeting. Finally, I just texted him something generic. *Call me when you get a chance.*

That was about eighteen hours ago and no call or text back. I hated it when people constantly checked and played with their phones, but I looked at my phone more in the past day and half than I probably did in a week. My dad threatened to throw it in the toilet if I looked at it one more time during dinner.

When I reached Tyler's locker, there were sophomores crowded around it and no sign of him, making me believe that Tyler was in full-on avoidance mode. I didn't have any experience with this.

If anyone were to ask me what I learned in psychology that day, I would have had to say, "I don't know. Some stuff." I had spent the whole period thinking about Art Appreciation and not because I was really interested in this sculpture unit we were doing. Tyler would probably stare straight ahead, pretending that I wasn't sitting a couple rows behind him.

I reached the art room before Tyler did with my stomach feeling like it was churning up something it didn't want to digest. As I slipped into my seat to take out a notebook I didn't plan on actually using, the bell rang and still no Tyler. I had felt nervous ever since I texted Tyler. Now I felt nervous and a little worried. Tyler would never ditch a class.

In Spanish class, there was finally some relief. The teacher spent the first ten minutes of class explaining how we were going to expand upon the travelogues we did last week and make a short video in which we "visited" the Spanish city we were assigned. I thought it would be helpful for more than one reason if I just took a trip to Valencia instead.

Señora Fannin led the class to the library, shushing a few along the way who forgot that there were still other classes going on. Allie looked up from the book she was reading as my Spanish class trooped through the entrance and gave me a small wave with her fingers. I nodded a hello back. I admired in her what I admired in Tyler. Confident and strong. Not seeming to give a shit about anyone. They made it look so easy when I knew it was anything but that.

I plopped my books down at what had become my favorite computer in the library, the one all the way at the end of the row. I searched Valencia and then watched as my teacher explained the assignment to someone who had been absent the past few days. Glancing at my classmates, it was pretty clear that no one was very focused on the assignment. I sauntered past the magazine rack, stopped at a shelf that contained new books, and straightened a stack of papers that were all over one of the copy machines.

As I approached the desk at the entrance, Allie hopped off her chair and shoved a bookmark in my face. "Would you like a complimentary piece of cardboard that would be perfect for reminding you of where you stopped in a book. They are courtesy of some author I've never heard of who's coming to visit the book club next week."

I smiled. "I'm good. I usually just fold the page down."

"Your loss. I don't hand these out to just anyone." Allie shrugged and placed the bookmark back on the stack. "Do you need something?"

"Uh, yeah," I hesitated. "But it doesn't have anything to do with the library or this stupid project I have to do for Spanish."

"I wouldn't be much help in Spanish, anyway. I took three years of Russian at my old school."

"Russian? That's cool."

"Yeah," Allie said. "They offered Spanish, French, Mandarin, and Russian."

"Why'd you pick Russian?" I moved the bookmark stack so I could rest my elbows on the counter.

"I thought the letters looked cool and I liked how it sounds like you're being mean even though you might be saying something like, 'You have the prettiest eyes I've ever seen.'" She batted her eyes at me.

If any other guy or girl would have used a line like that, I would have thought they were flirting with me. "I actually wanted to ask you something about your old school."

Allie hopped on a tall chair that spun. "Like what?"

"Was it big? I mean did a lot of people go there?"

Allie shrugged. "It was bigger than Lincoln, that's for sure. There were probably about eight hundred people in my class and over three thousand all together."

"Wow, that's pretty big."

Allie spun her chair in little half circles, craning her neck towards me if she turned a bit too far. "So, are you doing some sort of geography assignment on the demographics of neighboring schools?"

"No." I shuffled the bookmarks like they were playing cards. It was like I was back in front of the bathroom mirror, practicing coming out to my dad. "So...was it better at your old school or is it better here?"

"What do you mean?"

"I mean..." I wasn't sure what I meant. "I guess I wanted to know if you like it here."

"Now you're the welcoming committee? I'd say you're a few months too late," Allie smiled. "And it's okay here, I guess. It's high school."

I nodded, trying to figure out where to go from here so I could ask Allie what I really wanted to. "And there were teachers like Ms. Larson there? And SAFE?"

"And more." The way she said it, I could tell she really missed it.

"It seems like everyone was nicer at your old school." Señora Fannin was looking over the shoulder of someone and pointing to something on their computer screen.

"I'd say considering how many people went there, the ratio of nice people to complete assholes is more lopsided here."

"Hmm." Tyler and I never really talked about this or what it was like for him to walk the halls of Lincoln. Maybe because there was no need to say that it was really hard sometimes. Or maybe because we had each other. "Do you ever wish you weren't gay?" It was something I thought about when I was first trying to figure stuff out. But it hadn't crossed my mind in a while.

A thunderstorm rolled in on Allie's eyes. "What? Like it's a choice? Like why did I choose to be gay?" She slumped in her chair and crossed her arms, glaring at me.

"No, no, that's not what I meant," I stammered. "It's just..."

"Or, why don't I just stop acting like such a lesbo," Allie cut me off. "Maybe wear a cute little skirt and tie a ribbon in my hair?" She somehow raised her voice without yelling.

"Allie, stop," I said, my eyes darting to each corner of the library to see if anyone noticed what was going on at the desk by the entrance.

"Because I like the way I am. Fuck anyone who says anything otherwise." Allie hopped off the chair and became interested in a rack of returned books that suddenly needed to be rearranged.

I wished I had a baseball hat on so I could lower the brim over my eyes. "Yeah, fuck 'em. Saying that will make everything better, right?" I pushed myself off the counter.

"What?" Allie said, turning back to me.

Apparently I said that out loud.

I gripped the edge of the counter, taking a deep breath as I traced the grain in the fake wood veneer with my eyes. I followed it for about a foot before looking up at Allie. "Fuck 'em," I said. "Is it that easy?"

Allie shrugged. "I think so." There was still an edge in her voice.

I wanted to say, "fuck you" to Kevin, his dad, and probably even my coach. I felt an energy rise in me, like it was opening day and I was stepping onto the field for first time in my uniform. "It's okay, I can do this," I said to the counter top. My voice shook a little, not quite matching the way I felt on the inside.

Allie walked back to the counter. "Do what?"

"I'm gay." I was ready and wanted to say it. It was my choice. This was how it was supposed to work.

Allie smiled. "Good for you." She reached over the counter and patted me on the shoulder.

"Huh?"

"Feels good to say it, doesn't it? Two words. Five letters. Why is it so hard, huh?"

My hands went to my head to adjust a baseball cap that wasn't there. I put them in the pocket of my sweatshirt instead. "Because people suck. Really suck."

"Yup," Allie nodded. "Some people really do."

"And because it's me. Like it shouldn't have anything to do with anyone else but it's a big deal for some reason. Why does it have to be a big deal?"

"It's not a big deal," Allie assured me. "But you might see it on the news. You see it all the time when a celebrity comes out. Are you a celebrity?"

"I don't want it to be a big deal." And it wasn't a big deal until last week. I twisted my sweatshirt from inside the pocket. "I just want to play baseball and finish this year."

"Then do that." Allie's eyes glanced around me at something. "I think your teacher's on to you."

I turned to see Señora Fannin coming towards us. "Señora, hola. I was just getting back to work. I requested a book last week from another library and Allie was checking to see if they had it." It sounded believable.

Allie stepped behind a computer and began quickly typing. Her attempt to "check" on my book was admirable but unnecessary given how much time I'd already been standing at the counter.

Señora Fannin raised an eyebrow. "Really? Here I thought she might have been an expert on Valencia and helping you with your travelogue." She said the name of the city in a thick Spanish accent.

"Valencia?" Allie said the city's name in the same accent as my teacher. All these years in Spanish and my accent still sucked. "The Bioparc is incredible. It puts every zoo I've ever seen to shame. Just putting it in the same category as a zoo feels wrong."

"The Bioparc?" Señora Fannin somehow raised her eyebrows even higher.

"Yeah," Allie smiled. "I never liked zoos much anyway because of the cages and the two trees and some rocks that were supposed to double as an animal's natural habitat. But the Bioparc…wow."

I had no idea what Allie was talking about but my teacher seemed impressed. "Make sure Señor Lukas does some research on his own and not just ask you to tell him all about your trip to Spain," Señora Fannin said and then turned to me. "Why don't you try to get some work done on your own?" She gestured toward the computer where my books sat.

"Good idea." I nodded in agreement as my teacher went back to the class.

Allie clicked something on the computer screen a few times and leaned forward, resting her elbows on the counter.

"You've actually been there?" I asked. "What a crazy coincidence."

Allie shook her head. "I haven't made it overseas yet," she said. "But, you can find anything on the Internet."

"Good thinking." I laughed a little, taking a couple steps back.

"Maybe I should find out about this Bioparc for myself."

Allie shrugged. "It seemed kind of interesting."

I hesitated despite knowing Señora was waiting for me to get back to work. "I didn't plan on telling you. It just happened. You're one of like, five people who know."

"Does anyone else at school know?"

"Only one person up until last week." I lowered my voice. "And now it's getting…a little complicated."

"It's turning into a big deal?"

"I guess."

"Well, I won't tell anyone. I'll let the media outlets handle it instead," Allie snickered.

I had to smile. "They might want an exclusive interview with someone in the know."

"No comment. But I'll answer your questions if you want. I've got some practice at this…whole thing. You're not alone in this. You shouldn't feel like you are."

I believed Allie but the thought of Tyler walking away from his locker on Friday prevented me from fully appreciating what she said. "I've heard that before." I nodded a good-bye. "See you around." I walked back to the computer and sat down in front of the screen.

I had told Allie. True, she was probably more understanding than some people at Lincoln, but I made the choice to tell someone else and I didn't expect it to feel so good. I needed to talk to Tyler. But there was someone else I wanted to talk to first.

As I pretended to start my Spanish assignment, I decided that I was going to tell Mike after school today. Before the weight room, after, during our workout. I hadn't worked out the details yet but the longer I let Kevin hang it over me like it was something bad, something worth cowering about, the bigger deal it became. And if I were going to be on the news for anything, it would be for being the second player from Lincoln High School to be drafted into the pros. It was a long shot and probably not going to happen, but that was what would make the story so newsworthy.

CHAPTER 17
TYLER

I couldn't decide what hurt more. My face. My head. When David said he had no idea what Will was talking about and let me walk away from him.

A couple band-aids helped my face. Some ice helped my head. I didn't know what to do about that last one.

CHAPTER 18
DAVID

I found out that dodgball was a lot more fun without feeling like fifty-pound weights were tied to my ankles. My team had a shot at winning the period tournament, which meant there were five points extra credit and a bottle of water for each team member on the line. I caught every ball that came near me, causing my opponents to stare open-mouthed for a second before dragging their feet from the court.

This was how I usually felt before Coach Kelly called me to his office not quite a week ago. This was how I deserved to feel all the time, or at least as much as possible. Since I typically didn't get such a high from a PE class victory, I had to assume that I was still flying from seventh period when I talked to Allie. It was like the secret was slowly eating at me but I didn't even know it

I really wanted to tell Tyler about it, even if he didn't want to talk to me.

When the bell rang and I got caught up in a flood of students leaving the locker room. It carried me through the door and finally broke as I passed Coach Kelly's office. I glanced through the vertical window at the side of the door and saw Mrs. Carlson standing at the copy machine and Kevin sitting in a chair outside of Coach's office, hunched over, arms crossed, with a serious scowl on his face. Like a kindergartner who had to sit out of recess as punishment.

With the exception of some very clever jokes during the last workout session, Kevin had been quiet. Even if that scowl on his face wasn't about me, Kevin was pissed about something and whenever Kevin was angry, or even just a little upset, he quietly fumed until he just exploded. Many guys on the team referred to this mood as PMS and he PMSed most of the time.

"Hey, you're going the wrong way." Mike passed me in the hallway as he headed to the locker room.

"I just have to stop at my locker," I said. "I'll meet you in there."

"We're going to add weight today."

"I'm ready." I said, not just talking about the day's workout. As Mike waved, I couldn't tell if he was ready.

Out of habit, I walked by Tyler's locker, hoping I'd see his figure crouched at the floor of it, his head partially inside as he sifted through textbooks and notebooks. But when I reached the locker, all I saw were three sophomore girls dressed exactly the same. The girl in the middle was holding up her phone and giggling while the other two clapped and bounced on their toes.

"He likes you!" They squeezed their friend's shoulder.

The girl with the phone hugged her phone as much as it was possible to hug a four-inch piece of plastic. "What should I write back?"

I didn't wait to hear what her friends suggested and was almost to my locker when I ran into Allie. I smiled when I saw her. "Thanks for putting up with me in the library," I said.

"No problem. I was serious. Let me know if you ever want to talk more or anything. It doesn't always have to be a secret rendezvous in the library. They do let me out sometimes." She slipped her arm through the other strap of her backpack so it hung squarely on her back. "You should come to a SAFE meeting. We don't always get a lot done but you might want to meet some other people who wouldn't make you feel like a freak." Allie paused. "Well, they might make you feel like a freak, but it's only out of love."

"I don't think I'm ready for that." I shook my head. I told my dad. I told Allie. I was going to tell Mike. Maybe I worked better one on one.

"You know where the room is if you ever are." Allie gave me a little salute as she walked off.

"Took you long enough," Mike said to me when I came into the weight room and sat down on a crate near the leg press machine. "I had to get started on my own and was this close to asking Patrick to be my spotter for squats." Mike nodded at Patrick, who stood near the free weights, picking up the heaviest ones like he was testing to see if the weight etched on the side was accurate.

"I'm busy," Patrick said, struggling to pick up one of the largest weights. The weight room was empty otherwise.

"Sorry," I said. "I ran into someone in the hallway."

"Who?"

"Just someone I had to talk to." I shrugged.

Mike smiled slyly. "Your girlfriend? I could tell there was something going on between the two of you at the batting cages."

I rolled my eyes. "Shut up, idiot."

"Secret conversations. Meeting in the hallway. Sounds pretty serious to me."

If Patrick weren't nearby, I thought it would have been the perfect time to tell Mike that there was no possible way I would have a girlfriend and explain why. "I don't have a girlfriend. I'd tell you if I did," I said instead. It was true, even if that conversation was never going to happen.

"Whatever, Romeo. Spot me on this one, will you?"

"Of course." I lifted the bar from the slots and made sure it was steady in Mike's hands.

"This seems kind of heavy," I said as Mike adjusted his grip on the bar. "You got it?"

"Yep," Mike said quickly, already straining a little. His face was pink by the fourth rep, his left arm shook on the way up by the seventh, and on the last one, his elbow locked into place like it was refusing to do the lift again.

As I eased the bar back into the slots, the pink drained from Mike's face and his color was returning to his normal complexion. "Why are you standing there like some creeper?" Mike looked startled as he sat up on the bench and looked somewhere behind me.

Despite the fact that I already knew who was standing behind me, instinct made me turn. It was a given whenever anybody said something like, "Hey, what's that?" You had to look.

Rather than pushing the door open with such force that it bounced off the wall and announced his arrival, Kevin somehow materialized right behind me. "What do you think I'm doing here?" Kevin huffed, his mouth in a line and his eyebrows furrowed.

"Standing there like a creeper," Mike laughed.

"It looks like you're about to throw David in your van parked outside," Patrick added from his spot on the leg curl machine.

"Your boyfriend wasn't in school today, huh?" Kevin muttered as he shoved past me.

The image of Tyler's empty chair in Art Appreciation flashed in my mind, followed by Tyler's closed locker door amid the crowd of sophomores standing in front of theirs. "Why do you care?"

"Sorry." Kevin walked over to the leg press machine. "Coach told me to keep my distance from you. So I will." He held up his hands in a mock apology and sat down, making a show of not making eye contact with me.

"Are you okay?" Mike asked me.

I ignored Mike, my stare zooming in on Kevin, who was moving the pin down to add more weight. My entire body pulsated. I went from the bench to the leg press in three steps. "Did you do something to him?" Was it possible to lift someone up by their shirt like I had seen in so many movies? I wanted to grab the discolored collar of Kevin's T-shirt and find out.

Kevin pushed the weight up with a slight grunt. "Who? What? Your boyfriend?"

"Boyfriend?" I didn't turn around to see what Mike's face looked like.

"He was the one that ran into me," Kevin said.

"What. Did. You. Do?" My mind wasn't on Mike or anything else in the world.

Kevin threw his legs over the side of the leg press chair and stood centimeters from my face. "I did my best to get him to convince you to keep your faggoty ass away from everyone."

Mike stepped up like he was afraid to be caught sneaking up on me. "David, what the fuck is he talking about?"

I heard Mike but it didn't register that I should answer the question. All of my focus was on Kevin, that he hurt Tyler, and that Tyler wasn't in school today. "If I have to ask you again, I am going to kick your ass."

"You'd like that, wouldn't you?" Kevin took a step back as if I had a contagious disease and sneezed on him. "You just want to cop a feel on anything with a dick."

"That excludes you then." I breathed through my nose like a bull preparing to charge a red flag.

"You're gay?" I heard Mike spit out.

This time, Mike's question seemed to snap me out of my trance. I saw Mike's scrunched up, confused face. "Yeah," I said, knowing that Mike didn't need me to say anything. Shit, how many times did I want to tell Mike and now this was the way that he found out? Again. Kevin did it again.

"You…you like guys? Like, *like* them?"

As I slightly nodded, Kevin's face broke into a shit-eating grin. "He doesn't know? Your best friend didn't know? Oh god, this is awesome." Kevin looked like he wanted to high-five someone, most likely himself. "All you have to do is follow David's shitbox as he drives it to Homoville and you'll see quite a show when the track star gets out of the car."

"Shit." Mike took a step back. "Shit," he said a little louder this time, probably replaying our entire friendship in his mind: T-ball games, video games in his basement, double dates with Carrie's friends that never led to a second date.

Mike looked back at me. "Fuck you." He quickly walked to the weight room door, flung it open, and left without picking up the sweatshirt he brought with him.

"Would you like me to poll the whole team to see if they feel the same way as the Captain?" Kevin stared at me with arms crossed, like an umpire who had just kicked a player out of a game and was waiting for him to leave the field.

"I'm gonna go too," Patrick said to no one in particular as he rolled off the bench and headed for the door.

"Patrick, hey," Kevin called to his back. "Let's get your opinion on this. You want to make a "no fags allowed" clause for the team? Anyone who likes dick need not try out?"

Patrick continued to walk towards the door. "Shut up," he said without turning around.

Kevin's grin returned to me as I dumbly stared at the door close behind Patrick. "I'll take that as a yes. He's not exactly jumping up and down at the thought of having you check him out at every practice and every game."

Mike's "fuck you" echoed in my ears. That along with the thought of Tyler hurt or in the hospital or worse forced me to crouch and duck my head like a rugby player in a scrum. I lurched forward and caught Kevin around the waist. Both of us tumbled over the steel bar that connected the leg press chair to the machine.

"Don't fucking touch me," Kevin yelled when we landed on the stiff rubber mats that covered most of the floor.

I had to let go of Kevin while we were in midair and landed on my elbows a little off to Kevin's side, but I was able to spring to my knees and tackle Kevin again as he was about to get up. He twisted in my hold and managed to get to his feet. We two circled one another, with Kevin jerking his head forward in a weak attempt to make me flinch.

"You followed us? Why the fuck did you follow us?" There were too many kisses outside of Tyler's house for me to try to guess about when exactly Kevin saw us. I felt sick thinking about Kevin intruding into the world that was ours.

"It was supposed to be a joke you fucking sicko."

"You asshole. You fucking asshole." My voice grew louder with each word as I charged Kevin again, who crouched, ready for me this time. He threw his body weight into me and pinned me, winding up his pitching arm behind his head and releasing it like a catapult. Instinct made me scrunch up my face and close my eyes as if that would somehow deflect the punch. But it perfectly connected with my eye.

A series of small explosions went off in my head before pain spread across the left side of my face. I brought my hand to my eye like I was afraid it was going to fall out of the socket.

"You tell Coach that it was me, I'll really kick your ass." Kevin stepped over me on his way out of the weight room.

I heard the door open as I was still on my knees, blinking and holding a hand over my eye. When I heard the latch to the door catch, I let go of my face, expecting to see an eye in my hand. The area was already starting to swell, and it was getting hard to see from that side. I quickly blinked, as if that would slow the swelling down. When I brought my hand back up to my face, it felt wet and I immediately panicked. Was my nose bleeding somehow? Did eyes bleed? I didn't think so, but who knew? I looked at my hand and didn't see anything. It was only when my chest heaved and I choked out a sob did I realize I was crying.

CHAPTER 19
DAVID

My freshman year, I got a nasty blister on my right middle finger. Every time I gripped the ball to throw it felt like a small fire kindled directly on my fingertip. Eventually, I had to bat with my finger in the air, hoping the umpire didn't think it was a slick way to flick him off. I didn't tell my coach at first, feeling like a complete wuss for thinking a blister was an actual injury but then it got infected. This required me to go to the athletic trainer before practice to get the wound cleaned, bandaged, and taped to provide extra protection. I felt so stupid walking out of the training room with a piece of tape covering the top knuckle of my finger while other athletes got actual injuries taped or hobbled around the room on crutches, preparing to begin a rehab regimen. It probably looked ridiculous to everyone else. Really? A blister? Might as well just amputate it now. But, when the major aspects of the game required you to grip a ball or a bat, I eventually accepted that an infected blister was actually a debilitating injury.

My daily trips to the training room lasted about a week, and I got to know the athletic trainer, Mr. Litch, pretty well. As he wound a bandage around my finger he assured me several times that many major leaguers were placed on the DL due to similar injuries. When I sprained my wrist at the beginning of the season last year, Mr. Litch had known it was serious because I wasn't a regular in the training room. Some athletes spent their pre and post practice time there even though they didn't need to, pretending an old injury needed attention so they could avoid the boring routine of daily warm-ups and drills. So now, when I shuffled through the training room door, with my hand over my left eye, Mr. Litch looked up from the ankle he was taping and raised his dark eyebrows at me.

"How does the other guy look?"

"What?" I asked.

"It looks like you just got socked in the eye. What about the other guy?" Mr. Litch's tone was playful but his eyes were kind.

"No other guy, just a bar," I quickly constructed a story. "Mike was doing squats and I was walking past. I bent down to pick up my sweatshirt and bam…perfect timing."

"I'd say bad timing."

"I just wanted to get a bag of ice," I said, wanting to leave as quickly as possible. I knew from experience that the longer you waited to get ice on something the worse it looked. Mike had insisted he didn't need to put ice on his shin when he took a hard grounder off of it, saying it was just a bruise. The next day a purple welt the exact size of a baseball protruded from his leg and he had to wear a shin guard for a couple games.

"Sure." Mr. Litch nodded towards a large cooler. "You know where it is."

I fished for the biggest bag I could find and pressed the ice to my face. I couldn't help but release a small sigh as I felt the cold slowly start to spread over the heat that surrounded my eye.

"Good thing that happened now so you have a little while to heal," Mr. Litch said, going back to the ankle he was taping. "You might have been out for a game or two if that happened during the season."

"I'll have to be more careful," I said as I tried to spread out the bag as much as possible so it covered more of my face.

"Or tell Mike to be more careful," Mr. Litch smiled. "We'll blame this one on him."

I pushed open the double doors and a warm sun greeted me. It was shocking when I had been used to biting cold and snowflakes. I took my phone out of my pocket and watched the bars in the corner go from a couple little ones to completely full. Just as I was about to text Tyler, I lurched to a stop, almost tripping over my feet.

Mike sat on the trunk of my big, brown beast of a car, otherwise known as a shitbox according to Kevin. He slightly shivered in the T-shirt and shorts he was working out in. His Lincoln baseball cap from last season was pulled low over his eyes so I couldn't tell if he saw me or not. But, Mike looked up when I skidded through a small patch of gravel.

"What happened to you?" Mike nodded toward me.

I had lowered the bag of ice at the shock of seeing Mike. My reflection in a trophy case had told me that it looked worse than it felt with swirls of red and purple covering my puffy eyelid and lower eye. At least I could see out of it and I was pretty sure I was fine to drive home. It would look worse as it started to heal, but that wouldn't start for another day or two.

"Kevin," I said.

"Did you hit him back?"

Despite the few feet that separated us, I felt that we might as well have been on opposite sides of the Grand Canyon. "I tackled him first. He just got the first hit."

Mike nodded like he was watching film of batting practice and was analyzing the mechanics of his swing. He squinted. "Fucking asshole."

"Kevin or me?"

Mike leaned forward, resting his elbows on his knees. "Do you really have a boyfriend? Like not a friend who's a boy but a boyfriend."

My mouth felt as dry as a sandbox baking in the sun. "Yeah," I managed to say, surprised that the roller coaster feeling in my stomach was only that of a kiddie ride and not the ones that broke world records for speed and drops. This wasn't the way Mike should've found out. I wished I would have just done like I did on the patio with my dad and not given Kevin the chance to do this to me again.

"Who is it?"

"You know who it is. Tyler. From track." Saying his name reminded me that I was the reason Kevin hurt Tyler. Tyler got hurt because of me. My upper body jerked towards my car as if part of me could continue talking with Mike in the parking lot and the other part could speed over to Tyler's house. Texting or calling wasn't going to cut it, I needed to see him. But, I remained planted in the small patch of gravel.

Mike shook his head to himself. "For how long?"

I couldn't read Mike's tone. There was zero inflection or emotion. "Since the summer." It would be another blow to Mike. I knew it as I said it.

Mike reacted with a slight neck jerk. "That's fucked up."

"What is?"

"I had to hear it from Kevin? My best friend is…has a boyfriend and I have to hear it from that douchebag?"

I lowered my head, thinking about how to respond to Mike. "I wanted to tell you. I was really close a couple times."

"When? When I asked you to go out with Carrie's friend? When I wanted to know which girl you were taking to Homecoming? 'Actually, I think I'll just go with some guy!'" Mike sprang off the trunk and leaned against it, his arms folded tightly.

I looked around the parking lot, which was mostly empty since it was between sports seasons. I took a step towards Mike. "I was just getting used to everything myself," I said evenly, my voice stronger than it was before. It was getting annoying, people thinking they were owed some explanation about who I wanted to go out with. "And I asked how you felt about it and you made yourself pretty clear."

Mike looked taken aback. "When?"

"During lunch last week. You were working on that debate paper about the cake and told me you'd rather not know. So, I kept on letting you not know."

"What?" Mike looked like he was trying to take notes from a complicated lecture and was having trouble keeping up.

"I asked you how would you feel if someone on the team was gay and you said you'd rather not know."

"I didn't know you were talking about you."

I smiled in spite of myself, feeling a wave of calm spread over my body. "So you're okay? We're cool?"

Mike's eyes clouded. "I don't know."

"If you need some time, I get it. Completely," I said, taking another step forward and reaching out to put a hand on Mike's shoulder.

Mike jerked his shoulder away and turned his head to the side. My hand hovered in the air. I slowly lowered it, as if I didn't know how to place it back at my side. "Oh, okay."

"How can you expect me to just be okay with everything?" Mike turned back to me. "What did you think? That we can all go on double dates together? You, me, Carrie, and…"

"I don't know what I expected." I unlocked the car and threw my book bag and coat in the backseat. I slammed the door, something I rarely did since I wasn't sure the doors could handle the force. "Actually, no, that's not true. Maybe I knew that I should just shut up about it and start over next year. Kevin and his stupid dad, Coach, and now you."

"It's not that simple, David," Mike said. "Kevin announces to the weight room that you're gay and you think we can just go to the batting cages or play video games or…"

"Or what?" I pressed.

"Jesus Christ, David." He pushed himself off the trunk off the car. "We've had lockers right next to one another in the locker room for the past three years!"

"And we've been best friends for ten, so what?" My god, Mike actually thought I'd sneak a look at his dick after practice.

"So what?" Mike repeated, smirking. "Some best friend." He stalked away, without a glance back at me. When he got to his car, he slid into it and the car lurched into gear.

I watched the car whip out of the parking spot and speed off towards the exit, not bothering to slow down for the speed bumps that lined the parking lot. When I got in the car, I thought it was my heart that made my body feel like it was pulsating, but it was actually my throbbing eye. I tilted the rearview mirror to get a better look at the various shades of red and purple but bent the mirror away, hating the look of myself.

I punched the steering wheel with a yell. "Fuck!" I punched it again with my other hand and then again with the other like it was a speed bag and I was doing some weird boxing regimen in the front seat of my car. "Fuck!" I yelled again, giving it two final jabs before gripping the wheel with both hands and resting my forehead on it.

CHAPTER 20
DAVID

I blindly flew out of the parking lot, and not because of an injured eye, barely bothering to check if the road was clear so I could make the left turn. The stoplight in front of me changed from yellow to red. I slammed on the brakes. My body jerked forward against the tightening seat belt.

The muffled tune of the 1959 Chicago White Sox fight song still sounded peppy even though my phone was zipped up in my bag. Keeping an eye on the light, I rummaged through the little pocket with one hand until my fingers felt the phone. "Home" appeared on the screen and I had another nanosecond debate with myself. I didn't want to talk to my parents, but if I didn't answer, they would either expect a call back or I would have some explaining to do once I got home. And why were they calling any way? I swiped my finger across the screen and took a breath.

"Hello?"

"David!"

"Robert?" I took the phone away from my ear and looked at it, as if that would explain why my little brother was calling me. He rarely did and only when he needed something. The light turned green and I crept forward, holding the phone to my ear again.

"I got the mail..."

I rolled my eyes. "Good for you."

"No, let me finish." Robert said. "I got the mail and there was a really big envelope from Mankato!"

I almost dropped the phone. Everything about Kevin and Mike and Tyler went away for a second. "Really?"

"Do you think you got it?" I imagined Robert holding the envelope to the light in an effort to figure out what was inside.

"I don't know." Conflicting emotions battled for control over me. Relief as one of my prayers might already have been answered. But there was also Tyler.

"It's a big envelope," Robert reminded me. "They wouldn't stuff an envelope full of paper just to say 'you suck,' would they?"

"Probably not," I agreed, turning down a street.

"Are you almost home? I want to open this." I appreciated Robert's enthusiasm.

"Not yet, Rob," I said. "I have to go to Tyler's first."

"You see him all the time," Robert whined. "Don't you want to know what this says?"

I turned the car into a subdivision and pulled over to the side. "Of course I want to know what it says. I'll be home later. We'll open it with Mom and Dad tonight."

"Fine." Robert sighed and hung up.

CHAPTER 21
TYLER

I heard David's car before I saw it. The engine sounded like it should either be on a racecar or an SUV the size of a yacht. But it was just an old engine on an old car. He was coming here. There was no other reason for him to be in this neighborhood. Any other time, every other time, I got the cliché butterflies, but this time it was an anvil.

We have a porch swing outside of my house and I spent most of my day on that. Mom and Dad let me stay home from school and thank God they didn't try to miss work to babysit me. The deal was that I would go to school tomorrow.

After being inside the whole weekend, it felt good to be outside and not have to wear six layers. Plus, my face looked a little less like an artist's palette of blue and purple paint that swirled together. Slowly rolling my ankles back and forth to push the swing put me into some meditative trance where everything around me disappeared.

The engine jolted me out of the trance. Self-consciousness washed over me. My face didn't look like messed up paint but it wasn't pretty either. I didn't want pity from David. I wanted an "I'm sorry" or something that would indicate Kevin Kaminski didn't kick my ass for no reason.

CHAPTER 22
DAVID

I felt like some stalker, sitting in my car on the side of the street, peering over the steering wheel so I could see Tyler's house a few doors down from where I was. If I knew what was inside that envelope, I could share it with Tyler. But maybe Tyler didn't care to hear any news from me, good or bad. Maybe he wanted to break up because of everything that had happened. I felt hollow when I imagined my world without Tyler in it. My world would no longer be ours.

Sitting in the car, everything still held promise. The packet from Mankato could offer me the scholarship I'd been waiting for. Tyler was still my boyfriend. It seemed like a better option to just sit in the car, at least for a few more seconds. For those few seconds some things were still okay.

Finally I put the car in gear, and pulled away from the curb so carefully someone might have thought I was a brand-new driver behind the wheel for the first time. As the car inched closer to Tyler's house, the contents of my lunch inched their way up my throat. I parked along the curb when I reached Tyler's house because backing out of the driveway seemed like too much work if I needed to quickly leave. After putting the car in park, I checked my eye in the rearview mirror. It could have been worse if I didn't get ice on it. I turned the car off, hearing each click as the engine settled, and took the keys out. Before I could talk myself out of it, I took a deep breath, swung open the car door and stepped out.

"Are you just going to stand there?"

My eyes darted to the front porch swing where Tyler and I spent many cool evenings lazily swaying back and forth. He stood next to the swing in black workout pants, a long sleeve T-shirt from last year's state tournament, and an unzipped dark gray hoodie.

"You're okay," I said, not knowing what else to say but feeling a sense of relief. From where I stood, I could see some discoloration on Tyler's face but not how bad it was. There were no casts, crutches, or dramatic bandages you usually see in movies when someone was in a fight. Tyler leaned against the porch railing and I didn't know if it was out of habit or because he needed the support. I slowly walked up the driveway, keeping my gaze on Tyler's face as more details of it came into focus. Puffiness on one side. Colorful half-moons under an eye.

"You're here." Tyler held my stare as we neared one another. His expression didn't tell me much but the butterflies above his right eye moved as I got closer. Little scabs already started to form under the tiny strips. "What happened to you?"

"I came to ask you the same thing," I said, not stepping up on the porch, so Tyler stood a couple feet above me.

"How'd you find out?" Tyler asked.

"Kevin told me, sort of," I said. It took everything not to lay my hand on top of the one Tyler had curled around the porch railing. I settled for gripping the space next to it.

"Before or after he did that?" Tyler nodded at my face.

"Before."

Tyler just nodded and I felt lost. I didn't think we would engage in a heavy make out session right there on the porch after everything that happened but Tyler made no move to come closer to me. "You're pretty mad at me, huh?" I stuffed my hands into the pocket of my sweatshirt.

"Not for this." Tyler waved his hand over his face, indicating the bruises and butterflies.

I looked down and worked at a patch of dirt on the sidewalk with the toe of my shoe. "From before?"

Tyler just nodded.

"I was mad at you too," I said. It looked like Tyler raised an eyebrow but I couldn't really tell. "But I had all weekend to think about it and I'm not that mad anymore. I understand now…sort of."

"Before or after you found out about this?" Tyler, again, waved his hand over his face.

"Before."

"I thought about you all weekend too," Tyler sighed at the admission but when I was about to smile, he rushed on. "But not like that." The smile vanished from my face. "You told Will you had no idea what he was talking about when he asked if I was your boyfriend."

I couldn't remember his exact words, but that sounded about right. The look on Tyler's face, however, I remembered that.

"Not telling anyone is one thing. You and me having a secret makes everything seem more special in a way. But a flat-out denial that there's nothing here," Tyler waved his pointer finger back and forth between him and me, "I wasn't ready for that. And it sucked. I don't know exactly how, but lying is different than keeping a secret." Tyler backed up a couple steps to sit in the porch swing.

I got that. It was the same feeling I had with Coach Kelly when I was in his office. It would have been simple to tell Coach I wasn't gay but I couldn't bring myself to say no. "It felt like I took a line drive to my chest when Will asked me if I was your boyfriend," I said. "It's not an excuse, I know." Tyler nodded in agreement as I took a tentative step on to the porch. "And Ms. Larson had just talked to me…it wasn't a good time."

"I didn't tell her," Tyler evenly said.

"I believe you."

"Good."

"You have no idea who did?" I asked.

Tyler shook his head.

I leaned against the porch railing, hands in my sweatshirt pocket, trying to gauge if there was enough room for me on either side of Tyler. "I'll never deny it again," I said, believing it. "I don't want to. Plus, Mike knows and Patrick."

"Mike?"

This was why I was here. Not only did I need to know that Tyler was okay, but I needed him to know what had happened today. "Kevin and I got into it in the weight room. They were there." I shrugged like it wasn't a big deal but I could still hear Mike squealing out of the parking lot.

"How'd that go?" When Tyler turned to face me, he moved over the tiniest bit.

I just shrugged again and grabbed on to the chain of the swing, sort of hanging on it.

"I'm sorry about that, really. But now you have a good idea how I felt." He moved another inch over.

"I didn't know what to expect when I came over or if you'd even be here." I released the chain and slid into the empty space on the swing, relieved that Tyler didn't jump off or tell me to get off. "I seriously thought you were on life support or something."

"I think the goal was to scare, not to kill."

"Are you scared?" I put my hand on Tyler's knee, waiting and hoping.

"More mad that it happened. I didn't go to school not because I couldn't but because I didn't want to talk to anybody. I didn't want them to ask me any questions."

"I get that," I said.

"But, I'm glad you're here." Tyler lifted his hand off his knee and placed it on top of mine. I let it sit there for a second, feeling the weight of his hand on mine, before turning my hand over to embrace Tyler's.

By the time I got home, my mom was on her way out the door to do another second shift at the nursing home. Today was my dad's last day remodeling that basement. I knew he already had gotten the last check from that job, and he had no idea where the next one was going to come from.

"Dad and Robert started without you," Mom said, holding her coat in one arm and slinging her purse over a shoulder. "Grab a plate before there's not any left." As she was about to leave, Mom looked at me and stopped, with one foot out the door. "My god, David, what happened?"

My hand went to my face. Since leaving Tyler's, I'd actually forgotten about the red and purple circles around my eye. It didn't even hurt that much. "It was an accident in the weight room."

"What type of accident?" Mom pulled her foot back in the house, causing the screen door to slam shut. "It looks like someone punched you in the face."

A chair scraped the kitchen floor and Dad's heavy footsteps quickly approached. "Who punched you in the face?" he demanded.

"Mike was doing this lift in the weight room," I quickly said, sticking to my story from before. "My face got in the way. It's fine, seriously."

Dad stood inches away from me, looking over my face, which felt weird. I had to turn away. "Your mom's right. That doesn't look like something that would happen in a weight room."

"Well, it did." I laughed to myself. That, technically, wasn't a lie.

"Are you going to open this or what?" Robert came into the entryway with a bursting manila envelope.

My parents' attention shifted form my eye to the envelope's contents. An excited smile crossed my mom's face. "Yeah, hurry up and open that before I leave."

I remembered sitting in my car on Tyler's street, thinking about the promise the day held if I continued to sit there. With a glance at Mom and Dad, I grabbed the envelope from Robert's outstretched hand and tore it open before I could give it another thought. I held a stack of papers in my hand and read the top one aloud. "David, we are pleased to inform you that there is a spot reserved for you on the Minnesota State University-Mankato baseball roster. Welcome to the home of the Mavericks." I looked up at his parents and Robert, knowing I had a ridiculous smile on his face, but they had the same ones on too.

I went back to the letter. "Along with the spot, we'd like to offer you a scholarship that would cover…" I felt the smile disintegrate along with the bounce that had crept into my voice.

Shit.

My mom's face still held part of the smile. "What? What are they offering you?"

"A partial scholarship." I straightened the packet of paper and worked on stuffing it back in the envelope. "It covers most of the tuition and nothing for room and board."

"What's that?" Robert asked.

"A dorm room and food," Mom said.

"Well, how much could that cost?" Robert shrugged.

I tried to reseal the envelope with the adhesive left on the flap. "About ten thousand dollars a year. Maybe more."

"Ten *thousand*," Robert said.

After a few moments of loud silence, an overly cheerful smile popped onto my mom's face. "It's good news, though, right?"

I just nodded. It wasn't terrible news. Just not the right news.

"They think you're a really good baseball player. They want you to play for them." Mom ticked her sentences off on her fingers. "They're offering you something."

"But it's not enough," Dad said into his shoulder.

"But it's something. And if one school can offer you this, then maybe another will offer you this and more. You're still waiting to hear from Clearwater, right?" The cheerful smile was getting on my nerves.

"Whitewater," I corrected. "But they're D-3. They don't give athletic scholarships."

"Don't go throwing that away just yet," she said, motioning to the envelope. "We might be able to work something out."

"Like what?" Dad flatly said to her. "You got a bank account somewhere that I don't know about? A loan officer who's gonna think we have a decent credit score? Did your job just increase your pay by about two hundred percent?"

Robert gave me a look that said *Uh-oh*. It had been a while since Dad had gone on a tirade about work.

"Greg, stop it," she forcefully whispered as if Robert and I wouldn't be able to hear her. "We'll talk about this later."

Dad shrugged and ambled back to his place at the kitchen table. "There's not much to talk about." He plopped into a chair and served himself way too much rice before hunching over his plate.

Mom turned to me. “We’ll talk about this later.” She squeezed my arm. “Congratulations.”

After Mom slipped out the door, Robert and I walked to the kitchen and slid into our chairs. Dad didn’t look up as he continued to eat, chewing and swallowing so quickly that his plate was almost empty. I moved my food around feeling wiped out from the days of ups and downs.

“Maybe you could do some extra umping this summer,” Robert said. “Or you could call games for my league. I bet they pay more than the stupid park district.”

“That’s an idea, Rob,” I said just to make him feel better. Dad was being irritable enough for everybody, otherwise I would have said something about the stupid Rebels and all their awesomeness.

Dad pushed his chair back. “There’s nothing wrong with the stupid park district,” he said, disappearing down the hallway and closing the door to his bedroom.

CHAPTER 23
DAVID

The next morning, the schedule for spring sports tryouts was announced in the middle of the something about club fundraisers and other school activities. Baseball started on Monday. Five thirty. Softball got the early timeslot the first week and baseball would get it the next. Even though the date had been common knowledge among all the returning players for quite some time now, hearing it on the morning announcements made it seem more real.

I hadn't seen anyone from the team since Mike sped out of the parking lot. Actually, I did see Patrick when I got to school today but when we made eye contact he had ducked his head and sidestepped into the nearest bathroom, almost running into the wall. Patrick and I wouldn't have been considered great friends but we had been teammates as freshmen and then last year when Patrick was moved up to varsity. He rode the bench most of the season because the starting catcher was a senior.

Patrick was pretty funny and usually entertained everyone by drinking odd combinations of pop mixed with the spices and condiments on the table when we all went out for pizza after double headers. He almost threw up last year after drinking orange pop, iced tea, parmesan cheese, and ketchup. While he didn't exactly declare his support for me and march around the weight room waving a pride flag, Patrick didn't tell me to fuck off either. Which is pretty much what my best friend told me to do.

I ate my turkey sandwich on the way to the library, not because I had another paper to type up but because when I went to the cafeteria to see if Mike was at our usual table, he was sitting at a table with some of Carrie's friends and their boyfriends. He always said he didn't really like some of Carrie's friends because he thought they acted dumb and he just didn't get that. I guess he didn't find it all that annoying today.

Maybe it was too many movies and TV shows, but at some point during the day, I expected to see security guards drag Kevin down the hallway as he tried to free himself from their grasp and run away. Tyler decided to stay at home for another day and his parents didn't argue, but they did take him to Lincoln that morning so he could tell the dean, Mr. Landry, what Kevin did to him. All through my psychology teacher's lecture on various brain disorders, I imagined Tyler sitting in one of those damn plastic orange chairs, his parents on either side of him sitting in their own plastic chairs. I had only been in the dean's office once. It was sophomore year when a huge fight erupted in the locker room after PE and the dean wanted to get an account from every witness. Mr. Landry had taken careful notes during my brief deposition, and I knew he was doing the same while Tyler told his story.

Kevin was going to get suspended for at least a few days. He had to. And that suspension would definitely bleed into tryouts. Even though there was no debating that his son was at fault and responsible for Tyler's injuries, Scott Kaminski would still throw a fit about Kevin missing a day or two, if not more. But even without Kevin's dad buzzing in Coach's ear, I knew Coach Kelly would have a hard time cutting Kevin for missing part or even all of tryouts. His curve was that good and his change-up was expected to be lethal this year. That outweighs gay bashing and being a douchebag.

Even if the weight room were open today, I would have opted to skip it. It had nothing to do with Mike, Patrick, or anything baseball related. These free afternoons wouldn't be around next week with baseball and outdoor track starting. Even if the fight with Kevin never happened, and Tyler was at school today, I still would have skipped the workout to head over to Tyler's house. The few days left before spring sports officially started reminded me that in the fall Tyler would be starting classes at U of I and I would be…somewhere, but not in Champaign-Urbana. And not Mankato.

I stopped at my house first with every intention of running in and out so quickly that the screen door wouldn't even shut by the time I rushed back out, but my mom rushed up to me as soon as I walked in.

"Would you be able to pick up Robert from practice today?" She asked. "I'm going to do another shift tonight and can't go get him."

"I'm going over to Tyler's. Can't Dad do it?" I didn't like reminding my mom that Dad wasn't working at the moment and had all this free time, but if he was around then it made sense for him to get Robert.

"If he were home, I'm sure he would," Mom said, picking up her purse.

"Is he working on something?" I asked.

"Kind of." She looked away.

"Did a new job start up?" I never played Twenty Questions with my mom, usually because she never gave me a reason to.

"No, he went to a meeting." Mom busied herself by digging in her purse even though it looked like she was just moving things around.

"Where?"

"A meeting," Mom said again.

"Dad doesn't go to 'meetings'" I replied. "Even when he was working he never went to 'meetings.' What's going on?"

Mom stopped fidgeting in her purse and held her hair in a ponytail. "You can't tell him I told you. He's embarrassed for some reason and doesn't want you or Robert to know."

My stomach did a flip. "What's wrong with him? Is he okay?"

She must have sensed my worry because Mom walked over to me and put a hand on both my shoulders, looking at me squarely. "He's unemployed and has been for over three years."

"So he's at a job interview or something?"

"No, he's at a support group for people who have been unemployed for an extended period of time." Mom gave my shoulders a little squeeze before letting them go.

"Is this about yesterday and Mankato?" I needed to ask because I felt terrible that Dad felt terrible about the partial scholarship.

Mom shook her head. "This is his third time going. Although, I know he doesn't like that he can't help you out. *We* can't help you out." Her eyes were sad. "I'm so sorry, David."

I shrugged, not because I didn't care. I did. Plenty of my classmates were getting full rides to school courtesy of Mom and Dad. Even though I knew Mike was going to get a baseball scholarship to one of his choice schools, it wasn't like he needed it. This girl in my psychology class complained that her parents were making her pay for her own books. I would have gladly paid for my books and her books if it meant I didn't need to worry about any other costs.

"Your dad feels like he can't provide for us the we way he's supposed to. Like he's letting us down." Mom released her hair and tucked it behind her ears. "These meetings help him see that other people are in the same boat as him."

"That sounds like a good thing," I said. "Well, maybe not a good thing, but you know what I mean." I opened the pantry door and looked for something to eat.

"If he feels like he needs to go someplace for some extra support or help and talk to people who can fully understand what he's going through, I told him there's no shame in that." She glanced at the clock and went to the closet to get a Lincoln High School jacket that I outgrew my sophomore year. "I'm glad he finally decided to go. He had been talking about it for over six months, but just started."

"Thanks for telling me," I said.

"I guess he can listen to me say, 'There's nothing wrong with you' and 'Something will come along' only so many times." Mom shrugged on the coat and fastened the three middle snaps. The sleeves were too long and she had to push the cuffs up her forearms to keep them from covering her hands.

"So will you get Robert in an hour and a half? I have to get going. I said I'd be there by 4:00."

"Yeah," I said, not really listening, although I knew I committed to picking up my little brother. "I'm just going to Tyler's first."

A few moments after she left, I watched the van back out of the driveway, narrowly missing my brown beastly car, and disappear down the street. Mom wouldn't be home until close to midnight. She hadn't pulled a double shift like this in a while.

The news about Dad wasn't bad by any stretch, but it caught me off guard. Forgetting my rush to get to Tyler's, I went to the kitchen table with a protein bar and fell into one of the chairs, imagining my dad in a circle of people, hopefully on a chair more comfortable than the ones they have in the school's offices. I tried to picture the group. Some wore suits, unable to get out of the routine of putting one on every morning, while others wore jeans and T-shirts, their daily uniform for however long they'd been unemployed.

I wondered what Dad chose to wear to these meetings. His post-work uniform of a Sox shirt and sweatpants? A polo shirt to feel more professional? That was Dad's idea of dressing up. I glanced at the front door and noticed Dad's gym shoes were kicked to the side, but I didn't see his steel-toe boots. It seemed weird that he would wear them for anything other than work and doing a project around the house, but maybe he wore them for the same reason someone might wear a suit to the support group. Not because they came from work but because it made them feel like they had just come from work. Maybe having a place to go at a certain time reminded them of going to work so they dressed like they were.

I had seen enough movies and TV shows to know the basic format for a meeting for people dealing with various addictions. The circle of people stating their name, the chorus of "Hi [insert name here]," and then sharing the ups and downs since the last meeting. This group probably had a similar format. Maybe Dad would share how he had a good stretch of side jobs, a lot of word of mouth that kept him busy for most of the winter, but now just as spring was finally here, the beginning of what should be a carpenter's busy season, there was nothing. There was probably a lot of talk about mortgages, bills, and past due notices. And also some talk about kids who wanted to go to college and dwindling bank accounts.

I pushed my feet against Tyler's front porch, causing the swing we sat on to sway. "Dad's not really a talker," I said.

"Maybe he does a lot of listening."

"The winter was better than we thought it was going to be. I thought that would make him feel better."

Tyler rubbed the inside of my palm. "How long has it been?"

"About four years," I said, remembering the day Dad came home with the news that he would no longer have a job by the end of the week. With his knowledge and experience, I thought he would have no problem finding a job. But all this time later and Dad was still on the hunt…at least I thought he was. It didn't occur to me until that moment that maybe Dad had given up looking for steady work.

A strong breeze with a slight bite to it swept through the porch as Tyler burrowed his head into my shoulder. "That's a long time."

"And it seems like it's going to be even longer," I sighed.

We sat in silence for a few moments, lazily rolling our ankles in unison to keep the swing moving. Tyler laced his fingers through mine, my favorite way to hold hands. "Then it's a good thing he has that group."

"I just didn't think it was that bad," I said.

"Maybe the people in that group help him remember that he's not the only one. That there are other people out there struggling to find a job and take care of a family, just like him." It sounded so logical when Tyler said it. "Things don't have to be terrible to need a reminder."

"I know he's embarrassed about it," I said. "It's fine when he's busy and working on something but when the job is coming to an end or he's waiting for the next one to come along, he stays in his bedroom until Robert and I leave for school. Like he's jealous we have some place to go and he doesn't. Or maybe he doesn't want to remind us that he doesn't."

"That's sad," Tyler said.

I nodded. "It makes me kind of sad to think about it."

Tyler suddenly stood up. "Come on." He reached back to take my hand again.

"I have to get going soon," I took Tyler's hand. "I told my mom I'd get Robert in a little while." As I stuffed Tyler's hand and my hand into the pouch of my sweatshirt, I wondered how late I could be picking up Robert before he got really pissed and told Mom I forgot about him. "Where are we going?"

"I want to go somewhere with you," Tyler said, leading me across the street.

I raised my eyebrows to myself. "Some place you take all your boyfriends?"

Tyler stopped walking. "Some place I haven't been in a long time but now I want to go there and I want to go there with you."

I felt the smile fall off my face when Tyler turned to face me and I got a good look at the butterflies that arched over his eyebrow. The swelling on the one side of his face was practically gone, but there were still purple and yellow swirls under an eye and across part of his forehead. "I'll go anywhere with you," I said, knowing I meant it in every sense.

CHAPTER 24
TYLER

I smiled and squeezed David's hand, picking up my pace. "It's just a few blocks from here."

If I wanted David to understand that his dad needed support and that he had support, maybe I needed to take my own advice and finally tell someone about the thing I never thought I would ever tell anyone about.

David didn't say anything as I dragged him down the sidewalk. Since he didn't know where we were going, he had to let me take the lead and that seemed to relax him a little bit. We walked silently. David must have sensed my urgency. The only time we strayed from the sidewalk was when a group of boys about Robert's age came whizzing by on skateboards and we had to walk on someone's lawn for a few steps.

I kept my eyes on the passing cracks in the sidewalk and looked down a street before hurrying across.

"Are we having a race or something?" I heard the laugh in David's voice as we hurried to catch up. "You're going to win so don't worry about it."

"We're almost there."

Knowing the close proximity to where we were headed, I felt a dull ache stretch across the back of my shoulders. Another block to go.

"We're here." I stopped.

"We are?" David asked, looking around. There was sidewalk to our right and left, but right in front of us, the sidewalk abruptly turned into a limestone path that led into a forest preserve full of trees that were just starting to get their buds for spring.

The night it happened, the mass of trees coupled with the dusk sky made it look like something from a kid's nightmare. I thought it was ridiculous that I let myself think the forest was full of bad guys. As if on cue, another biting breeze rustled the branches and swirled around David and me.

I dug my fingertips into the back of David's hand. "Yeah, follow me." Clumps of tall, gray trees quickly surrounded us. Our shoes plodded along in an uneven rhythm on the path still wet from the winter. The sound alone made me want to run back to the sidewalk but David anchored me at his side. "The last time I was here, I was by myself," I said to the gravel ground. "It was almost two years ago."

"Really? This seems like a good place to do some running. Much better than the circles around the track," David kicked a larger piece of limestone further down the path. "I always thought that had to be kind of boring."

"Yeah, I thought so too." I nodded my head but it felt like it was detached from my body. The path looked long and never ending. I stared down as far as I could like there was a finish line somewhere in the distance.

I felt David's eyes on me. He stopped walking, forcing me to do the same. Standing in front of me, blocking the imaginary finish line, David looked me in the eye. "What happened?"

And I told him. Told him about the evening run that seemed like a good idea. How I wanted to try to run the whole twenty-mile trail before the end of the summer. About how it was getting darker but I thought I could do one more mile. About distant laughter that got closer as approaching feet slapped on the limestone. I had no idea how many. Shouts of "Cocksucker," "When did they start letting fags come here," and "How'd you like this up your ass?" About something hitting me in the back, right between the shoulders. And then something else. About skidding on the limestone and falling. About being crumpled on the ground when something else hit me. About getting up and running. And running. Running all the way home. About sitting on the porch. About not doing or saying anything.

No inflection. No emotion. As if I read from a teleprompter about something that happened to somebody else.

"Oh my god," David said, wrapping me in his arms. The bruised side of my face rubbed against David's, but it didn't hurt. David also put his head on my shoulder and I was grateful that we were practically the same height.

I wasn't sure how long we stood like that. Random breezes and distant voices coming from the path's entrance were the only things that indicated a passage of time. Eventually, David broke away from me but clutched my hand as we walked back to the entryway and out of the forest preserve that really did house villains from nightmares.

CHAPTER 25
DAVID

I didn't want to think about my phone in my pocket, urging me to check the time since I wasn't sure how long Tyler and I had been gone. Mom said I had an hour and a half and what I really wanted was forever. Or at least a couple more hours.

The thought of Tyler curled up in a ball on the ground helpless to defend himself from some stupid fucks was too much. Instead, I thought of when I stepped out of the weight room side door last summer, the one that led outside, and walked to a nearby drinking fountain. I would work out in the morning and ump games in the evening. The water in the drinking fountain was lukewarm and tasted a little funny. When I turned around, I saw Tyler rounding the track in a pair of blue running shorts and no shirt. His dark blonde hair even darker since it was soaked with sweat. He glided right by me, and I didn't wipe the water dripping down my chin. The stride. Arms pumping at his side. Everything about him looked confident. I not only wanted to be like him, I wanted to be with him.

"Nobody knows about that," Tyler said once we were back on the sidewalk and walking back to his house. "I never told anyone. Not even when I started going to SAFE."

"Did you want to tell them?" I don't know if I would have told Mom and Dad about anything that was going on with me if Mom hadn't caught me picking a fight with the kitchen cabinets last week.

"No. Just going there was enough to make me stop thinking about it for a little while."

"Do you have any idea who it was?" If Tyler could give me the smallest clue, maybe I could find them. I wanted to find them, tie them to a backstop, and hit line drives at them.

Tyler just shook his head. "I never saw them. Just heard them. And it was getting dark."

I shook my head, trying to comprehend what Tyler went through that night and then last week with Kevin. "Do you think about it a lot?"

"Up until a few days ago, not really."

"I'm sorry." I looked down.

"For what?"

"For you getting hurt."

"Don't be," Tyler shrugged. "I'm back to loving you again."

I tripped even though there was nothing in the sidewalk blocking my path. I glanced at Tyler, who kept on walking as if he just said the sky was blue. I smiled slyly and gave Tyler a sideways glance. "It took getting your head bashed on a bathroom sink to realize you love me?"

"I knew I loved you before I got my head bashed on a bathroom sink," Tyler said. "It took that to make me realize that I still love you."

"Cool," I said, feeling my cheeks get hot and a silly grin spread across my face. "I love you too." I'd never said it before but it felt natural. I liked it.

Tyler smiled at the sidewalk. "I was hoping."

We walked up Tyler's driveway and sat back down on the porch swing. I finally checked my phone. If I didn't leave in the next three minutes, I would definitely be late picking up Robert and I'd never hear the end of how I forgot him.

Tyler and I turned to each other at the same time and we laughed a little. Tyler kissed me first. Then I kissed his forehead, the butterflies above his eye, his cheek, and finally his mouth. We'd never kissed on the porch during the day before. Robert would have to wait just a little bit longer.

CHAPTER 26
DAVID

Tyler did go to school the next day and just like he predicted, questions and turned heads greeted him in every class. While it was pretty clear that Tyler got into a fight, no one knew who it was that threw the punches except for me and now Mr. Landry. I assumed Kevin didn't brag about it because he knew he would definitely get in trouble. Since there was no denying his role, Kevin's dad couldn't appeal the suspension or go to any higher-ups to insist his son was being unfairly punished.

Even with so many things still up in the air, I felt lighter knowing Tyler was back at school. I couldn't remember the last time I had ever enjoyed a period of Art Appreciation so much and it had nothing to do with the slide show and discussion of street art and graffiti as actual art.

At lunch, Mike again sat with Carrie's friends and their boyfriends. He happened to look up just as I walked by with my usual sandwich, ready to eat it on the way to the library and look up White Sox stats and predictions for the upcoming season. There were worse ways to spend a lunch period.

"Hey David," a guy named Jason looked at me from under a fringe of hair that almost hung in his eyes. I remembered him from the few times we all hung out together.

I nodded a greeting since my mouth was full, noticing that Mike seemed to grip the table as I approached.

"You want to sit with us?" Jason asked, moving his chair over.

"He can't," Mike said. "He's got a paper to write." He wound his ankles around the chair legs.

"Nope." I shook my head, looking directly at Mike. "The *1984* paper was due last week." The muscles in Mike's arms flinched. "But there is this Spanish project I have to work on. Thanks, though."

"All right," Jason said as I walked away. "See ya'."

If Tyler could survive an attack in the forest preserve and be in the same building with Kevin without hiding in the bathroom then I could stand up to my best friend. Even if I hated that I even had to stand up to him.

Tyler had to go to a short meeting about the outdoor track season and I was going to give him a ride home after so we could continue taking advantage of the precious free time that would be gone next week. After going to my locker, I slowly walked the hallway that led to the athletic wing of Lincoln, killing time until the end of Tyler's meeting.

"And that's when I said, 'Are those books really happy or do they like to have sex with each other? Is that why they're gay?'" An excited high-pitched voice came out from an open classroom door. I cocked an ear toward the direction of the voice.

Then I heard a polite laugh. "Good one, Anna. What did your teacher say when you said that?"

It was Ms. Larson. I was right outside her room. Sometimes I saw her standing outside of it but I hadn't seen her since that day in the library. She was erasing the day's lesson from the whiteboard and I remembered how she managed to fill the board with information almost every day. Ms. Larson always used a different color for each definition or note, insisting that a variety of colors made the board more interesting to look at. A girl sat on the center desk in the front row, swinging her legs. Even from out in the hallway, I could see that she had white canvas shoes with thick rainbow laces.

"He said that *The Scarlet Letter* could hardly be considered to have a cheery mood given how it's about the Puritans and that Logan should probably read the book so he could find a better word to use to describe it."

Ms. Larson put down her eraser. "Hopefully Logan heeds his advice. I think your teacher handled that really well."

The girl, Anna, hopped off the desk and began moving the desks around into a circle. "Well, I just wanted to tell you that story before everyone got here. I know I usually bother you with something that made me mad or how stupid people are, but today I had a good story and figured you would want to know about it." Anna cocked her head to the side. "Well, I guess there was some stupidity, but the good kind of cancels it out."

"I'm glad you focused on something positive. It's easy to get caught up in the negative," Ms. Larson said.

I wished I had been in Anna's class today, even though I read *The Scarlet Letter* last year and never wanted to read it again. But, I didn't think I'd have anything in common with Hester Prynne and the 'A' that made her an outcast and was surprised that I was able to connect with a single mother suffering through life in the 1600's.

I had no idea who this Anna girl was, obviously she was younger than me, but maybe if I had a class with her and had seen her rainbow shoelaces every day or met Allie earlier I wouldn't be dealing with a secret boyfriend with a busted up face, an angry best friend, and non-existent post-graduation plans.

"Hey, David." Adam strolled past me with a wave and whistled a nondescript tune like he was walking through a park in an old movie.

"Hi, Adam," I said to the empty hallway since he was already inside Ms. Larson's classroom by the time I responded.

"Adam," I heard Anna exclaim. "Ms. Larson got the permission slips for the dance. Are you going to go?"

"Probably." I saw Adam put his bag on one of the tables where I remembered doing science experiments freshman year. Adam then went to the whiteboard, settled on a marker color and wrote "agenda" at the top of the board.

Two girls approached me from the other direction, a short blonde in a Lincoln High School student council T-shirt and the other, a tall girl with brown skin that looked like she should be a ballet dancer. They walked in sync but were focused on their phones as they turned into Ms. Larson's classroom.

"Wow, you're just jumping in headfirst, aren't you?" Allie walked up to me, chuckling to herself. "Coming out to me the other day… joining the GSA today. Maybe you'll decide to hang up those baseball cleats and try out for the musical instead. It's *Oklahoma!* this year."

She had on her uniform of skinny jeans, a plaid shirt, and some band T-shirt. "No, I'm not going," I said. "I was just passing by."

"And stopped right outside the door in the middle of a really long step?" Allie raised an eyebrow.

I smiled. "No, the girl in the rainbows was telling Ms. Larson an interesting story and I might have listened in."

"Oh, you're just spying on us then."

"She's going to tell the story later on." I turned to face Allie. "You'll like it."

"What the hell happened to you?"

I had forgotten about my eye. It didn't look nearly as bad as I thought it was going to, but it probably still shocked someone who wasn't expecting it. "I ran into someone."

"Ran into someone's fist?"

"It ran into me." I shrugged.

Allie craned her neck to see the clock near the door in Ms. Larson's room. "Well, I think we're going to get started soon so I better go in. You know, new members are welcome any time."

"I've heard." I felt like I swallowed something without really chewing it as I remembered the last time someone invited me to a SAFE meeting.

"I know there's not a lot of us in there." Allie jerked her neck towards the lopsided circle that wasn't quite filled in with students. The two girls with the phones sat by one another. Anna stood at the board drawing something with one of the many markers. "But there are some of us and that's better than none, right?"

"True," I nodded, suddenly feeling a nervous energy pulse in my stomach, the kind I usually only got when I was up to bat with the game on the line.

"See you later," Allie said, ducking into the classroom and taking a seat on the opposite side of the girls.

Glancing at the clock, I guessed I had at least seven minutes before Tyler would be out of the track meeting. More than enough time. I rushed down the hallway, as if about to be late to class. The boy with the swoosh of hair across his forehead and the turquoise and black hoodie plodded towards me. "Hey, Will," I said, racing past him.

"Hey," Will looked at me. "How do you know my name?"

I didn't get a chance to answer because I was already too far away from him. I suddenly thought of something I needed to do at this exact moment. Something I should have done from the beginning and finally found the balls to do.

When I swung open the door to the athletic office, Mrs. Carlson put her hand to her chest and her eyes widened, but she quickly folded her hands on the desk and smiled a hesitant smile. I guess I scared her when the office door thudded off the wall as I opened it.

"Hello. David, right?"

"Uh, yeah," I walked up to her desk. "Is Coach Kelly in his office?" My hand beat against the side of my leg like I was in the middle of a crowd at a rock concert.

Mrs. Carlson looked at the closed door. "I believe he is. Would you like to speak to him?"

"Yeah." I continued to slightly bob up and down. "Can I go in?"

Mrs. Carlson glanced at the phone on her desk. "Well, he's been on the phone for quite some time but let me tell him you're here and see if he wants you to wait or come back later." She scooted her chair back. "David…Lukas is it?"

"Yeah."

"Have a seat."

While I bobbed my way over to the chairs opposite Coach Kelly's door, Mrs. Carlson poked her head inside the office and emerged a few moments later.

"Just give him a few minutes." She sat back down at her desk. "He's just about finishing up."

I took my eyes off of Coach Kelly's office door and saw Mrs. Carlson staring at me. Maybe the fading colors swirling around my eye caught her off guard. She pretended to be overly concerned about straightening the piles of paper on her desk, making sure not one corner was out of place. Maybe she thought I was pretty weird, bouncing into the office like a super ball but I'd never felt this way before. Not before giving a speech in class, not before a big at-bat, not even when I came out to Dad on the porch last summer. I had told him then that I didn't know how this worked and I still didn't. But what I was doing definitely wasn't working. It got me into a fight with my boyfriend, made me possibly lose my best friend, and let the biggest dick in school hold something over me that he had no right to.

Sensing that Mrs. Carlson would prefer if I looked somewhere else, my gaze fell on the shrine to Carl Howell who did get the call up to Triple A ball. Mike told me a few days ago and thought it would be pretty cool if everyone could take a little road trip to catch one of his games in Indianapolis where the team was based. Maybe they could even get Coach to drive one of the team vans.

That was before Mike didn't even want to sit in the cafeteria with me.

The sound of the door to Coach Kelly's office being opened pulled me back into the athletic office. "Coach, hi." I jumped up, waiting for Coach Kelly to officially say I could come inside.

"Oh Christ, you too?" Coach Kelly sighed.

"What?"

Coach Kelly opened the door a little wider so I could go into the office. "Get in here."

I stepped inside and stood next to the familiar plastic chair, opting not to sit down. I would lose my nerve if I did.

"Did Kaminski do that?" Coach Kelly leaned against his desk, his hands folded around the bottom of his belly.

"Do what?"

"I've been on the phone all afternoon with Mr. Landry. I'm assuming you heard about…an altercation of sorts took place between Kaminski and…someone on the track team last week." Coach shook his head like a frustrated parent.

"I'm aware, Coach." I felt my energy waver slightly and rushed on. "But that's not why I'm here. I came to tell you something."

"And what is that?"

"Well, Coach, I just want to say it to you. I know you know but it's not the same." The team pictures behind the desk caught my eye again and I wondered what this year's photo would look like. Coach Kelly was about to say something, but I cut him off. "I am gay, Coach. I am." Like a basketball that was slowly coming to a stop, I stopped bouncing. All of my energy went into those two little sentences and suddenly, I was tired. But I felt pretty good too. "And I don't know what Kevin and his dad wants to do with that but I want to play baseball. I need to play baseball."

Coach Kelly's eye twitched. "I know."

"Nothing else has anything to do with that."

I waited a second for him to say more, but Coach stopped after two words. He just leaned on his desk, holding his belly. I wasn't expecting a pat on the back or a high five, but I didn't know what to do with Coach Kelly's stare and silence.

"Well, I don't know what Kaminski and his dad can do," Coach finally said.

That sounded somewhat positive. I waited for Coach to go on.

"Anything else?" he asked

"Well," I started walking towards the office door and reached for the handle. "I guess I'll see you on Monday at tryouts."

"I shouldn't be telling you this but you're going to find out soon enough once it gets out. Kaminski got suspended for seven days for what he did." I couldn't read Coach Kelly's tone of voice. He didn't sound angry, or frustrated, or glad. It sounded like he was explaining why the infield fly rule was called.

"Good," I said.

"Who did that to you?" Coach jutted his chin at my face.

I brought my hand to my eye, feeling the tenderness that covered my eyebrow and cheek. It was healing but I guess it was still noticeable. "Weight room accident."

"Look David," Coach Kelly said, "you have a lot riding on this season and quite a few distractions have popped up for the last couple weeks. Kaminski and his dad aside. Do you think you can handle it? I've seen players sabotage themselves at the thought of a scout in the stands, let alone the prospect of playing college ball and…everything else you have going on."

"I had a good season for you last year, Coach. I plan on having an even better one this year," I responded, trying to figure out if Coach Kelly was being supportive or trying to get me to quit to get Kevin and his dad to shut up.

"I hope so."

It was one thing to bound into the office and make a declaration when it was just me and Coach. But practices, games, bus rides, and lunch breaks during double headers were going to be a completely different story. I might have felt brave in this moment, in the confines of an office with the door closed and only Coach Kelly around, but I had no idea what was in store once the season started.

Would Mike do the warm-up routine with another partner even though we'd always done it together? Would I get high fives after trotting back to the dugout after scoring a run? Would a school renege on their offer or not even make one on the grounds that there are many talented prospects and I "just didn't make the cut?"

I put a hand on the door handle and pushed down, but held the door shut for a moment. "Well, see you at tryouts, Coach."

"See you on Monday, 5:30. Be ready to go." Coach Kelly pushed himself off the desk and walked around to the other side.

"I will be." I pulled open the door and walked out of the office, remembering how I told Allie that I didn't want this to be a big deal. Coach not jumping up and down or kicking me out of the office meant it wasn't a big deal, right?

As the office door latched shut I thought that this what a

closer must feel like after only facing one batter and ending the game. The anticipation, the energy that builds up in your body for such a short time and then it was over.

"It took guts to go in there like that." Mrs. Carlson nodded towards Coach Kelly's door.

"You can hear everything going on in there?" I wondered what else Mrs. Carlson might have overheard.

"If it's really quiet in here. I try not to eavesdrop, but sometimes it's impossible," Mrs. Carlson explained. "I'm sorry if I was out of place by giving you that pamphlet."

"It's okay." I shrugged, honestly forgetting about that moment until just now, and headed for the door.

Mrs. Carlson carefully put down her stack of papers. "And I'm sorry if it was even more out of line to talk to Ms. Larson about you."

I stopped, midstep. "That was you?"

Mrs. Carlson distracted herself by putting a couple stray pens back in its cup and moving a picture frame on her desk a couple inches over.

"I have a nephew...You reminded me of him."

"He plays baseball too, huh?" I let out a fake laugh and swung open the door. "I hope he has an awesome season."

CHAPTER 27
TYLER

After a three-minute warm-up, I increased the speed on the treadmill to eight miles an hour, feeling the even rhythm of my feet slapping the rubber one after another. Track started tomorrow. Baseball started tomorrow. David and I had a lot to prove this season. I took third in State last year in the 3200 because my leg cramped up during the last half lap. That wasn't going to happen again. I'd been working on my final kick all year. At least the laps on the track last summer were good for that.

And David, he had a lot riding on this year too. More than just a scholarship that I wish I could magically find for him. I wish I could tell him everything was going to be fine but I never believed that line when someone said it to me. I don't think anyone does.

I turned on my running playlist. Looking at the beige basement walls reminded me that I was stuck inside, going nowhere like a hamster on a wheel. But if I looked between the machine and floor and turned up the bass of the electronic music I liked to listen to when I ran, the walls and the machine seemed to fade away.

It was easy to get lost in the noise and beat. And pretty soon my feet were moving on their own and my mind turned off. All I heard was the bass, pounding in perfect time with my stride.

The only image in my head was the upcoming curve followed by the last straightaway. Almost time for the final kick.

I increased the speed to ten miles an hour.

It was the best time to pass someone. I remember coming up on a guy in regionals last year who was already almost out of gas. When I passed him, he did a double take and I guess that took too much energy because I glided right by him and finished first.

The final kick was key. So much could happen in those last 200 meters. You could get a cramp. Someone might be losing steam. You could find out that you're capable of more than you ever thought.

Feeling my lungs start to burn and my legs begin to protest, I increased the speed to eleven miles an hour, focusing on that imaginary curve and straightaway.

Finish strong.

Finish strong.

Finish strong.

CHAPTER 28
DAVID

Because softball got the early time slot of right after school, I was able to go home before tryouts, which meant I could change into my practice clothes, organize my equipment there, and just go straight from my car to the field house before tryouts and straight from the field house to my car after. My plan was to get there four minutes early. Some of the guys would be there before then, and there were always a few that seemed to test the coaches' patience and slide in seconds before we were about to begin. I didn't want to be the first one, but I didn't want to be last either.

I would have liked to spend the down time with Tyler, but if it wasn't a downpour or below freezing, the track team now practiced outside which meant right after school. And Tyler would be jogging around the track in the hat with the little puffball on a string.

Walking into the quiet house made me antsy. Robert was at travel ball practice. Mom was probably at work, maybe putting in another double shift. I wasn't sure where my dad was. I hadn't been home this early in a while and didn't know how he spent his days now that there wasn't any work going on. Maybe he was meeting with someone about a prospective job. Maybe he was at another support group meeting. I didn't know how often they met.

I dropped my book bag on the kitchen floor, the thud reminding me that I could do homework during this time, but getting something to eat was more pressing. With the fridge kind of empty, I moved on to the pantry to see if the snack selection was any better. There wasn't much to choose from, not because there wasn't any money for food but because my mom hadn't had a chance to do some serious grocery shopping in a couple weeks.

"I finished the cheese at lunch."

I almost hit my head on the wall as I jumped out of the pantry. My dad stood by the kitchen table in one of his post-work/no-work uniforms. Today a black World Series T-shirt accompanied a pair of dark gray sweats. Since he wasn't wearing any socks, I guessed that Dad hadn't been out of the house today.

"That's okay." I picked a pear out of the fruit bowl. It only had a couple of brown spots on it. "I'm just killing time before tryouts."

My dad's eyes brightened a little even though the rest of his face and body looked like they were supporting several sheets of drywall. "They're today?"

"Yep," I said. We hadn't talked much since the packet from Mankato came in the mail. I added it to the pile of college materials in my room, unable to ignore the crinkled envelope from Sinni poking out from the middle. I'd looked inside the envelope from Mankato once more since the initial opening, thinking maybe I missed some information or the numbers would somehow add up to something different.

Dad leaned on the kitchen table with his hip. "How's everything going?"

I shrugged. "Okay, I guess."

"And what about our favorite all-star pitcher?"

Again, I shrugged. "Kevin got suspended. He's going to miss the first day of tryouts."

My dad smiled to himself. "His dad is going to let that happen?"

"He beat up Tyler and there really wasn't any way for him to deny it."

The smirk left Dad's eyes and was replaced by concern. "Tyler? Is he okay?"

I nodded. "It was a little while ago. Tyler's fine. He's pretty tough." Tougher than I thought. A lot tougher. Tougher than me.

"You didn't say anything about it. I'm glad he's all right." Dad pushed himself off the kitchen table. "Your mom made a list of stuff today. I'll go to the store tomorrow."

I threw the pear core into the trash and opened the pantry again, searching for something I might have missed on the first pass. "Is she working during the day tomorrow?"

"She actually has the day off, but I figure she's probably not going to bounce out of bed bright and early."

I spied a granola bar that probably fell out of the box some time ago because it was almost smashed into the corner of the shelf. It still felt somewhat soft so I decided to take a chance. "She's been working a lot."

Dad grunted. "Unlike some people."

"That's not what I meant." I couldn't keep the edge out of my voice, legit annoyed that Dad would think I would give him a hard time about not having a job.

"I know," he said, folding his arms. "But it's what I'm thinking."

Halfway through the granola bar and it suddenly tasted stale. "It's a little slow right now, but it will pick up once it really gets warmer." I knew Dad had heard it all before but I didn't know what else to say.

"Don't do that," he shook his head. "You need to focus on today and your tryouts and the season."

"I'm pretty sure I have a place on the team, Dad."

"But there's more riding on this season than others."

I could imagine the corner of the manila envelope from Mankato sticking out from in between two brochures. "Something will work out." I didn't even believe the words as I said them so I'm sure Dad didn't either, but he didn't seem to hear me.

"This guy I know, his kid is pissed at him because he can't send him to some fancy school and he has to go to community college instead." Dad kind of snorted.

"Who's this guy?" I asked.

My dad's hesitation was noticeable, but he just shrugged. "This guy I was talking to. He's been out of work for a few years too. He did something with computers and his job became obsolete. I don't know." Dad threw up his hands. "But, I can't even scrounge up a couple thousand bucks for community college."

"I haven't given much thought to community college," I said, clearly seeing the Sinni envelope with my name written on it.

"You shouldn't have to listen to your old man go on and on about this," Dad snapped. "You have to focus on tonight."

"It's only the first day. Probably a lot of calisthenics and boring drills." I walked back to the front door to get my backpack. Maybe I would do some homework. "Tomorrow will be more intense." Plus, Kevin would be there.

"That works out because I won't be around to bother you tomorrow."

"Because you're going to the store for Mom?" I gave my dad another chance to tell me about the support group meetings.

"I'll do that in the morning some time."

"Where are you going in the afternoon?" I tried again.

"For Christ's sake. Enough with the questions, David." He closed his eyes for an extra-long blink and roughly ran his fingers through his dark hair that had some white mixed in at the sides.

"Sorry," I said, not feeling the least bit sorry and walked to my room. My dad just got done telling me how I needed to focus on tryouts and the season and he was the one adding to the growing pile of distractions.

CHAPTER 29
DAVID

When I walked into the field house with my equipment bag slung over a shoulder and last year's cap pulled down over my eyes, a large group was already assembled in the center. All three levels of baseball tried out together even though certain players were already guaranteed a spot on varsity or junior varsity and there was a slim chance of any freshmen being moved up a level. However, this allowed coaches to see if an underclassman had the skill to play up and also gave the freshmen something to aspire to from the very beginning of their baseball careers at Lincoln.

With the exception of a couple nods of recognition from a couple guys, no one acknowledged me as I dropped my bag at the outer edge of the group and sat down. I felt like it was the first day of tryouts freshman year when the team's reputation for success and winning seasons was common knowledge and I had hoped I was good enough to make the freshman squad.

My teammates from the past three years, some longer if you counted Little League, fractioned themselves off into small groups of people that they hung out with and talked to outside of baseball. Even though I had known all of these guys for quite some time, Mike was really the only one I really talked to and hung out with when it wasn't baseball season. But now, Mike stood with Kurt and Alex, two back up players who sat on the bench a lot last season. Kurt had stood in the back row of team photos ever since freshman year because he was almost six feet tall in eighth grade. Everyone thought he played basketball. He might get some playing time this season since the starting third baseman graduated, but Alex was just a utility player who mainly got to play in doubleheaders.

Unless you counted the words we indirectly said to one another in the cafeteria last week, which I didn't, Mike and I hadn't talked to one another since he sped away in the parking lot. The only time I hadn't started a baseball season not sitting by Mike was my first year of Little League, before we knew one another. Maybe if I had found the balls to tell Mike before he heard it from Kevin he'd be sitting next to me, assuring me that it was going to be a kick ass season and none of the shit from the past few weeks mattered. He could have done that anyway.

Coach Kelly and the rest of the coaching staff walked out of the training room as Coach Kelly blew a whistle. "Ten laps around, gents!" He yelled. A few of the upperclassmen groaned at the idea of running. "That's a whole mile, I know. The same I run each morning when I get to school. Takes me eleven whole minutes. If I can do it and you can't, you probably should have worked a little bit harder in the off-season." Coach Kelly scanned the crowd and his eyes settled on me. "From what I understand some have been putting more time in than others. The weight room was a little empty the past few weeks."

At the mention of the weight room, Mike quickly looked at me. I was ready for it, catching Mike's glance like a routine grounder, seeing the ball all the way into my glove before Mike turned away again.

"Where's Kevin?" I heard someone whisper loudly.

"He's been out of school all week," was a response.

"Dude, he'd never miss tryouts, a practice, a game, anything."

"Maybe he doesn't need to be here because of his fancy scholarship."

"Nah, even if he didn't have to play he'd still show up just to show off."

"Well, he is part of the reason we went as far as we did last year."

"The paper did a whole thing about his private pitching lessons and his curve."

I guessed no one knew about Kevin's fight with Tyler.

Soon, the entire group of about seventy players jogged around the field house in a loud shuffle. I found myself sandwiched in a group of sophomores as the freshmen led the pack as they did every year, hoping to impress the coaches. "Do they ever move up any sophomores?" A boy in a Tigers cap asked me.

"Sometimes," I nodded. "I moved up when I was a sophomore. So did Mike and uh, Kevin."

"Cool! That means there's a chance then." Another boy smiled at the friends jogging around him. "Maybe all of us will make varsity this year."

They continued to excitedly speculate the odds of making it to the next level of their baseball careers but I drowned it out as I thought about Tyler and the countless laps he had run around this very track. And just as I imagined Tyler picking off one more runner in the final lap of his longest race, I saw him standing in the corner of the field house, his nose and cheeks bright pink from an outside workout. A yellow/greenish mark streaked under his eye and a scar over the other was the only evidence of what happened with Kevin. Similar colors circled my eye.

Tyler saw me as I approached a curve and we held each other's gaze until I couldn't see him anymore without turning my head all the way around. Right before he was about to disappear from my view, I could see the smallest of smiles form on Tyler's face. Something special just for me.

By the time I made my way back to that corner, Tyler had already left and I felt a little disappointed.

"Ask him," said one of the sophomores.

"You do it," whispered another.

I wasn't in the mood to give the swarm of sophomores a pep talk about their chances of being on varsity as an underclassman so I picked up my pace to break away from them but a couple kept up with me.

"Hey," said the one in the Tigers cap, striding along side me and lowering his voice so it was hard to hear him above the noise in the field house. "We, uh, we heard that someone on varsity is..." He looked at his friends, "…gay. Is that true?"

"Really?" I didn't break from the rhythm of my steady jog. I knew this was coming. I spotted Mike in the middle of Kurt and Alex, about fifteen yards ahead of me. Alex must have just said something stupid because Mike gave him a shove and Kurt laughed. "Where'd you hear that?" I looked straight ahead, my eyes following the lines that divided the lanes on the track.

The sophomore kept his voice low. "In the locker room. A couple of the varsity guys were talking about it. They said they don't want to play with someone who's…you know."

"Really?" I said again, disguising the hurt in my voice but feeling it in every limb of my body.

"So it's true?"

I didn't know this kid at all. He looked familiar, probably from tryouts last year or from the locker room. "It's true."

"Who is it?" The crew scanned the pack circling the field house, looking for the answer.

"Me."

The sophomores jogging with me stopped, creating a small pile-up on the track. "You?" they all said at once.

"Uh huh." I kept going so I didn't know what their face looked like but I felt their eyes on me. After a second, I heard the group start jogging again at a slower shuffle but I kept my pace from before. I still had three laps to go and needed to prove to Coach how I was ready and focused on the upcoming season.

CHAPTER 30
TYLER

Waiting to get a ride home from David crossed my mind, but sitting around for two hours seemed like a stupid thing to do. I wanted to tell him that I knew what it was like to wonder if someone knew or if you had to tell them, and then wonder why you even had to tell them in the first place.

One of my teammates drove me home but I didn't go inside my house right away. From the look of the dark house, it didn't seem like my parents were around anyway. I was about to sit on the stoop but opted for the swing instead.

I put myself into a trance by slowly swaying back and forth and thinking about David and what might be going on at tryouts.

Coming out was a never-ending process. Something you always had to do. I was out at my old school. And then I came to Lincoln, I had to do it all over again. When I went off to U of I in the fall, it would be the same thing.

If it mattered so much, it would be nice if it was the norm when introducing yourself to also state your sexual orientation. Like telling someone where you were from.

"Hey, I'm Tom from Cleveland and I'm straight."

"Straight? My brother is straight too."

"Hi, everyone. My name is Julie. I'm from Vermont and I'm bisexual."

"I've always wanted to go to Vermont! Cool."

"Tyler. Originally from Chicago and now some town you probably never heard of. Gay."

Simple.

CHAPTER 31
DAVID

When Patrick came red-faced and huffing and puffing down the last straightaway, Coach Kelly blew his whistle and unzipped a bag of baseballs. "Warm-up routine!" he yelled. "Partner up, let's go."

Out of habit, I immediately looked for Mike. We had warmed up together before every practice and every game except for the ones freshmen year when I had that nasty blister on my finger and for a week sophomore year when Mike had the flu. Mike went to get a ball but instead of walking towards me, he turned and positioned himself in front of Kurt, who was already waiting for the first throw. Last year, Mike told me he hated turning double plays with Kurt because his throws were always off.

Keeping my head down, I went to get a ball for myself, trying to come up with a plan before I reached the bag and had a ball in my hand. Throwing with a freshman or one of the assistant coaches would be so embarrassing.

"I'll throw with you."

I turned to see Patrick standing behind me, still breathing heavily from the run.

"You got a ball?" he asked, jamming his catcher's mitt on his hand.

"Yep," I responded, watching Patrick shuffle to a spot on the field house floor. When he got to the end of the line of partners, he gave me a small wave with his mitt, indicating that he was ready for a throw. A ridiculous wave of relief passed over my shoulders as I stuffed the ball into the pocket of my glove, and trotted over to Patrick.

I never had any desire to be a catcher before, but I would have liked to spend more time at Patrick's side with the pitchers and catchers than huddled in a line with the other infielders when warm ups were over. Two of the JV coaches hit balls to the players who were separated into two lines. I noticed Mike got in the back of the line that I was in and stood a few feet further back.

One of the coaches hit a grounder between two players and it was scooped up by a freshman who looked at his glove like he was surprised to see the ball in there. I took a couple steps forward, waiting for my turn.

"Maybe he's on vacation or something?" It was this junior who would probably be on varsity this year. I forgot his name.

"Seriously?" That was Kurt. "You think his dad would plan a family vacation during tryouts week?"

"I'm guessing he got suspended or something," Mike said in a tone that seemed proud to know something few others did.

I crouched in the ready position a few feet away from a junior who started the guessing game on where Kevin might be.

"Suspended?" Kurt laughed. "You think his dad would let that happen? I heard freshmen year he drew a dick on this frog diagram and Scotty got him out of that one on the technicality that it was biology."

"That's fucking hilarious," Alex laughed too.

With my body still facing forward, I craned my neck to keep an ear on the conversation but then I heard the sound of a ball connecting with a bat. The ball skipped to my left and I lunged at it, seeing the ball whiz just under my outstretched glove. "Shit," I muttered under my breath as the ball reached the back wall of the field house, bounced off, and slowly dribbled back towards me. Few things were more embarrassing in baseball than having to chase after a missed ball.

By the time I returned and rolled the ball toward the bag at the JV coach's feet, the conversation had switched from speculation over where Kevin was to which Chicago baseball team was going to have the best record this season.

Swings in the batting cage and at tees followed the fielding drills and the first day of my last tryouts were over. I did well in the batting cage, level swings and solid connections, perhaps thanks to Mike and our time in Grand Slam. Mike managed to get in the group that was on the tees while I was in the cage.

Most of the guys gathered up their equipment and dragged themselves to the locker room while I headed for the door that would lead me down the hallway into the parking lot. Either I was more out of shape than I thought or the day was tougher than I expected because I was exhausted.

"David," Coach Kelly called, "can you wheel the pitching machine to the equipment room for me?"

I looked around the field house. Everyone was gone except for the other coaches who were gathered around a clipboard, pointing at something and making notes. "Sure." I dropped my bag and maneuvered the machine so I was able to wheel it like a wheelbarrow. Coach Kelly led the way to the equipment room carrying the bags of balls and bats.

When he opened the door, a stench that rivaled the weight room's hit like Kevin's punch to my face. The door hadn't been opened too many times from last season and a stale, wet smell hung in the air. Dirty laundry mixed with sand and dirt. I tried to breathe through my mouth as I wrestled the pitching machine into its corner.

"You seemed distracted today," Coach Kelly said.

The memory of the ball just out of reach of my glove replayed in my head. "I had a couple of missteps in the field," I admitted.

"This is just tryouts," Coach Kelly had to walk sideways through the room since it was so small and flooded with equipment. "What about a game?"

"A game?" In a game that would have been an error.

"How do I know you'll be able to keep yourself together come game time?" Coach Kelly asked.

"Are you saying there's a chance I might not be on the team this year because I missed one grounder?" I couldn't keep the shock out of my voice. "Coach, you know I'm always ready come game time."

"I thought I knew that." Coach Kelly gave me a look that softened when he must have seen the distressed look on my face. "Look, David," he said dropping the balls and bats in an empty space on the floor, "this has nothing to do with…with what you told me earlier. It has to do with me needing to have complete focus on the field and up to bat. During games, during practice, and during the next couple days. If a player's head is constantly on something else and that affects his game, then that hurts the team."

"I know." I wondered if Coach Kelly would be having this conversation with me if he didn't know I was gay. If he would just chalk it up to some unexplained nerves and see how things went the next day.

"And Kaminski's going to be back tomorrow. Will you be able to handle that?"

At the mention of Kevin's name, my face hardened. "Do you think he'll be able to handle it?"

"He's going to have to," Coach Kelly said, squeezing past some softball equipment. "He's our best pitcher and we need his curveball."

"I have to too," I said. "Mankato offered me something but it wasn't enough."

"Really?" Coach Kelly stopped at the door and didn't open it. "I thought you'd have a solid offer by now."

"Me too." I looked sideways.

"A full ride is hard to come by," Coach reminded me. "Even for the most talented players."

"Yeah." He was right but it didn't make me feel any better.

Coach threw up his hands. "Well, now you can add that to your list of distractions."

"My head is in the game and there'll be no more flubs in the field," I told Coach. He had said distraction more in the past couple weeks than he had the past two years.

"Make sure it stays that way," Coach Kelly said, the gruff expression returning to his face. "I don't think that JV kid is ready to be a starter yet." He let the door slam behind him, leaving me to breathe in stench of years of baseball seasons.

Because of the unexpected detour into the equipment room, I

walked into the parking lot as other players were starting to filter out of the building. A few underclassmen were already seated on the pavement, waiting for their parents to pick them up. The group of sophomores that ran with me was huddled together off to the side of the door.

As I tried to clear my nose of the equipment room stink, I saw Patrick unlocking the door to his car. It was small and looked even smaller next to mine, which was a couple spaces down. "Hey, Patrick," I called, picking up my pace from a drag to an actual walk.

"Hey," Patrick responded with a small nod of his head.

I wasn't sure what to say next. It seemed stupid to thank him for warming up with me and desperate to ask him to be my warm-up partner again tomorrow. "Good job today," I finally said. "See you tomorrow."

"Yep, see you tomorrow," Patrick said, sitting down in the car and closing the door.

CHAPTER 32
DAVID

I leaned back against the locker next to Tyler's, hoping that the owner had already stopped by earlier in the morning so I wouldn't have to move. He looked really cute from this angle and I couldn't see any evidence of what happened with Kevin, who was back at school today.

"Want to walk me to English?" Tyler asked, closing his locker and standing up.

"Sure," I said.

We weaved our way through the stream of students clogging the hallway. "Coach is going to have me be the anchor in the 3200 this year," Tyler said.

"Is that a good thing?" I asked. "Doesn't an anchor weigh something down?"

"I never thought about it like that," Tyler said. "But in a relay race, the anchor is usually the best runner."

"Nice," I said as we had to separate for a second to let a herd of freshmen go by. They always walked in clumps.

When we were halfway up a flight of stairs, Mike came barreling down and almost ran right into us. He had a piece of paper in his hand and I noticed the logo from the University of Kansas in the corner. The excited look on Mike's face vanished as he looked from me to Tyler and back again. "I gotta talk to Coach," Mike said to the stairs below him before sidestepping and rushing off.

"So, he's obviously come around," Tyler said as we started up the stairs again.

"Not quite." I stiffly said. I turned back and saw Mike's practically empty book bag bouncing against his back. "He can't even share the good news with me?"

"Good news?" Tyler raised an eyebrow.

"He got a scholarship to Kansas. I know it. The paper in his hand was a letter from the school." I worked out a scuff mark on the speckled tile floor with the toe of my worn out sneaker. I was upset that Mike didn't tell me about Kansas and jealous that he even had news to share.

"Very observant," Tyler said. "You're like someone on one of those detective shows." The warning bell rang, telling me I had a minute to get to Psychology. "There's still time for you to get something." I hated the look on Tyler's face, like he felt sorry for me.

I shrugged again. "I already did get something."

"What?" Tyler asked. "That's awesome. Why didn't you tell me?"

"It's just some stupid letter from some guy in the athletic department at Sinni," I said, embarrassed that my news was so lame in comparison to Mike's. Two of the sophomores from yesterday hurried by and looked away when they saw me.

Shit. Everything about me sucked.

"That doesn't sound like a 'stupid' letter," Tyler said. "You have to tell me more about it later. See you in Art." He walked toward a classroom. "A whole period about Michelangelo's David. Not my favorite David, but should be interesting, right?" He raised his eyebrows at me.

I couldn't help but smile. "It sounds very…interesting." At least Tyler still didn't think I sucked.

Keeping a steady powerwalk pace, I knew I could make it to Psychology in about twenty-five seconds, all I had to do was avoid the couples strolling side by side, taking up almost the whole side of the hallway.

When I pulled back into the parking lot that evening, I saw two large, similar SUV's occupying the two spots nearest to the entrance.

One was beginning to rust along the bottom while the other looked like it was just detailed or driven right out of a showroom. I sat in my car, staring at the SUV's. While I had given too much thought to Kevin being at tryouts today, I never thought of his dad. I didn't see Kevin at school today but that didn't mean much since I usually didn't see him during the day.

A knock on the window jolted me. I still had my seatbelt on so my arms flailed but the rest of me stayed locked in place. Outside, Tyler waved, flashed me a smile, and then hurried off to catch up with his teammates. I waved back even though Tyler was long gone.

In the field house, it was a similar scene to the day before. Players gathered in their usual groups and Mike with his new best friends, Kurt and Alex. Before now, he never even sat with them when everyone went out after doubleheaders. I spotted Patrick walking in from the locker room, dragging his bag of catching equipment behind him.

The only difference today was that Coach Kelly looked over some notes on a clipboard with Kevin's dad peering over his shoulder. And then there was Kevin standing a few feet off to the side, his arms folded like he was a little kid who just got yelled at for something.

I sat off to the side of Patrick, keeping an eye on Kevin, his dad, and Coach Kelly.

"Scott, come on," Coach Kelly looked up from his clipboard. "I've told you before that spectators are definitely welcome at games. But practices are for players and coaches only. The same applies to tryouts."

Kevin's dad maneuvered himself so he was standing squarely in front of Coach Kelly. In his khaki pants and striped polo shirt, he looked like he was about to spend an afternoon playing golf. "You told me you were going to take care of this." His raised voice shushed several of the conversations circulating around me. I suddenly felt like I needed to retie the laces hanging off my glove.

Coach Kelly lowered his clipboard and clicked his pen before putting it in the pocket of his workout pants. "And I have."

Loud whispers replaced the discussions about baseball, school stuff, and weekend plans. "What's he talking about?" I heard someone whisper.

"What's going on?" whispered someone else.

"It doesn't look like it," Scott Kaminski retorted, glaring at me.

Even though my head was down, I raised my eyes and looked at Kevin's dad. He looked less intimidating without his sunglasses on. A couple of the players around me must have thought they were the intended targets of the glare because they self-consciously looked around and nervously laughed.

"Look," Coach Kelly said. "If you'd like to, we can step into the training room for a minute and have a conversation. And we can also talk about how your son is lucky he's not going to be penalized for missing tryouts yesterday." At the mention of his name, Kevin huffed and turned his head so his chin was almost touching his shoulder.

Coach Kelly nodded at the JV and freshman coaches next to him. "Start 'em up in three minutes. Stragglers run extra."

"Fine," Scott Kaminski answered, breaking his glare only for a moment to give Kevin a stern eye. As he led the way to the training room and walked past me, he said, "I don't care how good you think he is. The baseball diamond and the locker room is no place for a fag."

"We're talking in here, Scott," Coach Kelly said pointing to the training room.

I sucked in a breath as if punched in the gut. My whole body tingled from the imaginary effects as the whispers swirled around me.

"Did he say 'fag?'"

"For real?"

"Who is it?"

Several heads looked around the herd of players as if they would be able to spot the person when they saw him. Kurt and Alex joined in the search, ignoring Mike's list of Kansas's accomplishment over the last few seasons.

Patrick sat with his arms resting on his knees, his head cocked in my direction. "Jeez, what's up his ass?" He raised his eyebrows at Kevin's dad and Coach Kelly who were just entering the training room.

I tried to give Patrick a smile of thanks but was too distracted by the four sophomores I jogged with yesterday who were whispering to the people around them. I couldn't make out what they were saying. My shoulders were so tense I couldn't move them.

Kevin sauntered to the part of the group that was as far as possible from me. He started talking to two other starting pitchers.

"Hey, did you hear..." I heard one of them say.

I didn't need a crystal ball to tell me what was about to happen.

"Fuck no, man. I'm no homo," Kevin blurted out for all to hear. The buzzing of everyone talking stopped as Kevin pushed one of the other pitchers in the shoulder. He caught his balance in a step or two and laughed.

"Watch your language, Kaminski," the JV coach flatly said over his shoulder.

"Yeah, watch your language Kammie," someone in Kevin's group imitated the coach.

Everything seemed to happen very slowly. Necks turned in Kevin's direction. So many eyebrows raised. As Kevin turned, he raised an arm and extended his pointer finger. He opened his mouth.

Not again. This wasn't going to happen again. "It's me." Two words. Five letters. I let out a breath.

But then, also in slow motion, the necks swiveled to the other side of the group and stopped when they got to me. Except for Mike, who looked at the floor and the four sophomores from yesterday.

"Whoa," I heard Patrick whisper to himself.

"You?" Kurt looked at me like I hadn't showered in a month. "Seriously?"

"Gay?" someone whispered. "Like guy on guy?"

"Like butt sex," someone replied in a whisper.

"Yeah," Kevin said, jutting his pointer finger in my direction. "He's the fag, right there."

"That's enough, Kaminski!" the JV coach yelled.

My breath quickened and came in short bursts. I couldn't do anything to slow it down. With the exception of Mike and Patrick, every eye in the field house was on me, including the JV and freshman coaches. I couldn't see them, but I could feel them.

More whispers. They sounded so loud.

"Did you know?" Kurt asked him.

"I, uh," Mike stammered.

"Since last week," Kevin answered for Mike. "It kind of *came out* in the weight room."

"Oh," Kurt said, looking sideways.

I couldn't have said anything even if I could think of something because of this crazy breathing. My whole upper body moved with each inhale and exhale. I could barely move my neck so I was stuck looking at the small bumps in the field house floor I had never noticed before.

"Hey, man," I heard Patrick say. "Are you okay?"

A loud and long whistle pried all the eyes away from me and somehow also snapped me out of my weird trance. "Ten laps, gentlemen!" The JV coach clapped. "Let's go."

When no one moved, the freshmen coach blew three short whistles. "Let's go!"

Everyone snapped to attention and hurried on to the track. Patrick nudged me. "Come on," he said. I straightened my elbows and knees, feeling like they had been stuck in a cast for the past two months. With the two coaches staring at me, I shuffled past them.

My goal was to not get lapped. I managed to plod along and if I kept this pace I wouldn't have to talk to anyone for the next ten minutes.

What the fuck just happened?

It wasn't the way I would have planned it. Harder than telling Allie in the library but strangely easier than telling my dad last summer.

I heard people say they thought the world looked different and they looked different after having sex for the first time. As my feet slapped against the track, I wondered if the same happened after coming out. Like all the way out. I didn't think I looked different, but I definitely felt different. Like my fly was open and everyone was looking at my junk.

At least no one ran out of the field house. No one called for me to clean out my locker right then and there and supported Kevin's no-fag clause.

As I rounded the curve, about to finish my second lap, a bang caused me to almost trip over my feet. I looked ahead and saw Kevin's dad stomp out of the training room and swing his arm out so the door bouncing against the wall wouldn't hit him. Coach Kelly followed behind him, catching the door before it slammed into him. He calmly walked over to the other coaches while Kevin's dad continued on a path that would lead him out of the field house. That door opened, letting in a stream of track team members. He appeared not to notice since he didn't break his stride and plowed right through them.

CHAPTER 33
TYLER

Some tall guy in khaki pants shoved his way through everyone and almost ran right into me. I managed to slide right by him and into the field house. He could have been a coach but I'd never seen him before and he was stomping around like he just got kicked out of class. He even muttered something about something being a bunch of bullshit.

A few guys glanced at one another with confused smiles and laughed at the guy's tirade. I joined in but the smile left my face as soon as I saw David coming around the curve and jogging towards me.

He didn't appear to be physically injured. No blood or anything. But his face looked pained. Like each step hurt even though there wasn't a trace of a limp. I tried to send him a telepathic message. *Please look at me.* And he did just that as he labored by me and started his next lap.

As more baseball players passed by, I walked to the other side of the curve, trying to keep an eye on David. Mike passed by, running in between two guys in an exaggerated slow motion like it was the end of a race in a movie.

And then there was Kevin a few paces behind him. The icy feeling from the last time I saw him filled my chest and I was embarrassed by the jerk in my legs that told me to go to the locker room. But I stood my ground, needing to see David as he made his way around again.

He was on the straightaway, coming towards me. His stride choppy and his arms close to his chest. If I focused all my attention on him, he would know that whatever happened, I was here for him. He had come so far in the last couple weeks. So much further than he had in the past six months.

I wanted to jump on to the track and run alongside him.

CHAPTER 34
DAVID

I must have looked like shit because Tyler gave me the look I saw on TV shows, where someone is dying in a hospital. When I saw he was still in the field house, waiting for me to complete another lap, I did my best to shake the stiff feeling from my legs and relax my arms so they were easier to swing at my sides.

I wished I had time to plan for this. To prepare for it. But how? Like a speech for class and print out articles about the gay NFL player or about the major league players who said baseball was ready for an out and proud teammate? Maybe the major leagues were, but I wasn't so sure about Lincoln High School.

As everyone finished their laps and some dropped to the floor in exaggerated exhaustion, I felt my plod slow to a trudge as I approached the final straightaway, so much so that Patrick managed to catch up with me. I sat down in the exact spot I was in just ten minutes ago. Tyler still stood off to the side of the track but after a few seconds, he turned and went to the locker room. Of course I understood that he had to go but I felt safer, less exposed with him there.

Coach Kelly stood in front of the group for a moment. He inhaled like he was about to say something but didn't. He quickly glanced at me and then looked back out over the group. Again, he opened his mouth and after standing there with his mouth open for a moment, he said, "Let's warm up, gentlemen."

"Hey," a small freshman called to another. "I'll be your partner." He glanced at me and looked around as if searching for a place to hide. "Not like that. I mean with the balls." He shook his head. "One ball. A baseball."

"I get it," I said to him. "You're going to warm up."

"Yeah," he said, looking even smaller.

"I'll grab a ball?" I said to Patrick. Phrasing it as a question left room for him to back out.

Patrick nodded. "Sounds good," he responded and slowly backpedaled a few paces to an open area.

Knowing I still had a warm up partner actually relaxed some of the tension in my shoulders. I used that feeling to propel me forward, keeping my eyes on the bag and the ball resting right on top. There was nothing special about this ball but the slight scuff mark on the top gave me something to focus on.

"Dude, get your hands off the balls," Kevin sneered from behind me.

My hand froze on the scuffed ball but I quickly gripped it. "I just need this one," I evenly said.

All through tryouts, I felt the stares. Apparently this was how it worked. At least this was how it worked when you're part of the baseball team at Lincoln High School. When I was in eighth grade, this girl had cancer and when she came to school with her bald head, I couldn't help staring. She had sat in her desk, looking down and didn't move for the entire class. I wanted to find her and say I was sorry.

I felt eyeballs burrow into my shoulder blades during fielding drills where the JV coach stood at home plate, barking out situations. When we broke up into several smaller ones to do timed base running, the staring continued as I rounded first and headed for second. The feeling made me run faster. The sooner I crossed home plate, the sooner I could disappear at the back of the line. Looking up, I saw Coach Kelly glance at his stopwatch. This was going to be my fastest time ever.

I kept my eyes on the plate as I rounded third. Only ninety more feet to go. My brain must have been moving faster than my legs because my left foot somehow kicked my right calf and I knew what was going to happen even before my arms outstretched, bracing for the fall. Through my sweats, the field house floor burned my knee as it skidded on it. I rolled a few feet, landing in a tangled heap in front of everyone. My knee burned. My elbow tingled.

I got up as quickly as I could, ignoring how my sweats were stuck to my knee.

Feeling like I was in a sauna, I managed to hobble the remaining fifty feet as the snickers and whispers swirled around me.

I traced a line on the floor with my eyes so I wouldn't look at anyone.

"Not your best time, Mr. Lukas." Coach pressed a button on his stopwatch and didn't look up as I limped past him.

At the end of tryouts, Coach Kelly gathered everyone for the last time. After today, the three teams would practice separately and some of the players would be told they didn't make the cut. "The list will be posted outside of the athletic office tomorrow morning by seven o' clock," Coach Kelly said. "Thanks for your hard work these past two days, gentlemen. If it is any indication, this is going to be one hell of a season for us. At every level."

Coach Kelly clapped his hands and rubbed them together a few times before folding them over the gray Lincoln T-shirt that stretched over his belly. "All right, that's it. Listen to the announcements for practice info. Be prepared to go outside because as soon as it's dry we're going out the first chance we get."

Many of the freshmen and sophomores, plus a few juniors, hurried to the locker room, wondering about rosters and pitching rotations for the freshman and JV team. I overheard Alex telling Coach about a wedding he had to go to over part of spring break that was out of town. Mike walked past me, very interested in a loose thread at the hem of his T-shirt. I packed my equipment bag like I was arranging things in a suitcase and trying to make the most out of the space I had.

"Hurry up," Kevin loudly whispered to several of the pitchers gathered around him. "Before he gets in there." It was hard to miss Kevin jerk his head at me.

"Oh," said one the pitchers who was on JV last year and was probably going to make varsity this year. He stared at me for a second and hurried away.

Kevin's voice dripped with sarcasm, slightly louder than necessary so anyone in earshot could hear him. With the other player, I heard embarrassment. As if all of them wanted to the grab every set of boobs that walked by. Little did everyone know that I had no plans of going into the locker room today or any other time we had a late practice. I could avoid the issue a little while longer. But now I was "the gay guy" on the team and while that was a very important part of me, there was so much more than just that. I hoped that maybe, just maybe some of the guys would think of the diving stops, the perfectly laid bunts, and pizza at the end-of-season parties when they looked at me. It might be a tall order considering my "best friend" seemed unable to remember ten years of friendship.

I tried to ignore Coach Kelly as his head popped up when I was on my way out, but he called me over.

"Quite a spill on the base paths today," Coach said.

"Yup," I said, doing my best to hide the slight limp I still had. When I tore my sweats from my knee, I think some skin came with it.

"He's looking for a reason to have me kick you off," Coach Kelly said to my back.

I froze but didn't turn around.

"If he had been at tryouts the past couple days, he might have one. Don't give him one."

Hoping my crappy car would be some sort of safe haven like it had been so many times before, I marched right through the group of underclassmen waiting for their parents. As I took the keys out of my bag, I heard someone approaching me, quick steps dragging on the gravelly parking lot. The noise made me think of Tyler running out of the forest preserve. I fumbled with my keys and couldn't find the lock.

"I don't go around advertising everything about myself either."

"Huh?" My hand froze on the door handle. Patrick stood on the passenger side of my car, resting his arms on the top of it. He still wore his cut off sweatpants from tryouts and didn't bother putting on a sweatshirt or jacket before coming outside.

"I have two moms."

"Two moms?" I sort of remembered Patrick taking a picture with two women at the end-of-the-season awards night last year. They didn't come to too many games. "I thought one of those ladies was your aunt or something."

"Nope. Two moms and no dad." Patrick thought for a second. "Well, I guess technically there's a dad but neither of them know who he is."

"Okay." I nodded. Two moms.

"I'm not embarrassed by them or anything." Patrick adjusted the bag slung over his shoulder and straightened up, as if ready to get going. "It's just nobody introduces themselves to me as, 'Hey, I'm Some Guy and I have a mom and a dad,' so why should I? They're just my parents."

Exactly. They're just Patrick's parents. I love Tyler. Tyler loves me. "Thanks for telling me that."

Patrick shrugged like I had thanked him for putting our ball for warm-ups away. "No problem." He walked to the next space over and unlocked his tiny car. "Those sophomores were going around the locker room yesterday, saying stuff about the gay guy on varsity."

"I told them while we were running around the track," I said, not surprised.

"You did?"

"Yeah," I smiled. "I just said, 'Hi, I'm David. I have a mom and a dad and I'm gay.'"

Patrick laughed a little. "They didn't say your name or anything. They were just talking loudly among themselves."

"It doesn't really matter now." In my three years of playing ball with Patrick, the most in- depth conversation we had was when the Sox's season got off to a pathetic start and we wondered which trades needed to be made in order for them to at least have a decent pitching rotation. "How do you think the season's going to go?" I asked, hoping Patrick would be honest with me.

Patrick shrugged. "You heard what Coach said. Hopefully we make it to State this year."

"Yeah," I said, looking into my car so I could throw my bag in the passenger seat.

"You just have to make sure you get a good pair of cleats," Patrick said. "We're not scoring many runs if our fastest player is falling down between third and home."

If it had been anybody else, I would have been pissed. "They're in my bag," I assured him. "Ready to go."

"Good because I bet the season will probably be a little rough at the beginning," Patrick went on. "But I think it will be a good. We all know what we're doing out there. Especially Kevin and his curve, huh? So, we should do pretty good."

"You think so?" I asked.

"Kevin is an asshole. Nothing is going to change that."

"So, I should just expect him to be an asshole?"

"Count on it," Patrick said, sliding into his car and shutting the door.

"Count on it," I said to myself. Kevin would still be an asshole even if I weren't gay or if he never found out. Something to remember. Just as I was about to close the car door, I saw Mike getting into his car a few spaces down. "Hey," I called to him, unsure what I would say next.

Mike looked at me without turning his head and barely breaking his stride. "You trying to turn Patrick gay too?"

"Come on, Mike," I said. "You know that's not true."

"Well," Mike said, stopping only because he got to his car. "I guess I don't know a lot of things." He managed to get in and start the engine in one motion before peeling out of the parking lot.

CHAPTER 35
DAVID

Two freshmen I recognized from tryouts the past two days ran by me when I walked into school the next day. Judging by the direction they were headed in, I guessed they were on their way to check the list of names posted outside the Athletic Director's office.

I remembered getting to school early on this day of my freshman year because Mike and I had begged Mike's dad to drive us to school instead of taking the bus so we could see the baseball roster as soon as it was posted. Both of us knew our names would be on the list, we had a good feeling, but we still wanted to see it for ourselves. Sophomore year, Mike and I harassed my mom for a ride. Since we had taken fielding drills with the varsity team, we were anxious to see if we'd spend the season there or on JV. Junior year, Mike drove us and we had gotten to school just as the warning bell rang because we had stopped for breakfast sandwiches at the convenience store.

As I waited to fall asleep the night before, I didn't have the knotted stomach that I did when I was a freshman. Instead, I thought of this scene from a TV show I had seen a few years ago. Something major had just happened, so the main character called her best friend who called her boyfriend who called his best friend and so on and so forth. The scene was mainly a series of shots of characters picking up the phone but it did a great job of showing how quickly the news spread throughout the student body. And how sometimes the news changed as it went from person to person.

I wasn't sure if any scene like that took place in the towns surrounding Lincoln High School after everyone had gotten home after baseball tryouts.

Kurt and Alex walked by me when I got out of the athletic wing and I raised my hand to wave at them, but the two of them looked away, suddenly very interested in whatever was on their phones. I lowered my eyes, my hand still up in the wave position.

"Hey," a vaguely familiar female voice said.

I looked up and it took me a second to place the girl with dark brown hair pulled into a loose ponytail, wearing a black T-shirt that said *Know Gays Aloud* in a bright red font you might see on a sign posted outside of a child's fort. I glanced at the shirt, smiled to myself, and caught sight of the rainbow wristband circling one wrist and noticed that the white canvas shoes still sported their thick rainbow laces.

"Uh, hi," I said, lowering my hand.

"This is weird." Anna looked around the almost empty hallway and back at me. "I thought you were saying hi to me so I said hi back."

"Oh, right," I said. "I didn't realize I left my hand up."

Anna laughed. "What?"

I had to smile too. This was turning into a ridiculous conversation. "I was saying hi to a couple of my…teammates when you came by and I must have left my hand up." I offered Anna a real wave this time.

"Well, hi to you too." She mimicked my wave.

Just then Kevin came up behind Anna. He wore his Yankee cap backwards even though hats weren't allowed in school. "Checking the roster?" he asked, seemingly unaware that Anna was practically standing between him and me.

I wanted to rip the cap off Kevin's head and stuff the stiff beak into his mouth. Instead, I just shook my head. "I don't think I have to. But you seem to think you need to."

Anna sidestepped out of the way like a cartoon character tiptoeing past a huge sleeping dog. "Nice waving at you," she said to me before tiptoeing away.

Kevin rolled up the sleeves of his University of Illinois long sleeve T-shirt. "Just wanted to check it out, that's all."

"Have fun." I turned, but Kevin grabbed my shoulder and spun me around. I shook his hand off me.

"I don't care what the roster says. Even if it says they somehow managed to put you back on the freshmen team. No one's going to want a cocksucker hanging around." Kevin stood inches from my face.

I ignored the slight tilt Kevin's head had to do to look down on me and pushed him in the shoulder. He took a few steps back not because of the power of the shove but because he was probably surprised I had the balls to do it. "No one wants an asshole on the team either and somehow they keep you around."

Kevin's brown eyes would have glowed red if they had the ability. His next move might have been to charge me if more students hadn't started to filter into the building as it got closer to 7:45. "Don't ever put your fucking gay-ass hands on me again," Kevin said through gritted teeth.

"Same goes for your fucking straight hands." I turned away again. It wasn't quite the "fuck you" I had wanted to say to Kevin a few weeks ago, but it was pretty close and it felt pretty damn good.

As I marched to my locker, I felt Kevin's eyes follow me down the hall. I sharply turned to go up a flight of stairs and was taking them two at a time when Carrie, Mike's girlfriend, started coming down.

Carrie stopped on the landing and grabbed my arm. I glanced at the purple fingernails gripping my arm.

"David!" Carrie said, shaking my arm as she spoke.

"Carrie," I responded. I liked Carrie, but I probably would have never hung out with her if it weren't for Mike.

"I uh…I heard," she finally said.

"About what?" People were going to know. People I didn't tell were going to know. It was part of the big telephone game played over and over again. But, it wasn't the top story on the news, so at least there was that.

Carrie let go of my arm. "Since some people are probably going to say some stupid shit, I want you to know that I think it's kind of cool you're being open about it."

"Uh, thanks," I slowly said, thinking about how I wasn't so open a few weeks ago. "Did Mike tell you?"

"Nope. Natalia did. But I guess this explains why Mike has been really weird the past few days."

Sometimes it was hard to keep track of who was with who, but I remembered Alex going out with Natalia at some point, maybe at the beginning of the year. "Weird?"

"Yeah, it's like he's been somewhere else. But the news from Kansas seems to have him back in this world." Carrie adjusted the bag hanging off her shoulder. "Does everyone know?" She asked in a lowered voice.

I wasn't sure what she meant by everyone. Everyone on the baseball team? Yes. Everyone in the school? Probably not. More people than who knew yesterday? Definitely.

"I just started telling people," I said.

"That's great." Carrie took a step down. "Really, I mean it." She continued down the stairs, her many bracelets jangling against one another like bells.

"Thanks, Carrie," I said to her swinging long hair.

As I unpacked my book bag in front of my locker, I had the feeling that had become too familiar the past twenty-four hours. The one from tryouts yesterday where eyeballs burrowed into my back. When I turned around, all I saw was a crowded hallway with no one looking in my direction at all. But on my way to Psychology, this guy in a Slayer T-shirt who I had a class with last semester shoved into me. "No homo, dude." He held his hands up with a laugh.

While sitting in Art Appreciation and not really listening to the teacher go on and on about performance art, I tried to untie the knots my insides were in. I had Facetimed with Tyler the night before from my driveway as soon as I got home. He sat on his bed in a pair of flannel pants and the team shirt from last year's cross-country team.

"Are you okay?" Tyler had asked me after I told him everything. Well, everything except what Patrick told me in the parking lot. I wouldn't have liked it if Patrick went around talking to other people about me so I didn't do it to him.

"I don't know." I had trouble finding the words. "I feel lighter I guess. I didn't know it was weighing me down so much."

"I was going to say something about your horrible posture the other day."

"Smart ass," I said.

"You have a sexy ass."

"Thanks." I smiled to myself.

"And how's your knee?"

I relived the moment I fell during tryouts and sprawled out in front of my teammates. My knee felt sore. "I won't be on the DL or anything."

"And what about you? Are you going to be okay?"

I tried not to think about my long limp to home plate but the snickers that followed me to the back of the line echoed in my ears. They would have laughed about the fall even if I weren't gay. "Probably."

There had been a couple seconds of silence. Tyler glanced off to the side and I wondered if it was time to say goodbye.

"So," Tyler had slowly said. "What should I say if someone asks me if I know the new gay guy at school? Because you know, all of us gays know each other."

I had tried to imagine what it was like for Tyler to not say anything about our relationship with anyone at school. "Well, you know me, right?"

"I do," Tyler had said. "I really know you."

I was thinking about the sly grin on Tyler's face as he said that when there was a knock on the Art Appreciation classroom door. The hairs on the back on Tyler's head were sticking out every which way, probably from his hat. As much as I wanted the temperatures to rise I also knew that warm weather would force Tyler to retire his puffball hat for the season. I wouldn't get to see Tyler wear it nearly enough next winter when he was away at U of I.

Without missing a beat in her lecture about a woman who sat in a museum exhibit for days to send a message about human interaction, Mrs. Berns swished past my desk in her long skirt and dropped an envelope in front of me. I hadn't even noticed the student worker deliver it to her and leave.

The only thing on the envelope was my name scribbled in black ink. I couldn't quite place the handwriting but it did look familiar.

I saw Tyler turn his head slightly, his eyeballs all the way to the side so he could try to see what the envelope was all about. With a short fingernail, I tried to open the letter without making any noise, but each little tear sounded like someone was ripping open a bag of candy in a movie theater. Mrs. Berns even stopped talking long enough to look at me, silently asking me to stop.

I dropped the letter in my open bag and waited for the bell to ring.

During lunch, I sat at my favorite computer rereading the letter from second period. As I left him at the door to his sociology class, Tyler had said, "I want to know what that's all about." To which I responded, "It's probably a formal invitation from Ms. Larson to join SAFE now that another gay is officially roaming the halls of Lincoln."

"Maybe it is," Tyler said, ignoring my sarcastic tone. "If it is, I'm jealous. No one ever sent me a personal invite."

The envelope wasn't from Ms. Larson. Inside was a thin piece of paper, apparently quickly torn from a pad because of the jagged top edge. On it, Coach Kelly had scrawled. "Just got off the phone with Anthony Rowen, head coach over at CNEI. Check your mailbox for more info."

I actually raised an eyebrow when I read the short message. Seriously? Sinni?

On one hand, I was grateful that Coach was still rooting for me but on the other hand, I didn't want to recognize that my college plans had been reduced to Sinni. The stress of not having any concrete plans was always present but I hadn't given it much thought the past few days with everything that was going on.

After dropping the envelope back into my bag, I started aimlessly searching for things. *Baseball scholarships to real schools. How to pay for college. Salary for minor league baseball players.* I didn't even look at the results, just typing in words and hitting "enter," feeling helpless and annoyed. Then I looked around the library as if concerned someone might be over my shoulder, monitoring my searches and typed in "College of Northeast Illinois."

I quickly navigated my way through the website and found the page for the baseball team. There was Coach Rowen's picture in the top corner. Square face with an equally square jaw and buzzed brown hair. But he was actually smiling in the photo, so much so that it showed the wrinkles at the corner of his eyes. In the team photo, the players looked happy to be playing there, a couple grins were sprinkled among the stereotypical stare downs at the camera. The uniforms were blue and black with brand new hats that had perfectly shaped beaks. Photos featured all the typical shots of players diving and sliding, the same I'd seen on every other college site he'd visited.

I wasn't sure why I'd expected something else, like the team would be playing some sort of stickball in the parking lot while wearing the grass stained gray pants each player borrowed from the park district during my Little League days. This looked like a real team. I recognized a player from Lincoln who tore his ACL halfway through the season a couple years ago.

"Doing some window shopping?"

I turned to the chair next to me and saw Allie plop down in it. She had decided to forego the button-down shirt and just sported a Beatles T-shirt with her traditional skinny jeans. Aside from a couple waves in the halls, I hadn't really talked to her in a while.

"Some of those guys are pretty cute," she said, raising her eyebrows. "Not that I'm an expert or anything."

I quickly collapsed the window and tried to gauge if Allie saw anything on the screen besides the "cute guys." The various photos and stats for the players hopefully drowned out the CNEI banner across the top of the page. "Do you ever go to class or do you just live in the library?"

"I am doing research for my sociology class." Allie faced her computer with her fingers poised over the keyboard. "We're studying deviant behavior and breaking society's norms."

"Okay, so you have one class," I said.

"Thinking of going to Sinni?" Allie nodded towards my computer, which now displayed the Lincoln High School coat of arms.

"No," I quickly said. "Maybe."

"So, what are you doing next year?"

"I'm not sure yet." I clicked the icons on the desktop, making them bigger and smaller, darker and lighter. "I had a couple of ideas, but they fell through."

"That sucks."

I shrugged. "What about you?"

"Both of my parents went to U of I," Allie explained. "So, I'm going to UIC."

"Cool," I said.

"So, how's it going since the last time I saw you here?" Allie asked, typing while still looking at me.

"You didn't see the story on the news last night?" I asked in an exaggerated shocked tone.

"No," Allie turned to me like I was a girl with some hot gossip. "What'd I miss?"

"My best friend won't talk to me. My boyfriend got beat up. And I told everyone at tryouts yesterday that I'm gay." I spilled everything to Allie, unsure how she had that effect on me.

"Wow, that's a lot. Are you okay?"

I shrugged a shoulder. "Better than I thought."

"Is your boyfriend okay?" Allie stopped typing.

"He's a lot tougher than me." I liked how it felt to talk about Tyler with someone at school.

"You're kind of tough," Allie assured me. "Does baseball have the late time slot again?"

I nodded. "Probably for the next week and then we'll switch with softball until it gets warm enough to go outside."

"We're having a speaker at our meeting tomorrow. Some guy who founded a hotline for kids. He didn't come out until he was in his fifties." Allie went back to typing. "You can come if you want."

"Interesting but I'll pass, thanks though."

"Your turn, Allie." A girl with super straight, long black hair who had a glittery scarf knotted around her neck tapped Allie's shoulder.

"Thanks," Allie said as the girl sat down at a nearby computer. "Conference time with the teacher. Gotta tell him my idea about cannibalism for this project." She grabbed her notebook and stood up. "And seriously, some of those guys are really cute. Imagine being cuddled up next to one of them during those cold early spring games."

"I have a boyfriend," I reminded her.

"It's okay to look." She laughed as she walked toward a man in a sweater vest.

I rolled my eyes at Allie's back, wishing I somehow would have met her sooner. When I saw that she was seated at the table with her teacher, I clicked on the Sinni baseball site that I had collapsed. Allie was right, some of the guys were kind of cute, but I was pretty sure none of them would have a puffball bobbling off their hat during the first practices of the season. Doing another scan of the library to make sure no one was looking at me, I scrolled through the players' biographies and noticed that the current second baseman went to the school that Lincoln beat last year in order to advance to the playoffs.

CHAPTER 36
TYLER

The series of equations and element symbols blurred together. I had done two of nine questions and my teacher was going to go over them soon. She sat at a laptop behind her desk, oblivious to the whispers going on in front of her.

I wasn't whispering or doing much of anything for that matter. David was out, for real this time. It was what I had been hoping for ever since we got together. While that didn't mean we were going to make out in front of my locker, at least people would know that was why another senior was hanging out in the sophomore hallway.

"Did you hear what happened at baseball yesterday?"

I stopped scribbling in the corner of my paper and cocked my head in the direction of the whisper that came from a seat off to the side of me. It was Tara talking to Corey. I didn't know them very well even though we'd had a few classes together. Tara played volleyball and Corey wrestled. That was about all I knew.

"What? About David Lukas?" Corey moved his arms to the edge of his desk.

"Yeah," Tara whispered. "My friend's boyfriend is on the team and she said that he stood up and announced to everyone that he's gay."

"Seriously?" Corey whispered back. "He just stood up and did it?"

"Uh huh." Tara nodded as if confirming important information.

I started scribbling again in case my teacher decided to look up and check if everyone was working, keeping an ear on the hushed conversation next to me.

"And then when they were running, someone came up and tripped David and he fell all weird," Tara went on. "Everyone started yelling stuff at him while he just rolled around in pain."

My eyes rolled.

"He got hurt?" Corey narrowed his eyes. "Really?"

"It was probably a hate crime or something like that," Tara said.

This was getting ridiculous. With my teacher still engrossed in whatever was on her computer screen, I leaned over and whispered to Tara and Corey. "That's not what happened. At all."

Corey and Tara looked at each other, as if surprised they were overheard. "How do you know?" Corey asked.

"Because I talked to him last night and I know that's not what happened," I evenly said.

"Well what did?" Tara asked like she didn't believe me.

"He just fell, that's all."

"What about the shit they said to him?" Corey leaned toward me.

"People always say shit," I said.

Tara and Corey leaned toward each other, talking in quieter whispers than before, occasionally looking in my direction. Apparently they moved on to a different subject because I heard Tara say something about prom.

I hadn't thought about prom and possibly going with David since our fight in the hallway. Maybe it could really happen. Maybe it didn't have to just be a fantasy.

I'd never seen him in anything except jeans or workout clothes. He would probably looked really hot in a tux, if he agreed to wear one. Maybe they had tuxes with the White Sox logo on the bowtie and vest. I would be okay with that.

He probably didn't dance. We could just hang out by ourselves, like we usually did. Only this time we could hang out by ourselves in a room full of other people.

CHAPTER 37
DAVID

Both the van and my dad's pickup truck were in the driveway when I got home after school. I hoped my mom would be rushing out to do another second shift and that maybe Dad had something to do that would get him out of the house until practice. I even waited in the car for a few minutes, giving them time to fly out of the house and into their cars, but the front door remained shut.

I knew Mom would be thrilled about the news about Sinni while Dad would probably grunt because he couldn't provide something better for his son. I hadn't talked to my parents very much in the past few days mainly due to my mom's busy schedule and my dad being in a bad mood. I did see Mom this morning before going to school and she asked me with a cautious smile how tryouts went and I just nodded and said, "Fine." They were over and I was on the team.

When I finally did go into the house, Robert stood at the sink, halfway through a peanut butter and jelly sandwich. Of course, my whole family would be home today.

Robert licked some jelly off the back of his hand and then wiped it on his T-shirt. "What's that all about?" He nodded toward the kitchen table.

In the center of the table, probably perfectly placed there by my mom, was a large, flat envelope from Sinni. My name and address were handwritten and Rowen was written above the return address. "Sinni, huh?" I shrugged. When Coach had said to keep an eye on the mailbox

I had no idea that meant to expect something today.

"Are you going there?" Robert asked, his mouth full of what was left of his sandwich.

I swiped the envelope off the table. "Where are Mom and Dad?"

"Mom's in the shower. Dad's in the garage."

Dad being in the garage either meant he was looking for something to do to keep busy or that maybe he was organizing his tools for a job that was starting up.

I carried the envelope to my and Robert's room as Mom stepped out of the bathroom in pajama pants and a long sleeve T-shirt that was from Robert's middle school. The comfortable clothes meant she was done with work for the day.

"David," Mom smiled when she saw me. "Did you see what I left in the kitchen for you?"

I held up the envelope and nodded.

She wrapped her arms around herself. "Well?"

I looked at the envelope like it was a test I was pretty sure I failed. "I don't know. I haven't opened it."

"Why not?" Dad asked, stepping in from the garage. He wore jeans with holes at the knees and a T-shirt that had so many stains on it, I couldn't tell what it originally looked like.

"I just got home," I said. "And does it have to be a show? It worked out pretty well last time when everyone got to see me find out that Mankato thinks I suck."

"They don't think you suck," Mom said. "They just didn't give you everything you thought they would."

"Because they think I suck." I didn't care that I was being all whiny and complaining. It was easy for Allie to try to convince me that a couple cute guys would make up for the fact that I was destined for Sinni. She was all set to go to the UIC.

"You open it." I thrust the envelope into Mom's hands. I went into my room and sat at the foot of my bed, looking at the streaks my feet made in the carpeting as I slowly ran them back and forth.

I heard Dad's heavy footsteps walking closer, followed by Robert's quick ones, and the envelope rip. A moment of silence and then a gasp.

"David!" Mom exclaimed. "It's an official offer. Tuition and fees completely paid for." The towel on her head loosened and fell to the floor.

"Yeah, I had a feeling," I said without looking up.

"You knew about this?" Dad asked, stepping into the bedroom.

"Kind of."

Mom stood in the doorway, scanning the letter. Her eyebrows furrowed. "This says they hoped you received their first letter and had a chance to consider CNEI among possible places to continue your education." She held out the letter to me. "What's that about?"

"They sent me a letter a few weeks ago," I shrugged, wishing everyone would get out of my room.

"Why didn't you say anything?" Since I didn't take the letter from her hands, Mom let it hang at her side.

"Because it looked like some stupid generic letter they probably sent to everyone. It didn't seem important." I didn't want it to be important.

Mom picked up her towel and slung it over her shoulder. "Well, I think it's pretty important and I can't believe you don't." She placed the envelope next to me, with the letter from Coach Rowen on top.

I narrowed my eyes at it, trying to read the contents in one glance. I was able to gather that Rowen had been to a couple Lincoln games over the past couple seasons and was impressed by my skills and speed. Coach Kelly had sent him my reel a couple weeks ago. Rowen hoped I would consider becoming a Bobcat if I didn't already have plans for the following school year. Please get in touch as soon as possible.

I didn't know Coach had done that. "Can we talk about this later? I want to do some homework before practice."

My dad's demeanor changed at the mention of practice. "Season officially starts today, huh?"

"Yup," I nodded.

"How's that going?" my mom tentatively asked.

"It's just the beginning of the season," I said. "Lots of drills and boring stuff."

I noticed my parents eye one another. "That's not what I'm talking about," Mom said.

A filmstrip of the last two days played in my head. Coach's concern about me being distracted. The sophomores. Mike's letter from Kansas. Kevin. His dad on the lookout for any reason. The team. Patrick and his two moms. "It's going better than I thought it would." Which was true.

"Is that jackass bothering you?" Dad asked.

Jeez, my dad made it sound like Kevin and I were getting into fights on the playground during recess. "He bothers everyone."

"You know what I mean."

"He behaved himself yesterday," I said. "As much as anyone can expect him to behave himself. And I think Coach made it clear to his dad that the team is not going to be fag-free even if he doesn't like it."

"Don't say that," Mom sighed.

"What? It's good news isn't it?" I looked at my dad and gave him an "am I right?" look and noticed the splashes of paint on his tattered jeans and the tan flecks that dotted his hands and forearms. "What are you painting?"

Dad looked at his hands. "The people with the basement I just finished?" I nodded so Dad knew that I knew what he was talking about. "A hallway and the master bedroom."

"I thought you didn't like to paint," I said, remembering how often he cursed himself when trying to not get any paint on the ceiling.

"I don't," Dad agreed. "Are you done in there?" He turned to Mom and jerked his head in the direction of the bathroom. When she nodded, he said, "I'm going to take a shower." He picked at the flecks on his hands on his way out. "This'll never come off."

After Dad left the room and closed the bathroom door behind him, Mom stood in the doorframe. "This isn't bad news. I don't know why you're acting like it is."

I grunted a little, unsure how to explain to my mom that it's not that the news was bad. It just wasn't the news I wanted.

"One of my coaches played for CNEI," Robert piped in from behind my mom.

"Real inspiring, Rob, thanks," I said. "Maybe one day I can coach an overpriced travel team too."

"They have a lot of stuff." Robert sounded offended. "Actual batting cages inside that roll up and down. It costs a lot of money for stuff like that."

"My mistake. It's worth every penny."

"Leave your brother alone." My mom gave me a look I hadn't seen in a long time, which forced me to mumble out an apology to Robert. "This is what we've been waiting for, isn't it?" She gestured to the paper on the bed.

"*We've?*" I looked at her. "Yes, *we've* been waiting for this. Aren't we so excited that David sucks so bad that the only place that wants him is stupid Sinni. Not Kansas, not U of I, not Mankato. Nowhere."

Mom rewrapped her hair in the towel and snapped her head up. "I'm not going to tell you that getting a scholarship to CNEI is the same as getting a scholarship to one of those schools. I would love to be able to send you to any school you want." She paused. "As long as it wasn't too far away. But I can't. We can't. And you know what? A lot of other kids' parents can't either."

I lowered my eyes, feeling like a complete asshole and remembered trying to talk to my dad about him going to the unemployed support group. Paying for college on top of everything else had to be a popular topic.

Mom picked up the letter that still sat by my side and waved it in my face. "And I bet those kids would do anything for this. Anything." When she dropped the letter, it fell to the floor. Mom stalked out of the room and I heard her walk the three feet to her bedroom and shut the door.

The only sound came from the shower stream coming from the bathroom across the hall and Dad's groans as the shower pelted his body. He always liked the spray to be on the strongest setting.

"What?" I rolled my eyes at Robert who was leaning on the doorframe.

"I had to sell a million candy bars and do this stupid home-run-a-thon to play baseball and they're going to let you play on their team for free?"

"Yep." Even my little brother was giving me a hard time.

"That's pretty awesome," Robert said.

CHAPTER 38
DAVID

The good news was that the first practice of the season was predictable. I already knew Mike would continue to avoid me by sticking to Kurt and Alex like they were the ones who played Little League with him for years. Of course, Kevin didn't half ass anything, always on a mission to prove over and over again how awesome he was. And thankfully, Patrick warmed up with me again. The drills were the same as last year but held some excitement since it had been about a year since we last did them. I even welcomed the exercise I hated as a freshman where we had to field grounders with a piece of particle board cut into the shape of a mitt strapped to our hands. I looked each grounder all the way into my body and used two hands.

I didn't know if the whispers I heard were directed at me or just in my head.

By the end of the week, I stopped feeling like my fly was down. Kevin's dad stayed away and he was quiet ever since that last day of tryouts. Well, I guess his dad would be quiet providing I didn't grab a teammate's ass or let a grounder go between my legs.

The following week brought a warm streak, where the fields dried out a little and temperatures climbed all the way into the mid-forties but it felt even warmer when the sun was out. When I headed to school on the day the mercury finally hinted that spring was here to stay I knew I'd have an early practice and was jittery all day. Maybe because there was really no way for baseball to be an indoor sport. We could do hitting drills and fielding drills on the smooth field house floor, but it doesn't compare to being out on the dirt.

Sure enough, when I took a detour past Coach Kelly's office on the way to my locker, the information was already posted. On a plain piece of white paper and written in his hurried handwriting was "Varsity baseball WILL practice after school today." 'After school' was underlined several times.

"I can give you a ride home," I told Tyler as we waited for Art Appreciation to start. Yet another reason why practicing outside was so great.

"Maybe you can stay for a little while," Tyler suggested.

"I'll be all sweaty and gross," I said.

"So will I," Tyler pointed out. "Besides, we've seen each other all sweaty and gross before, remember?"

I smiled, always happy to remember the summer before when I would see Tyler running his laps. "Good point."

I had to run all over the place after school. My PE class just started a weight lifting unit, which coordinated nicely with the start of the baseball season, but the weight room was the furthest you could get from the locker room. I decided not to change into my jeans and just run out to my car in my PE shorts and T-shirt. After getting the bag of warm practice clothes, I had to fight the stream of students coming out of the doors because I needed to get back in. I dug through the bag on my way back to the locker room, double checking what I had even though I couldn't do anything if I discovered I had forgotten a sweatshirt or an extra pair of socks.

The athletic part of the locker room was a blizzard of athletes from three different sports coming and going, bags being thrown into lockers, equipment bags being packed, and many athletes applying several layers of clothing. Except for the volleyball team who could practice in their shorts and T-shirts in any weather.

I didn't even see Tyler, although I did look for him. Most athletes chose lockers based on where their teammates were and Tyler's was near the entrance while mine was in the middle. I quickly peeled off my PE

T-shirt and exchanged it for a long sleeve T-shirt of the construction company my dad used to work for and then slid out of my PE shorts so I could put on a pair of sweats. As I grabbed my cleats and turned to head out of the locker room, I almost ran into Alex, who quickly covered his bare brown chest with his jacket, the way a cartoon character would when he discovered he was suddenly naked.

"Seriously Alex?" I said, ignoring the squirmy glance to either side of me.

"Whatever," Alex huffed, still holding his jacket over him.

I shook my head, wishing Alex knew I wanted to check him out as much as he wanted to check me out. In my socks, I slid over the locker room floor and out to the field house. I pushed open a side door in the field house that was closest to the baseball diamond and sat off to the side of it to put my cleats on.

Robert didn't think that I knew he had slept with his glove under his pillow the night before his first travel ball practice, but I did. I had seen it dangling from underneath the pillow when I had gotten up that morning. I had smiled at the thought of Robert being so excited. But, at this moment, I felt the same excitement. In my opinion, the season officially started today when I would first set foot in the familiar territory of second base and hear the dirt and sand crunch as I shuffled to my right or left.

Who knew where I would be next spring and if I would be going through the same ritual but Coach was right about what he said at tryouts. This team had the ability to go far and I felt the possibilities as I laced up my cleats and double knotted them. I hoped there would be some sort of batting practice today because the sound of a bat squarely connecting with a baseball on a cool day was comparable to a singer hitting that high note at the end of a song. It just sounded awesome and impressive.

"Hey, Coach," I said, leaning his bag against the bench in the dugout.

Coach Kelly had a cloth band wrapped around his head to keep his ears warm and it looked like it was going to pop right off his head. He had an old Lincoln windbreaker zipped all the way to his chin. "Mr. Lukas," Coach nodded at me. "You get in touch with Rowen yet?"

"Not yet," I stiffly said. I'd seen the large envelope from CNEI everyday ever since it arrived and got added to the college pile.

"Well, don't wait too long."

"I won't," I responded, busying myself by taking my glove and bat out of my bag. I was getting used to the idea that Sinni could very well be my only option and didn't hate the idea but didn't exactly like it either.

"We're doing base running today." Coach Kelly walked to the equipment box behind the backstop. "Stay on your feet this time, okay?"

My cheeks were probably already red from the cold so if they got any redder at Coach's comment, he didn't notice.

Gradually, the rest of the team made their way to the dugout, filling it with more equipment bags and giddiness about finally being outside. It wasn't long before Coach Murray, the assistant coach, blew his whistle and barked out, "Four laps around the perimeter."

"We're still running even though we're outside?" Kurt said.

"What's your point?" Coach Murray asked.

Several players grumbled as they got to their feet and started trotting to the right field fence. Cleats sloshed when landing in a patch of grass that had not yet recovered from the winter. Everyone's breath came out in small clouds that swirled together as we made our way through center field, toward left field, and finally back to home plate.

The captains led stretches, which meant Mike and Kevin sat in the middle of the circle made by the team, each facing one side. Mike sat directly in front of me but kept his eyes on Patrick who sat on my left. I wondered if he knew how Carrie felt or if he'd even talked to Carrie about anything that was going on.

It was a practice that would have been monotonous had it been in the middle of the season when all anyone wants to do is just get to the next game. Situational fielding drills, bunting practice, and then diving practice for the fielders while the pitchers threw to the catchers behind the dugout.

I dove to my left, stretching out my glove as far as I could and managing to snag a grounder before it whizzed under it.

"Good stop, Lukas," Coach Murray said as I tossed the ball back to him.

A streak of cold, wet dirt seeped through the side of my sweatshirt and clung to the long sleeve T-shirt underneath. No doubt, my mom would ask me to start doing my own laundry again.

"Nice grab," a junior named Cameron said to me as he joined the back of the line. "I didn't think you were going to get it." Cameron's primary position was shortstop but he probably wouldn't get much playing time there so the coaches were working on turning him into an outfielder.

"Thanks."

The small interaction with Cameron added to what I felt at the end of the practice the other day. While Kevin would never stop being a douchebag and Mike would hopefully stop being weird after a little while, I had spent more than half of my senior year being so anxious for no reason. Maybe I should have given more credit to my team and everyone at Lincoln High School. How would this year have been different if it started by holding Tyler's hand when I entered the building back in August? Maybe that would have been too much. But maybe I could've at least acknowledged that he was my boyfriend, and an awesome one at that.

When we ran bases at the end of practice, I felt myself holding back, overly concerned about getting the proper footing as I rounded each base. As I ran past Coach, he raised an eyebrow at his stopwatch unimpressed.

"He was faster when he was straight," Kurt sneered when I was behind him in line. Real clever of him.

The second time, I quickly hit my stride and tagged each base without even thinking about it. Visualizing Kevin's face as home plate, I squarely stomped on it and had to catch myself on the backstop in order to slow myself down. I had to look down and smile as I saw Coach look at his stopwatch in disbelief. It had to be my fastest time ever.

"Maybe I'm faster now, huh?" I said to Kurt.

He looked away.

At the end of practice, as everyone walked toward the locker room, the track team came in from an opposite door, so the two groups met at the locker room's entrance. The volleyball team was still putting away the poles and nets from their practice.

As the noise in the locker room increased with the amount of people coming into it, I heard Alex loudly say, "What the hell?" It was followed by loud laughter and then, "That's fucking hilarious!"

I didn't give it much thought but then I saw several of my teammates gathered around my locker. I felt like I was on one of those cheap carnival rides that spun really fast and the floor had just dropped out from beneath me. I shoved my way through the people that blocked my path and unintentionally pushed someone I didn't know out of the way so I could see what everyone was looking at.

Someone had duct tape a jock strap to my locker and in a thick black Sharpie marker drawn an arrow pointing at the cup along with the message, *Looking for some serious dick.*

What the fuck.

I grabbed the jock strap and yanked it from my locker. Then, I realized I was holding *someone's* cup in my hand and hurled it across the locker room. A couple guys got out of the way in mock fear of being hit by it, which started up the laughter again.

The message was still on my locker, which looked even worse without the context of the jock strap, if that was even possible. I felt like I was in a movie and the camera was spinning around me to capture the crowd of faces. Kevin was doubled-over laughing the kind of side splitting laugh that would probably give him an ache soon. "Man, I wish I thought of that," he managed to gasp out.

Kurt and Alex had nervous smiles on their faces, their eyes darting from side to side, like they were trying to swallow the laugh that wanted to explode out of their mouths. Patrick darted out of the locker room. Mike pushed his way through the crowd, not looking at me or anyone else, and opened his locker as if he was the only one in the room.

"You're the gay guy?" Someone from the track team asked me, looking me up and down.

"I told you he was," another guy said.

"No." I heard Tyler's voice before I saw him. "He's one of the gay guys." Dressed in black running tights and a red Under Armor shirt, I soaked in the sight of my boyfriend. Wind burned cheeks. Matted hair from the puffball hat clenched in his hand. Eyes focused on me.

The locker next to me slammed, startling me and everyone else in the locker room. Mike slung his bookbag over a shoulder and headed out. I watched him leave, but just as Mike was about to open the door, Coach Kelly stomped in, tracking in mud because he still had on the old sneakers he wore outside for practice. Mike jumped back upon seeing Coach and quickly slid past him to leave.

Coach Kelly marched through the small crowd, glanced at my locker, to me, back at the locker, and then looked over the track and baseball teams. "Everyone grab what you need and get out of here," he ordered.

It took everyone a second to react but they all obeyed, many simply grabbing their book bags without changing clothes or putting on jackets. The noise and people swirled around me, seemingly moving at a fast pace while I stood still. I had to touch my locker in order to get my car keys, and I didn't want to do that.

In less than a minute, everyone was gone and Coach Kelly and me were the only ones left. It seemed loud in the locker room even though something in the boiler room was the only noise. "I'll tell the maintenance crew about this immediately," Coach told me. "It should be gone by tomorrow morning. Before anyone comes in for first period."

I nodded, kind of numb and unable to tear my eyes from the locker like it was a bad car accident.

Coach Kelly stood for another moment. "If you hurry, you should be able to make it out of here before the volleyball team comes in and sees you standing there." He shrugged when I didn't say anything. The writing was so dark and so big. "I'll try to find out who did this." Although his face was sincere, Coach Kelly didn't sound very hopeful about the prospect.

"Fucking idiot," I yelled after the door had closed behind Coach.

In order to open my locker, my hand had to be mere centimeters from the word "dick" and I felt dirty for almost touching it. It took me two tries to lift the handle. As I got my stuff together, the effects of the gravity carnival ride slowly wore off. The thing with those gravity rides was that you go on them knowing the floor was going to drop out. You expected it. Well, I had gotten on the ride and was stupid enough to think that just because it had made a couple of uneventful rotations, that meant nothing was going to happen even though the ride started spinning faster and faster. I swallowed a scream rising in my chest, feeling like I wanted to throw everything in my locker at the wall.

Just as the volleyball team was coming in, I left the locker room and walked toward the parking lot with my head down, looking at my feet going one in front of the other. After doing this for a few seconds, it looked like my feet weren't part of my body anymore. The hallways were empty for the most part, which was a good thing because I wasn't looking where I was going. I had walked the path from the locker room to my car so many times I could have done it with a scarf tied over my eyes.

"Hey, look where you're going, All Star."

I stopped and looked up to see Allie. "Hey," I said, putting my head down again, ready to resume my blind walk to the car.

"Well, that's not a very enthusiastic greeting," Allie said, following me to the door. "Shitty day?"

"It wasn't that bad until about five minutes ago." I didn't slow down but Allie kept pace with me.

"School related? Boyfriend related? Or stupid douchebag related?"

"That last one," I muttered, not in the mood to describe what had just happened. I pushed open the door.

Tyler was sitting off to the side of the door, hugging his knees, but he quickly stood up when he saw me come out of the building.

"Hey," Tyler said. "I didn't know how long you'd be."

"I wasn't about to do a handwriting analysis or collect DNA samples," I grumbled.

"Huh?" Allie said, raising an eyebrow at me.

I noticed Allie and Tyler glance at one another. "Do you guys know each other?" I waved a hand from Tyler to Allie.

"Library girl," Tyler nodded at Allie with a smile.

"Calculus guy," Allie nodded back as if this were a formal introduction. "And boyfriend?"

"Yup," Tyler said, a smile spreading on his face.

"Well, give this one some extra loving tonight. He seems pretty upset about something." Allie kept walking when Tyler and I stopped at my boat of a car.

"Do you need a ride?" I asked.

Allie shook her head. "I have my own wheels, thank you." She walked over to a lamppost and unlocked the chain that was looped around an expensive looking bike.

I opened my door and then climbed over to the passenger door to unlock Tyler's. We sat for a little while, staring at the dashboard.

"I'm sorry," Tyler finally said.

I narrowed my eyes, staring out the driver side window. "I don't know why. You didn't do it."

"True. But that doesn't mean I don't feel bad that it happened."

I continued to stare, noticing how different the scenery looked since that afternoon when I gave Tyler a ride home after the first day of open gym. No more snow sloshed at the curbs. The grass actually looked alive in some places. I felt a pull at my right hand, which I had put in the pocket of my hooded sweatshirt after turning the car on.

"What did your coach say?" Tyler asked as he ran his finger over the calluses on my hand.

"He's going to get someone to clean it up before school starts tomorrow," I said to the window so my breath made a cloud on the glass.

Tyler gave my hand a squeeze before wrapping my fingers in his. "Do you want me to go with you to tell the deans about it?"

"Nope," I said, making another small cloud.

"Are you going to tell the deans?"

"Nope."

"You thought it was a good idea when I did it," Tyler pointed out.

I finally turned from the window and faced Tyler, noticing that there was still a small scar above his eyebrow but the butterflies and bruises were long gone. "That was different," I said. "Kevin beat the shit out of you."

"It wasn't *that* bad."

"He deserved to get suspended." I ignored Tyler. "He deserved more than that."

"I was wrong that day in the library." Tyler's tone changed. "About how all we need is each other to get through stuff like this."

I furrowed my eyebrows. "What else is there?"

"We need each other," Tyler assured me. "No doubt, we need each other. But, David, you're the only one who knows what happened to me two years ago and not saying something sooner was a big mistake."

"What are you talking about?" I demanded. "I go tell the deans about my locker and they'll point to the little rainbow flag hanging in their office and that makes everything okay?"

"I'm not even talking about the deans," Tyler sighed. "I'm talking about Allie."

"What about her?" I asked, following a car into the parking lot with my eyes and then watching it pull up in front of the door so two small freshmen could climb in after throwing their bat bags in the trunk.

"It's nice knowing she's there, isn't it? In the library, in the hallway. Just in the building itself. What if she wasn't? What if she never moved here this year?" Tyler pressed.

My first thought was that another library worker probably wouldn't have let me in that day I needed Tyler. Most of them seemed like such kiss-asses. And then there was when I was doing research that turned into coming out to her. She was the first one to know besides my family. "These past few weeks would have been a lot harder," I admitted, feeling like I was in a class where the teacher was forcing me to answer questions. I released Tyler's hand to put the car in gear and steer my way out of the parking lot. "I don't know if now's the right time to make me feel better about today. I want to be mad about it for a while. It was fucking embarrassing, Tyler."

"I'm sure it was," Tyler agreed. "I'm sure it still is."

"I fucking touched someone else's cup!"

Tyler laughed and tried to suppress it when I shot him a glare. "It sounded funny when you said it," he said.

I navigated the streets to Tyler's house without even thinking about where to turn and when to brake. "This is not how I imagined the end of my senior year."

"No?" Tyler asked as if he were shocked I would say such a thing. "What could you possibly want to be different?"

"A clean locker door in the athletic locker room." I released the steering wheel with one hand to tick off the items. "A full scholarship."

"You did get a full scholarship," Tyler reminded him.

I shook my head. "You know what I mean."

"That Kevin never saw us together and never said anything?" Tyler asked.

I had to slow down because the stoplight turned yellow. "Yes, but because he's an asshat. Not for any other reason."

Tyler seemed to accept that answer because he settled into his seat and leaned over to put his head on my shoulder. Tyler must have really wanted me to feel better because there was no way he was comfortable bent over the center console like that.

CHAPTER 39
TYLER

"I'm calling to make you feel better," I said, FaceTiming with David while sitting on my bed. My AP Calculus book made for a great footrest.

"You think you can do that?" David responded. I could see him walking into the short hallway in his house and turning into the room he shared with Robert. The phone dropped to his side so I got this weird angle of Robert sitting on the floor reading some sports magazine. David nudged him with his toe. "Out."

Robert huffed and made a face as he stalked out of the room.

David turned the phone upright again and I could see the tips of his short brown hair were still wet from a shower. When he sat on his bed, I saw his fleece pants with White Sox logos all over them.

"I'm going to try," I said. Part of me wondered if David needed the night to just be by himself but I hoped I knew him well enough by now to be certain that he would be stewing over what happened today and wasn't doing much homework either.

"If you can, you'll get a prize." David turned his pillow vertical so he could lean against it.

I smugly smiled. "A prize? Interesting. What sort of prize?" Several thoughts sprang into my head, one of which made my face warm and my stomach drop a little.

"I'm not sure yet," David said. "We'll have to find out if you're successful."

"Okay, here goes." I quickly glanced at my laptop that was off to my side. It was probably pointless to make David feel better about the dick on his locker but maybe I could make him feel better about Sinni. I squinted at my computer screen. "So, did you know that Mark Bewhurlly went to community college too?"

David furrowed his eyebrows, clearly unimpressed with this information. "Who's that? Did he play for Lincoln?"

"No, he played for the White Sox for a while." I scanned the information on the screen to make sure I was getting this right. "Do I know something about the White Sox that you don't know?"

"Nope, because you're making it up. No prize for you."

"No, no," I insisted. I put my phone down on the bed but tried to angle it so David could still see me. I picked up my laptop. "It's true. He won two games during the 2005 World Series and even closed one of them. First time in the history of the sport that happened."

A loud laugh came from David as he shook his head. "Do you mean Mark Buehrle?"

"Huh?" I doubled checked the name. "It doesn't look like that at all."

"I'm willing to bet Mark Buehrle never had a cup taped to his locker," David said.

"We don't know that for sure," I replied. "There are assholes everywhere. Probably even where this Mark guy went to school."

"Maybe." This cheering up thing wasn't going well.

"I bet D1 schools are crawling with assholes," I added.

"Well, I won't have to worry about that," David said. "You will, though. And we already know U of I is up one asshole for next year."

I studied David. His damp hair. The faded black of his T-shirt. How soft his pants looked. "I know I'm not going to say anything that will magically make everything better," I said. "But maybe think of Sinni as a place to start. Not a place to end up."

David shrugged, unconvinced and unmoved.

"What if Mark Buerhle didn't go to community college because he thought it was pointless or stupid?"

Another shrug accompanied by an eyebrow raise. "You sound like my mom."

Fail.

I ran my feet under the covers to feel the cool sheets. It had been so long since David and I were tangled up on my bed. I stared into my phone as if David were really in front of me. "I liked you before I knew where you wanted to go to college. And before I knew you were some awesome baseball player. I'll be able to say 'I knew you when.'"

David smirked. "When I had a dick drawn on my locker and felt like almost everyone on the team wanted nothing to do with me."

"Yep," I responded. "And I also knew you when you somehow got through this with the help of your awesome boyfriend."

David turned his head away from the phone but I managed to catch a glimpse of the smile he was trying to hide. "My boyfriend is kind of awesome."

Some success.

CHAPTER 40
DAVID

The next morning, I thought about checking to see if Coach followed through on the clean-up effort but decided against it. If the marker was still there, I didn't want anyone to see me looking at it and I didn't want to go through the day wondering if it would still be there when I went to practice. If it was still there at the end of the day, I wasn't sure what I was going to do, but I had the day to figure something out.

While I stood at my locker looking through some psychology notes for a quiz I had that day, I felt like someone was staring at me. I whipped around and saw Mike standing there, nervous, like I was a girl he was working up the courage to talk to. He had his hands jammed into his jean pockets and managed to look at the floor with one eye and me with the other.

"Hey," I said, unable to hide the surprise in my voice.

"Hey, uh," Mike shifted from one foot to the other.

"Are you sure you want to talk to me?" I gestured to the crowded hallway. "What will people think now that they know I'm looking for some serious dick?" Being mad felt better than being embarrassed.

"Yeah," Mike said, still looking down. "I wanted to let you know that it's not there anymore."

I furrowed my eyebrows.

"I wanted to put my practice clothes in my locker before school and saw it wasn't there." He stood off to the side of me and it was hard to hear him over the morning traffic in the hallway.

"Oh." A small wave of relief replaced some of the anger. "Do you know who did it?"

Mike shook his head. "Nope."

"You didn't see anything?" I pressed, suddenly concerned with the perpetrator now that I knew I didn't need to worry about my locker anymore.

"Nothing."

"I thought maybe you would have since you and your new best friends were almost late to practice yesterday," I said, remembering how they had to hustle from the field house to the baseball diamond.

"New best friends?" Mike looked confused. "Kurt and Alex?"

I nodded.

"They're not my new best friends."

"My bad." I turned back to my locker to pretend to look over my notes.

Mike was still standing behind me. I could feel it. I didn't know whether to be grateful that Mike was actually talking to me or be pissed that Mike had spent so much time not talking to me.

"See you at practice," Mike said before disappearing into the stream of students flooding the hallway.

After scarfing down my sandwich and guzzling a drink in the hallway, I found myself standing in front of the athletic director's office. I slowly opened the door and tossed my empty sports drink bottle into a nearby recycling bin.

"Hi, David," Mrs. Carlson beamed when I came in and smiled like I was a relative she hadn't seen in a long time. "How are you?"

"Okay." Actually, I'd been better. "Is Coach around?"

Mrs. Carlson glanced at the phone on her desk, which didn't have any lights blinking on it and then to the closed door. "I'm pretty sure he's available." She pushed back her chair and softly knocked on the door before poking her head inside.

I stood off to the side of Mrs. Carlson's desk, again taking in the shrine of Carl Howell and thinking about how he was doing in spring training and getting ready for the upcoming season as a Triple A ball player. In the fall, there would be a new 8X10 photo of Carl in his current team's uniform and then another frame of a collage of action shots from the season. Despite how impressive the professional uniforms looked and the small stadiums that sat hundreds, I had read enough magazine articles and seen enough news stories to know that the life of a minor league baseball player was eons away from anything resembling that of a major leaguer, but every guy always said they wouldn't have traded it for anything. Many had regular jobs in the offseason since minor league contracts didn't involve millions or even thousands.

Above Carl's shrine were several rows of photos of players who played a sport in college. Next year there would be a photo of Kevin in his Illini uniform, complete with the stupid tough-guy expression, and Mike in his Kansas gear. After a quick scan of the wall, I noticed an absence of CNEI navy blue. I had to snort to myself. Even my school didn't consider it a real college. If they did, they'd have to clear the wall designated for the grainy and sun-bleached team photos from Lincoln's earliest days.

"He says you can go in," Mrs. Carlson broke into my thoughts.

"Thanks." I ducked past her and went into Coach Kelly's office.

"We're starting to make this a regular thing," Coach Kelly said from behind his desk. He must have had a meeting this morning because the top button of his short sleeve dress shirt was buttoned, making his neck look like it had a bad sunburn.

"I'll be quick, Coach," I said, closing the door behind him and ignoring the plastic chairs. I didn't think I'd be able to sit in one of those for a long time. "I just wanted to thank you for taking care of the…of my locker. I heard it was cleaned up before school started."

"Well, I can't take the credit," Coach Kelly said. "The guy in charge of maintenance told me it was already covered up with some white paint by the time he got there. It was still wet so he said he would go over it with the yellow tomorrow morning."

"Someone already painted over it?" I immediately wondered who did it. Tyler? Patrick? Another maintenance guy who took it upon himself to do something?

"It's all covered up," Coach assured me. "Rather poorly, if you ask me. But at least it's gone, right?" He sounded like he was talking about a fly that was buzzing around his office.

"Yeah," I said, not really listening.

"Did you make a decision about Coach Rowen's offer?"

"I'm still thinking about it," I said absently, consumed with the image of a hastily painted square on a sheet of yellow metal.

"Still?" Coach seemed shocked. "They're not going to wait around for you, David. They have a roster to fill too."

"I know, Coach," I headed to the door. "See you at practice."

I quickly changed into my PE uniform so I could look at my locker before class. It had been on my mind all day, and I just wanted to see it. This meant a foggy afternoon of classes. Maybe there was a pre-calculus quiz tomorrow. Maybe there was a study guide to go along with the next chapter of *Brave New World.* My teacher did hand something out at the end of class but that might have been a flier about a college talk we were going to next week.

The fog vanished when I stepped into the athletic part of the locker room. I immediately spotted my locker. The glaring white paint stood out like a bleach stain on a favorite hooded sweatshirt.

I studied the paint job feeling like a detective on one of those cop shows my dad liked so much. The coat of paint was thick and in a lopsided square with small drips running halfway to the floor. Big drops clung to the locker. The white paint covered an area that was way bigger than necessary. Whoever did it was in a rush. Not that I expected the paint job to be worthy of a discussion in Art Appreciation class.

Everyone seemed uncomfortable at practice. It was like that girl in the eighth grade, the one who had cancer. No one knew what to say to her. We wanted to say we were sorry or say something to make her feel better but we couldn't come up with anything so we just pretty much avoided her. Any eyes that met mine quickly looked the other way. Only Kevin said something, shifting his position in the group while they ran and whispering loudly, "Keep your eye on your dick." He got a couple snickers in response.

Coach Kelly made a poor attempt to find the culprit by gathering up everyone after their mile run by saying something about how it would be in the best interest of the team if everyone did their best to minimize any outside shenanigans and report anyone who was creating or adding to existing distractions. During my two seasons playing varsity ball, I had never known Coach Kelly to be so concerned about distractions and probably only heard him use the word once when a group of the guys' girlfriends came to one of the home games and screamed like they were at a concert when one of them came up to bat.

Patrick caught me shaking my head and rolled his eyes at Coach, causing me, again, to be grateful for Patrick's presence on the team and to regret not getting to know him better sooner. I knew it was a given that Patrick would warm up with me, the same way I used to know that Mike and me would warm up together. Maybe we could continue the routine next year if I decided to go to Sinni. If.

With the first game just a week away, barring snow, rain, or extremely cold temperatures, Coach Kelly wanted to work on situational fielding. While the players who weren't in the field lined up behind home plate, I checked out the dirt around second base and halfway between first and second, where I would spend most of my time. It was still wet between the bases so my cleats made pronounced tracks in the dirt, but a drying agent was dumped around second base causing it to be pretty slippery. I dragged my feet through the sandy stuff, trying to spread it out.

"Kaminski," Coach Kelly called. "Get with the others by the plate. Let Junior take some in the field." Junior was the nickname given to the sophomore pitcher who was moved up to varsity. He was tall and skinny and would probably only see playing time during the bottom of a doubleheader.

Kevin looked up from the pitcher's mound that he had been sitting on. "Why? He's not starting next week."

"Because he needs the practice in case he needs to bail you out," Coach yelled from the sidelines. "Get in line!"

"Nobody on, nobody out!" Coach Murray shouted from behind a pair of sunglasses.

Everyone in the infield and outfield crouched in the ready position. A hard, fast ground ball shot toward second base. I angled back at it, seeing Mike out of the corner of my eye. "I got it, I got it, I got it." I heard Mike say as he stretched out his glove and threw the ball to first base from his knees.

"Good grab," Coach Murray called, getting ready to toss and hit another baseball as Kevin put his head down, ready to race down to first. "Nobody on, one out!" This time it was a hit between third and shortstop. Kurt was able to field the ball deep in the infield, but didn't have enough time to make a clean throw to first.

"All right," Coach Murray said, "runner on first, one out. Watch out for the bunt."

The corners took a few steps in and I cheated a step over to second base in case I had to cover it. Coach Murray tossed the ball in the air and nudged a bunt to the right of Junior who flailed off the pitcher's mound.

I sprinted the few steps to second base. "Right here, right here," I yelled, holding my glove out to give Junior a good target. The top of Kevin's batting helmet barreled toward me. Junior did a sidearm toss that got away from him, forcing me to jump in order to catch the ball. I felt the ball land in the pocket of my glove. Just as my brain told my other hand to get the ball out of the glove to attempt the double play, my feet were knocked out from under me and the ball flew out of my hand.

"What the hell?" I sprang up, glaring at Kevin who was standing up, dusting the drying agent from his pants.

"What?" Kevin imitated my tone. "Just trying to break up the double play."

"By slicing me with your cleats, dumb ass." My shin stung. There was definitely a gash from Kevin's cleats.

"Lukas!" Coach Murray pointed his bat at me. "Language!"

"You did go in kind of high," Mike said from a few feet off the second base bag but I was sure the wind drowned him out.

I pressed my mouth into a thin line glaring at Kevin while he stood on top of the base like he was king of the mountain. My arms shook at my sides.

"Give him a break, Coach," Kevin rolled his eyes. "He's just so distracted by everything that's been going on lately."

Before I knew it, my arms extended in front of me. "Shut up." I pushed Kevin off the base.

Kevin stumbled back but quickly recovered to lunge at me. "I fucking told you not to touch me." He pushed me back. I stumbled back a couple steps but quickly recovered.

"Kaminski! Lukas!" Coach Kelly bellowed from in front of the home dugout. "Get your asses over here!"

I stalked off the field, keeping my eyes on Coach Kelly. Someone whispered "Oooo" like the characters do in a sitcom when someone gets into trouble.

Kevin huffed behind me, grumbling to himself. "Make *me* run the bases and get pissed when *I* do *my* job. It's how you play the game."

The tendons in my neck and jaw tensed.

"Next in line, get on second." Coach Kelly waved an arm toward second base. "Alex, you take over at the position." Alex hurried from the end of the line to grab his glove. Without another word, Coach Kelly marched around the fence and behind the dugout.

Coach took deep breaths in and out like he was doing some sort of childbirth breathing technique. In the few steps it took me to reach him, I realized this could be the end of my baseball career at Lincoln. Scott Kaminski was looking for a reason and this could be it. Coach couldn't kick me off the team for being gay but he could for any other reason he might think of, including swearing at and pushing a teammate.

Coach Kelly turned like a drill sergeant marching past recruits during inspection. "What the hell was that out there?"

"A spike to the leg." I crossed my arms, feeling my left shin throb. If my place on the team was in jeopardy, then Kevin's was too and I planned on taking him down with me.

"Clean play, Coach," Kevin smirked.

"Shut up, Kaminski," Coach Kelly's neck snapped to look at Kevin. "If anybody slid into one of our guys like that I'd charge the field and get him thrown out."

Kevin narrowed his eyes. "Just trying to break up a double play," he muttered.

"Not like that," Coach Kelly said before turning to me. "And you. Are you going to respond like that if an opponent slides into you? You lay a hand on another player and you're done. How many times have you told me how badly you wanted to play this year and you wouldn't have any trouble on the field?"

I couldn't hold Coach Kelly's stare, embarrassed that I let Kevin get the best of me again.

"Our first game is coming up and I need to know that this team is together. That we have one another's backs. How are we going to do that if we're cursing at one another and pushing each other?" Coach Kelly paused as if he expected Kevin or me to answer but both of us just shifted our weight, staring at the dirt. "I don't care what you two think about each other. I really don't. But I need to know that if you need to throw the ball to second, you're not going to whip it at his head or worse." Coach's stern eyebrows straightened into a quizzical look. "Did you pull that stunt in the locker room?"

"What? With the cup?" Kevin asked, still pouting.

Coach nodded. I tried to look at Kevin without moving my head, looking for a sign in his body language.

"Hell no," Kevin said. "I'm not going to touch somebody else's junk."

"You didn't do it?" Coach pressed.

"Nope."

"You didn't?" Coach asked again.

"No," Kevin said, this time with a slight whine.

Coach Kelly looked from me to Kevin and back. He was thinking about something but I wasn't sure what. He believed Kevin didn't write on my locker and I did too. Kevin would have slipped if he did do it. "You're going to run."

"Run?" I asked

"We have to run the bases again?" Kevin whined.

"Nope." Coach Kelly shook his head. "The perimeter of the field. Not the baseball diamond, the whole field. Together." With his pointer finger he gestured to the grassy outfield and soggy infield of the JV diamond that was behind the varsity diamond. The JV players stood all over the field, doing drills at various stations.

"The whole field?" Kevin asked as if Coach had just said we had to run ten miles.

"How many times?" I asked, wanting to get this punishment over with and get back to second base before Alex got too comfortable there.

"As long as it takes," Coach said. "You can stop when you can really tell me there is not going to be another episode like that one out there again."

"It won't happen again," Kevin quickly said.

"I don't believe you." Coach Kelly said and walked back onto the diamond. "Get going gents. I've got all week."

CHAPTER 41
DAVID

Kevin sprinted ahead of me so he was a good twenty-five yards ahead of me for most of the first lap. By the way he shook his head and made small grunting noises, I knew he was talking to himself. Probably damning me to hell for making him run like he was a bench player who committed too many errors.

At first, I didn't mind the running too much. It actually calmed me down. But with each crack of the bat, I did my best to watch the play through the chain link fence that circled the field. A clean play looked so effortless from a distance. Alex dove for a ball that I knew I could have nabbed without the dramatics. I should have been on the field instead of running behind the backstop of the JV field as all of the JV players paused to look at the two varsity players jogging by.

Even if Kevin had never seen Tyler and me together and none of this had happened I still would have been counting down the days until I'd never have to see his face again. If it bothered him that much to be on the same team and breathe the same air in the locker room as me, then Kevin would have to be the one to walk away. One thing the past couple months taught me was that not everyone was a douchebag and very few people were as big a douchebag as Kevin. If only I had come to that realization sooner.

Kevin slowed as he approached the varsity field backstop and eventually stopped when he got to the dugout. I trotted a few paces behind.

Coach Kelly stood at the dugout's entrance with his arms folded and his belly blocking their way in.

"You're done?" Coach Kelly asked.

"Yup," Kevin said, making a move to get past Coach, but he didn't budge.

"I'm never going to see crap like that ever again this season?"

"Nope," Kevin responded.

"Never again," I confirmed.

Coach Kelly looked around the perimeter of the field, having to squint when he got to the JV field. When his eyes got back to Kevin and me, he said, "Take another lap. Just to be sure."

Kevin's mouth dropped. "What? Another one?"

"If you two can make it around the field together without killing one another, I'd say you're ready to rejoin practice."

Coach Kelly had never been one for team-building exercises and stuff like that and now he suddenly thought they were a good idea?

"Fine," I said. "Let's go." I didn't look back at Kevin as I started up again.

"You better catch up, Kaminski," Coach Kelly said and I saw him leave Kevin standing at the dugout entrance. "More than enough time left for a third go-around. Maybe even a fourth."

In a matter of seconds, Kevin was at my side and the only sounds were cleats hitting the dirt and our huffing and puffing. I wasn't sure I could keep this pace for a third lap. Coach wasn't expecting us to turn the final corner as best friends, but I didn't know what he wanted us to get out of this.

A small pack of four track runners approached Kevin and me at a quick pace. Despite the similar black running tights and long sleeve T-shirts, I easily spotted Tyler. We locked eyes as the distance between us decreased. Tyler's eyeballs shifted to Kevin and then back to me, his eyebrows furrowed in a silent question. I just rolled my eyes at Kevin, hoping to convey to Tyler that this was not like the last time he saw me running when I looked like I was dying.

"What a stupid sport," Kevin huffed as the runners passed. "Running around in circles for hours. What's that all about?"

I remembered the exact same conversation I had with Robert a couple months ago. Of course Kevin wouldn't realize that baseball players ran around in circles too. "How many more of these are we going to do?" I asked.

"I'm walking off if Coach makes me do another lap." Kevin slightly pulled ahead of me.

"Great, let's go again."

"Fuck you."

"If it makes you that sick to be around me, feel free to leave." A surge of confidence rose in me.

"I'm not the only one who thinks you're fucking sick." That hit me in the chest. There was no hesitation in his voice or any hint of stumbling. He believed what he was saying and had no problem saying it.

"I'm not the only who thinks you're a fucking asshole."

"Yeah, well fuck all of them. They're just jealous." Kevin pulled slightly ahead.

"That must be it." I set my mouth in a firm line, breathing heavily through my nose. I picked up my pace so I was ahead of Kevin as we approached the dugout and Coach Kelly standing outside of it. "We're taking another one, Coach."

"I'm done," Kevin shouted.

"Doesn't seem that way," Coach Kelly said.

I heard Kevin grunt loudly in frustration, followed by quick steps to catch up. "What the fuck? You want to get me alone or something?"

"Yeah, I do," I said. Seeing Kevin jerk to a stop and glare at me wiped away any fatigue I felt. My legs no longer felt like sandbags were tied to my ankles. My arms swung at my side, relaxed. I jogged in place at Kevin's side. "I have something I want to tell you so follow me." I started running again, at a slower pace so Kevin could catch up.

"Just say what you want and get it over with," Kevin said when he caught up with me. He glanced back at the field where runners stood on all of the bases and Coach Murray tossed a ball in the air, ready to hit it. "I don't want to have to tell my dad I spent the entire practice running with you."

I rushed on, not having the time to address every stupid thing that

Kevin had ever said. We would be running for the rest of the season if that were the case. "I want to say thanks for being a complete shithead and telling Coach about me and Tyler." As Kevin sharply drew in his breath I knew he had a comeback but I cut him off. "I'm completely serious. If you weren't such a dick, I would have never done the thing that I should have a long time ago. So thanks for forcing me to do it." I kicked up my heels, ready to take off like a character in old cartoons. "Prick."

I didn't have to look back to know that Kevin had stopped running and was just staring at my back as I found a sudden burst of energy that would allow me to finish this lap and probably five more.

I was riding high for the rest of practice that I barely noticed the sloppy paint job on my locker as I opened it and got dressed. I didn't even think about my locker and the mystery asshat who destroyed it until I walked past Mike's car and saw what was on the backseat. A small can of white paint that I recognized from when Mike bitched over the summer about having to paint the garage door. It was for these three rectangles on the door that intersected like the Olympic rings. A large paintbrush stiff with a gob of white paint rested next to the can on an old T-shirt. I peered into the window as if looking at some strange animal in a zoo enclosure.

"Hey!"

I took a startled step back and saw Mike standing at the trunk of his car. "Oh, hey," I said.

Mike opened the trunk and tossed his bags in it. When he slammed the trunk down, the car shook a little. He deliberately walked to the door with his head down. I had to step back so Mike didn't run into me. Without saying anything, he opened the door and sat down.

"Your dad would have been so pissed if the garage door turned out like my locker," I said.

"He was pissed about it anyway." Mike didn't look at me. He just sat in the car with the door open and his hands on the steering wheel like he was about to drive away with the door open, but the engine wasn't on. "He'll probably make me do it again this summer before I leave for Kansas."

I couldn't stop the jealousy that struck me in the gut.

"Your boyfriend's coming," Mike flatly said.

"He is." I turned to the door and picked out Tyler's blonde head from the small herd of athletes leaving the building. Even though it was a strained conversation, I wondered if something inside of me would always smile when someone said "your boyfriend."

Mike grabbed on to the door handle. "Well, see you around." He somehow managed to close the door, start the car, and drive off all in one quick motion.

Tyler stood with his elbows resting on the top of my car. I hadn't washed the brown boat since the first snowfall and the gray film of salt and dirt got on Tyler's coat.

CHAPTER 42
DAVID

I walked with Allie to the next SAFE meeting, having no intention of going, but there was something I needed to do. It had been bothering me for quite some time.

"You were actually the topic of conversation at last week's meeting," Allie said, elbowing me.

"What?"

"Your name didn't come up or anything, but your baseball locker did. No one knew it was yours except me," Allie assured me. "Maybe Adam knew. I'm not sure."

"Weird," I said, not sure how I felt about people I didn't know talking about me, even if they didn't know they were talking about me.

"Will saw your locker and shared it with the group," Allie explained. "He seemed pretty proud to be able to contribute something."

"What was Will doing in the athletic locker room?"

"He's on the freshmen volleyball team."

"Oh. I didn't know," I said.

"First game today?" Allie asked, stopping at the classroom door like I was dropping her off at home after a date.

"Last first game of my high school career," I said.

"So melodramatic," Allie said

Anna came toward us from the other direction. "Hey, Allie."

"Hey," Allie nodded back, playfully tugging on the rainbow

necktie that Anna had hanging around her neck.

"Hi," Anna excitedly turned to me. "Are you here for SAFE?"

"I just need to talk to Ms. Larson for a minute." I craned my neck to peer into Ms. Larson's classroom and saw her in the back putting away beakers and test tubes. The dancer girl and the short girl were already inside, dragging the desks into a circle.

"Well, anyone can come, you know," Anna rushed on. "Gay, straight, bi, whatever." She ducked into the classroom and went straight to the whiteboard and began drawing a series of stars in all the different colors.

"Put the caps back on the markers this time, Anna," Ms. Larson said, walking to the front of the room. When she got to the door she smiled at Allie, but it froze on her face in a weird plastic way when she saw me standing next to her. "Hi, David."

"I was just walking with Allie," I said.

Ms. Larson's genuine smile came back. "I didn't know you guys were friends."

"The library brings people together," Allie said. She waved goodbye to me with a half salute like she usually did. "I hope you score today." Chuckling, she went into the classroom and began straightening out the desks so the shape resembled more of a circle.

Ms. Larson stepped into the hallway and closed her classroom door halfway. "How are you doing?"

"Good," I quickly said. "Better. Not bad."

"Those all sound okay," Ms. Larson said.

I saw Will approaching in his black hoodie with the thin horizontal stripes, blowing the swoosh of hair off his forehead. That kid had amazing timing. "Uh," I began, thinking about what I wanted to say. "Sorry I got so pissed - I mean mad. There was a lot going on."

Ms. Larson smiled at the speckled tiles in the hallway and then looked at me. "I might have been pretty pissed too. Some teacher you haven't talked to in forever pops up out of the blue..."

Will slid between Ms. Larson and me without saying anything.

"Hey, Will," I said.

Will stopped, looking at me from under the curtain of hair that hung over his eyes. "You know me?"

I shrugged. "Not really. But I know your name, so, hi."

"Hi." Will turned to Ms. Larson. "I have to catch the bus for our game so I can't stay long."

"That's fine. Leave whenever you need to," Ms. Larson said.

Will walked into the classroom to be greeted by a shriek and hug from Anna.

Ms. Larson glanced back at the scene and smiled. "I think I have to get the troops settled and get this meeting started. Thanks for coming by."

"I'm glad you're doing this," I said, gesturing to the scene inside the classroom with Adam at the board, Anna dragging Will to a desk near her, Stacey and Monika listening to music from the same phone by sharing earbuds, and Allie sitting on a desk like she was hanging out on a park bench.

"This?" Ms. Larson repeated. She also surveyed the scene and then shrugged. "Whether there's five of them or fifty, I'll keep doing it."

"Good," I said with a small nod as I headed off toward the locker room. Tyler had said that he was going to come to the game after his practice was over and that turned the flurry of little kid Christmas excitement into a full-blown blizzard.

All through warm-ups, the game, and the final team huddle just behind third base, Scott Kaminski's glare hovered from the top corner of the bleacher furthest from the dugout. Despite the clouds that hid the sun for minutes at a time, he wore his dark sunglasses. I couldn't help glancing at him when I jogged out to second base for the first time. I couldn't see his eyes from where I stood, but I bet they focused on me.

There would always be people wearing sunglasses when it was unnecessary or just because they thought it looked cool or intimidating. But, at least on this particular day at this particular game, there were more people not wearing sunglasses than who were.

"Batter up!" the umpire behind the plate called, causing me to instinctively crouch in the ready position.

Kevin raked his cleats around the pitcher's mound a couple more times as the opposing batter, dressed in green and white, strode to the left batter's box and settled in. He swung at the first pitch, a line drive straight at me. Without even thinking, I raised my glove in front of my face and clamped it shut.

One out.

Cheers from the crowd in the bleachers.

A good way to start the season.

CHAPTER 43
TYLER

David looked hot in his uniform. I had no idea red knee socks and white pants that went just below the knee were so sexy. Or maybe people were just hotter when they were being honest with themselves.

An inning was about to start when I got to the baseball diamond so I mainly watched David stand around, moving his head from left to right as he followed the ball into the first baseman's glove. I had told him I was going to be at the game but didn't know exactly when I would make it.

The bleachers weren't full, but most of the spectators sat at the ends of the rows and I felt weird having to climb over them or asking them to move. A few people sat on the top row, one of which was this man who had on sunglasses even though dusk was approaching. He looked pissed about something.

I ended up standing off to the side of the bleachers, furthest away from the dugout so I wouldn't distract David. He'd told me how his coach was extra worried about that.

Aside from Homecoming football games, which I went to my first year at Lincoln because it seemed like something you were supposed to do, I'd never been to any other sporting events outside of track. The only reason I was here was to see my boyfriend play baseball.

As the umpire yelled, "Batter up," Kevin dug his feet into the dirt around the mound. Scanning the rest of the players crouched with their gloves brushing the ground, I settled on David who stood up as the umpire called the first pitch a ball. He paced in the base path for a couple seconds before getting ready as the next pitch was thrown.

On the second pitch, the batter connected and it looked like the ball was hit straight up in the air. Everyone on the field looked up and did a little dance, their feet shuffling to where the ball might land.

"I got it, I got it," David called and the ball somehow landed squarely in his glove. He tossed the ball to Kevin without looking at him amid claps and cheers from the bleachers.

David wouldn't want to wear a tux, White Sox logos or not. He wouldn't want to be in a room packed with people he wasn't fully comfortable being around because he was just beginning to be comfortable with himself. But maybe we could do something else. And not the same routine of just the two of us, hidden away from everyone, even though I did enjoy that and looked forward to it all week.

CHAPTER 44
DAVID

With my uniform unbuttoned and a thick red long sleeve T-shirt underneath, I leaned my dirt-covered knees against the shiny black material of Tyler's running tights. We sat on the same bleacher that Kevin's dad did until Coach Kelly brought the team together so we could grunt *Lions* in unison before heading off the field. I took a detour to the bleachers instead, in no hurry to get to the locker room.

"Undefeated so far." Tyler elbowed me in the ribs and nestled into my side with a smile that was usually reserved for swaying on the swing on his front porch.

"And I'm batting over three hundred," I said like it wasn't a big deal but I felt Tyler's head move and noticed the puzzled expression that crossed his face. "One for three," I explained. "A double and a sacrifice bunt. Not bad."

"Sinni is lucky to have you," Tyler said. "I know it wasn't your first choice or not even one of your choices, but you can always transfer in a year or two."

"Maybe you can put in a word for me with the coach at U of I. Then we can go to the same school, maybe get an apartment off campus." It would take a lot of Little League games to cover the cost of apartment living for a school year and tuition but I was in the mood to daydream.

"And play on the same team as Kevin again?"

"A price I'm willing to pay," I said.

"Wow," Tyler said, sitting up and turning to face me. "You must really like me."

"I do," I said. "I really like you."

"And I really like you too." Tyler smiled. "And since I really like you, there's something I want to ask you."

I straightened, noticing how Tyler hesitated. It was a familiar tone heard around this time of year. The question being asked to girls from guys even though the big dance was still over a month away. Please don't ask me to prom. I liked our weekends together in Tyler's room. Couldn't we just keep doing that?

Tyler had to notice the strained smile stuck on my face as he took my hands in his. "I wanted to ask you if…if you would go to prom with me."

I felt the smile get even tighter. It meant a lot to me, really. Sometimes, it still surprised me that Tyler wanted to be with me. "Prom?"

"Prom," Tyler repeated. "But this is a different prom. Lake Park's GSA is having one."

"A prom just for gay kids?" I asked, not knowing there was such a thing.

"Gay, ace, trans, straight. Pretty much anyone who wants to come."

"Really? I don't know." I tried to imagine walking into the dance with Tyler. Nobody would be looking at us because we were the gay guys but I'd only gone to one dance during high school. Homecoming freshman year. Mike and I had spent most of the time by the snacks and punch. "I've never worn a tux before."

"It's not that formal," Tyler tried to assure me.

"Not that formal?" I laughed. "Last year, Mike bitched because he had to wear a tux and not just a nice shirt or something. And Carrie got this dress that probably cost close to what Robert spent to play baseball."

Tyler laughed a little. "Mike would fit right in at a GSA prom. A nice shirt is appropriate attire."

Anna. Will. Probably Allie too. She'd probably ask me to slow dance with her.

"That might be cool," I finally said.

"Yeah?" Tyler's whole face smiled as he put his head on my shoulder.

"Yeah." I leaned my head against his.

"Cool."

The sun dipping closer and closer to the outfield fence reminded me that it was getting late. I had told my mom that I would come home right after the game. My dad had wanted to come. He'd never missed an Opening Day, but with the slight rise in temperature came some work. So rather than seeing me play my last first game of the season, Dad was helping another unemployed carpenter build a shed. They had met at the support group meeting that he still hadn't told me anything about. The guy even had a son in college who had a partial tennis scholarship.

When I sat up, Tyler turned and faced me so I got a chance to study his cheeks that turned pink whenever he was in the wind or the sun for even a short amount of time and moved on to his eyes, big and blue. Only the slightest hint of a scar from his fight with Kevin. You wouldn't see it if you didn't know anything about it. My black eye was long gone.

Tyler narrowed his eyes at me with a little smile. "What?"

"I have to go but I don't want to." I stood up before I could convince myself not to. "Everything is too perfect now."

"Nothing is perfect." Tyler followed me down the bleachers. "But it can be really good."

"I know," I said, heading toward the field house doors. "I'm still trying to figure out how this works."

"Me too." He probably thought I didn't notice his hand reach towards mine.

"Really?" I asked, thinking of that confident runner from last summer that ran lap after lap around the track.

"Yeah. I really have no idea."

I zeroed in on Tyler's hands slightly swinging at his side, his fingers curled into a loose fist. So many times I fought the instinct to take his hand. But this time, I didn't.

ACKNOWLEDGEMENTS

This book wouldn't be in anyone's hand if I did not get placed in Mr. Mark Maxwell's Expository Writing class my junior year. I can trace every step I've taken from that first day of school. Thank you, Mr. Maxwell, for being so thoughtful, supportive, encouraging, and patient.

A huge hug and thank you to my agent, Tina, for being excited about this project when I shared the first five pages with her and she asked where was the rest. Another big thank you and hug to Sam at Trism Books and my editor, Erica, for believing in this project and helping me make it better than when it first came into her hands.

More thank yous to Jim Klise, for that snowy walk in the woods at Ragdale, Story Studio for helping this writer grow and grow, and SCBWI for giving this writer exactly what she needed and so much more.

For their support, feedback, babysitting services, and/or fuzzy feelings, the following people deserve a special mention: Michael and Elda Robbins, Lori Rader-Day, Ozge Gunday, Joyce Zeiss, Sumeet, Iyengar, Lauri Wade Higdon, Josh Feinzimer, Maureen Ritter, Carl Hauck, Rachel Anderson, Kathy Olson, and Katie Larson.

To Virginia, my favorite girl in the world, and Wallace, my favorite guy under thirty-six: you are my everything. I hope I make you proud.

To Matt. Thank you and I love you. I hope that encompasses everything I need to say.

ABOUT THE AUTHOR

With a BA in Screenwriting and MFA in Fiction, **Kim Oclon** taught high school creative writing and film, in addition to the classics. There, she was the co-founder of her school's first gay-straight alliance. As an active member in the LGBTQ community and SCBWI representative, she has combined her passion for storytelling and giving a voice to the LGBTQ community in her writing. Kim lives in Dundee, Illinois with her understanding husband and two silly children. Connect with Kim online at www.kimocolon.com